Jay and Adam have been sharing a flat, and a bed, since they moved down to Adelaide after high school a couple of years ago. Neither man considers himself gay or mentions the sexual nature of their friendship to anyone else.

Their arrangement doesn't stop Jay from casually dating random women he meets through work and both men seem happy with the way things are. That is, until Adam meets April, a damsel in distress that latches herself onto Adam in a way that he doesn't mind at all. Jay sure does, though.

As Adam gets closer to April, the friendship between the two men starts to unravel and for the first time in years, Jay is facing a life without Adam. If he wants to save their friendship, he will have to offer Adam a lot more than a spot in his bed. There's only one problem, Jay doesn't believe in love.

COMING IN

Michelle Ogilvy

Published by
NineStar Press
PO Box 91792
Albuquerque, New Mexico, 87199
www.ninestarpress.com

Warning: This book contains sexually explicit content which is only suitable for mature readers.

Print ISBN #978-1-947139-09-1
Cover by Natasha Snow
Edited by Jason Bradley

One

JAY KNEW IT was going to be a hard night. Adam had come by the store to pick up something for dinner, and he'd been mumbling to himself again. It was becoming a habit with him. Ever since Adam had started the new semester, he'd been complaining about this one subject. It didn't seem to make any difference what Jay said or did. There was only one thing that could distract Adam. Not that Jay had a problem with providing that kind of distraction—it was the bitching and moaning that preceded it that had him dawdling to get home.

This would be the third year that he and Adam had been flatmates in Adelaide, and Jay could picture exactly what he would find when he walked through the door. He pasted on a smile and braced himself. Sure enough, Adam was sitting in the middle of a pile of textbooks and handwritten notebooks spread across most of the floor space with various highlighters and pens strewn throughout the mess.

The more stressed Adam got, the less likely Jay would be to see the floor, or the bench in the kitchen area, or pretty much anything in Adam's room. Jay always drew the line at any of that shit ending up in his own room. His aim for the night was to get Adam in there where the other man couldn't torture himself over whatever went wrong that day.

At least now Jay didn't have to worry about Adam literally pulling his hair out from stress. Adam had starting cutting his hair short after he'd started at uni. The new hairstyle had broken the stress-pulling habit, so Adam had kept it. The muttering had gotten worse, though. Jay wasn't even sure that Adam knew he was doing it half the time.

"So, what sludge have we got for dinner tonight?" Jay asked, making sure to keep his tone light. Adam didn't look up. "It was your turn to cook, remember?"

"Oh, right. I forgot. I bought some stuff." Adam gestured vaguely towards the kitchen area. Jay couldn't bring himself to call an area bounded by benches rather than walls an actual kitchen, like it was a separate room.

"What are we in for? Pizza? Lasagne? Reheated puke?"

"It was rice."

"In puke?"

"In... I don't know." Adam finally pulled his head up from his books and looked at Jay. "It was weeks ago. When are you going to let that go?"

Jay shrugged. "When it stops being amusing."

"I'm too tired to joke around, Jay."

"Fridays." Jay shook his head and sighed dramatically. "I'll just go ahead and nuke us something then."

"It's my turn," Adam said, not moving from his position on the floor.

"I'm not sure you're trusted with the microwave, Adam. Do we really have to have the reheated puke joke twice in one night?"

"That wasn't my fault, bakeboy."

"Bakeboy? Maybe you should take a break from the study. I think it's fried your brain. That's the lamest insult I've ever heard. Come on, Obsesso, come get some grub."

"Obsesso?" Adam was trying not to laugh. Jay could tell.

"I think that's about at the same level as bakeboy. Figure I'll keep all my best insults until you're feeling more up to it."

Adam huffed but got up off his butt and onto the stool at the kitchen bench. He watched as Jay put the dinners in the microwave.

"You shouldn't stand in front of those, you know," Adam said. "They'll give you cancer."

"The sad thing about that is that you wouldn't cry at my funeral," Jay replied.

"What do you mean?"

"The way you're going, you'll die from an ulcer long before I die of cancer."

Jay moved away from the thing anyway. Their microwave was large, old, and temperamental. Or just plain mental, depending on how generous they were feeling towards it on the day. The clicking noise it was making was certainly a new development.

Adam heaved a large sigh, and Jay turned his attention back to his friend.

"Do I dare ask what the evil wench did today?" Jay asked.

"It's just that she expects so much," Adam replied.

"I hear ya."

"Where did she get such high expectations anyway?"

"Germany." Jay's comment barely rated a glance.

"It's not like we're all overly efficient geniuses."

"I've always been partial to lazy dimwits, myself."

"It's like that stupid subject is supposed to be the centre of our universe."

"Unhealthy, that."

"If we don't spend at least three times as much effort as we do in other subjects, we barely pass."

"That's what I've heard."

"I just don't have that amount of time."

"Another credit?"

"I never got a C in anything before I took her class."

"Well, there was PE. You weren't real good at PE."

"I know it's a big joke to you, Jay, but it's *my* life."

"I don't think uni's actually counted as life." Jay was trying for a smile, but all he got was a glare. "Geez, if it bothers you that much, *do something*."

"Like...?"

"Hmm. Leave it with me. I'll think of something," Jay said as the microwave beeped. "And dinner is served. Enjoy your cancer in a bowl, Obsesso."

Adam didn't say anything, but he was finally smiling. The first step in Jay's plan. The crucial point would be after dinner when Adam would want to go back to studying. If Jay could prevent that happening, at least for the night, Adam might have time to get over whatever issues he'd had that day and look at the problem afresh in the morning. Otherwise he would be obsessing over it all night.

When Adam had finished eating, he dumped his dishes in the sink and started making motions towards the pile of papers and other paraphernalia in the lounge. Jay threw out the first distraction he could think of to prevent a return to study mode.

"Hey, it's Dan," he said, directing Adam's attention to the window and a view of their neighbour. "Out for another night of debauchery."

"I don't know how he does it," Adam said, coming over to stand next to Jay at the window.

"Of course not. You barely leave the flat for anything but uni. Practically a hermit. You'll end up one of those old men who stay at home all day waiting for some kid to kick a ball into your yard so you can yell at them from the porch."

"Fuck you."

"If you insist." Jay grinned and pressed his lips to Adam's.

"My assignment. I have to go over the comments," Adam mumbled around Jay's tongue.

Jay ignored him. Adam needed this way more than he needed to chastise himself over comma placement or whatever minor issue the professor was cracking down on that week.

Jay had never been afraid of hard work, but Adam made everything harder than it needed to be. Including Jay. Which is how they had started this little dance of theirs in the first place. Now, it was simply a part of life.

Everything about Adam was familiar now, from his long, slightly crooked nose and deep brown eyes to the toenails that he never seemed to trim frequently enough. No matter how many times they did this, though, Jay didn't get tired of looking or touching. The women that shared Jay's bed on occasion, they never lasted long. But Adam was his mate. That was something completely different and lasting.

Yet, each time Jay leaned in for a kiss with Adam, there was always a moment as their lips met when he wondered if this would be the night that Adam pushed him away. When Adam finally questioned why the hell they were doing this. Whether this really was a 'mates' thing to do. But Adam never questioned.

Jay was glad of it. The guy needed a release, with all the pressure he put himself under. Jay didn't mind providing a helping hand. And by this point, he knew all the right buttons to push until Adam let go and surrendered to the demands of sensation and impulse. Just the way Jay liked him.

THE ALARM WENT off at 3:30. As usual, Adam had latched onto Jay like a drowning man while they were sleeping, but Jay had learnt how to extricate himself enough to roll out of bed.

"Turn it off," Adam moaned, pulling the sheet over his head.

Jay leaned over and switched the alarm off. Then he yanked the sheet from Adam's head, put his mouth to Adam's ear and said, "You could always sleep in your own room."

Adam groaned and pulled the sheet back up again. Jay grinned and sauntered out of the room to have a shower. A typical Saturday morning.

THE EARLY MORNING shifts usually meant that Jay had a long afternoon nap so that he'd be functioning on Saturday night. On this particular night, though, Jay kind of wished that he was sleepier. It was the only thing he could think of that would have made the night more endurable.

It felt like Tammy had been yapping in his ear ever since he'd picked her up a few hours ago. You would think that somewhere in all that noise, he would have found some commonality to latch on to, some topic to discuss rather than talk at each other. Even some peace and quiet during the movie would have been welcome. But no.

He had not anticipated the night going this way when he'd asked her out earlier in the week. Of course, his attention might have been slightly lower than her mouth when he'd thought that a good idea. She was hot, for sure. He was starting to think that he might need to expand the criteria for a date, though.

Maybe he should just offer to take her home and end the misery. On the other hand, she was the one who'd suggested going back to his place. Maybe they could find some commonality there. Like a shared need for less clothing.

He was in two minds about which option to choose, but when driving, a destination is usually a pretty good idea, especially seeing as the two options were in opposite directions. For the moment, his little mind was winning.

"What made you want to be a baker, anyway?" Tammy said. It took Jay a second to realise it was an actual question, and he should respond. By that point, she'd moved on. "You don't seem like someone who's into looking after people. The smell must be just delicious, though. I love the smell of baking. Is that what it was, the smell? I know that—"

"There's less traffic in the morning," Jay interrupted.

"Huh?" the girl said.

"That's what I like about baking. We start early so there's less traffic when I go to work."

Tammy just looked at him for a few beats. Then she shrieked in his ear. Startled the hell out of him.

"Isn't it gorgeous?" she exclaimed, staring out of Jay's window. "Spunky."

"Spunky?" People still used that word? Jay grimaced. He glanced over and saw one of those dumb hatchbacks that looked as if the tail had been lopped off.

"You know, cute, zippy, sporty, lush—"

"It's crap." He cut her off before she could think of another twenty or thirty adjectives.

"What do ya mean it's crap. It's not crap."

"Zero to a hundred takes a month," Jay explained. "It's got average suspension. Understeers. You'd pay through the nose for petrol. And a mate of mine said his air-conditioning barely cooled his left... hand."

"Seats looked comfy, though."

God. If the seats looked comfy, it must be roadworthy. Obviously cars were not going to be their common ground. Jay was still betting on nakedness.

JAY HAD TOLD Adam that he'd be bringing someone home. He'd hoped it would force Adam to rein himself in a little. Even so, Jay held his breath as he opened the door to the flat. Adam was back to studying, sprawled across the lounge room floor again. It appeared to be his usual level of overachievement, though, rather than the disaster area from the night before so Jay figured a mental breakdown wasn't drastically imminent.

"Can I use your bathroom?" Tammy asked.

"Through the hall, on the right," he replied.

Tammy smiled and headed through. While she was gone, Jay went over to the fridge to grab a couple of Cokes, leaving boot prints on several sheets of paper on the way. When he turned, Adam was right behind him. He offered Adam one of the Cokes before he got any grief about how important the papers had been.

"How's it going?" Adam asked.

Jay leaned in conspiratorially. "My advice: don't engage. She'll go into an hour-long monologue about her long-term goals, then segue into what yours should be."

"I don't know. She looked in a pretty big hurry to me."

Adam's statement prompted a grin from Jay.

"I bought the biggest Coke they had and kept shoving it at her. She must have a bladder the size of an elephant," Jay said.

"What was she? Talker? Toucher? Popcorn hogger? Not..." Adam widened his eyes, "a mobile phone answerer?"

"Talker. Through the whole movie. I swear she didn't even close her mouth to sip. How is that possible?"

"Could explain the whole elephant bladder thing, though."

"I gotta start dating out of Woolworths." Jay shook his head mournfully, and Adam laughed.

Jay made this statement frequently but never took his own advice. Adam always maintained that this was due to laziness on Jay's part. But it wasn't laziness, it was practicality. Why bother looking for girls when they threw themselves at him on a daily basis at work?

Neither man noticed Tammy coming back.

"Got any Coke?" she said from the other side of the kitchen counter.

"Adam just drank the last of it, but I'm sure we can find you something." Jay turned to the fridge, mouthing "elephant" to Adam. Adam hid a smirk and headed to the lounge area.

"So, you want it here or in my room?" Jay asked when he emerged from the fridge with a can of Solo. "It's a little overcrowded in here."

Tammy looked over into the lounge area and saw Adam step into the small circle he had made inside of all the junk he had around the room. It might have been less than the night before but was still a remarkable amount of junk for a normal person.

And then Adam started mumbling to himself. They heard "the internet," said scornfully, with a snort of disbelief. Jay frowned. Maybe it was worse than he'd thought.

"Yeah. Okay," she said.

Jay led her to his bedroom. He was still frowning as he closed the bedroom door, his mind half on Adam. He should probably check in on Adam later, make sure the guy wasn't stressing out too much again. The frown dissipated a little when he turned around and found a bare-chested Tammy waiting for him on his bed.

"Not one for small talk?" he said. That surprised him.

"Just come over and show me what you've got, big boy." She patted the bed, and Jay went over and kissed her. Hard and long, savouring the silence. Then he started to kiss down her neck.

"Kinda sparse in here. Don'cha even have a picture of your mother?"

Jay groaned inwardly and made his way back to her mouth.

JAY WAS LYING peacefully in bed after Tammy left when he felt a body slide in behind him. Then breath warming the back of his neck.

"Well?" the body asked. "It couldn't have gotten worse with elephant bladder, surely."

"Ugh. If she would've shut up for more than three minutes at a time, it might have helped."

Adam laughed, and Jay would have hit him with a pillow if they hadn't been lying on both of them. He tried a palm instead, but Adam still snickered.

"She seemed..." Adam paused. "Inquisitive."

"Inquisitive?" Jay said. "Was she quizzing you on the way out? God, what did she ask? It wasn't 'do you have a picture of your mother' was it? You probably would have liked that."

"Showing her pictures of my mother? I don't think I want to hear about the kinky shit you get up to, Jay. Actually, she saw the cans there for recycling and asked me why we use Heinz baked beans instead of SPC. I'd never really thought about it."

"'Cause SPC are crap. Now go to sleep, ya big wanker."

"That probably would have been a shorter conversation," Adam acknowledged. "Going to Ash this weekend?"

"Gotta work."

"You have to go down there sometime, you know."

"No. I don't," Jay said. He felt Adam turn away and knew Adam was disappointed.

Adam was always more disappointed when Jay didn't go than Jay's own family was. Strange boy. Jay had never understood his friend's attachment to their lame-ass hometown. Jay would be completely fine going the rest of his life without setting foot in Ashdon Harbor.

"Adam?" Jay murmured.

"Mmm?"

"Why is it that I only seem to attract women that I have absolutely nothing to say to these days?"

"Dunno. Maybe you just attract women with bad taste in men," Adam replied.

Jay slapped Adam again, using the opportunity to pull Adam towards him so that Adam's front was right up against his back.

"You still feeling stressed?" Jay asked.

Adam sighed, burrowing his forehead against Jay's shoulder.

"Take that as a yes," Jay said.

"Thanks for reminding me about it," Adam mumbled.

"Oh, you were looking for distraction? I can do distraction." Jay nudged Adam off his shoulder and rolled around so they were facing each other. "Besides, I think I've come up with a solution to your problem."

"Oh yeah?" Adam said, as Jay started with the promised distraction, slipping his leg between Adam's thighs.

"You know I always come through for you," Jay said, his hands wandering over Adam's body.

"Mmm. What's your solution?"

"I'm gonna buy you a watch."

"Which will...?"

"You're always saying time gets away from you. Can't do that if it's strapped to your wrist. Only logical."

Adam made a noise somewhere between a groan and a laugh, mixed with a little arousal as Jay's wandering hands found a particularly sensitive spot. "That may be the stupidest joke you've ever made," Adam said.

"Doubt it. But stick with me, kid. They'll only get worse."

Jay could feel Adam laughing, probably against his better judgement. But he wasn't tense anymore. Mission accomplished. Still, while Jay was there, he might as well finish what he started.

He pulled Adam closer, hot skin against his, Adam's erection evidence that tonight wasn't going to be the night Jay would be pushed away. Emboldened by the encouragement, Jay grabbed the back of Adam's head and kissed him stupid.

He fully intended to lick his way down, tracing the path his hands had already made on Adam's body, and do something with that hard-on that Adam had so graciously supplied for him. But, for the moment, he was content staying right where he was, Adam's tongue playing with his and Adam's fingers digging into his cheeks, keeping him close.

He didn't have to work in the morning so there was no need to speed things up. They had all the time they could want. And there was nothing Jay wanted more than to replace the taste of Tammy with Adam's familiar flavour.

Two

ADAM HAD BEEN walking along, minding his own business, when it happened. Just coming off another late night in the library. Then, smack, a girl slammed into his chest.

She put her arms around his neck and whispered, "Please. That man. Just pretend you know me."

Behind the girl, a man was sitting at the bus stop bench, staring blearily at them. The guy was obviously drunk, and had a definite unsavoury vibe to him. Whatever he'd been up to had frightened the girl enough that she'd thrown herself into the arms of a stranger.

"Meg," Adam said loudly. "Didn't know you were in town tonight. Do you want a lift home?"

"Thanks, Davis."

The girl flashed Adam a dazzling smile, and he almost wished he was Davis and knew more about her. She was probably two or three years younger than him, with long blonde hair that she kept pushing back from her face. Adam had always had a thing for long hair. He didn't know what it was, but every flick she made to move it back went straight to his groin.

"Is your car around here?" she said.

Oh. Crap. She was expecting him to actually give her a lift. Was that a good idea? He *could* do that. And she seemed like she needed the help.

Adam pointed vaguely down the incline ahead of them. The girl started to walk down there, and Adam followed.

"So, where are we headed tonight?" she asked.

"Home. That is, I was going home." Adam cursed himself for sounding like a sleaze, but the girl just curved her lips in a sexy smile. Or maybe she was laughing at him tripping over the gravel on the embankment.

"And where is home, Davis?" she said.

"Adam."

She tilted her head in a question.

"My name's Adam. Adam Pearson."

"Well, pleased to meet you, Adam Pearson. My name's April. But you—" She touched Adam lightly on the chest. "—can call me Ms Williams. We do hardly know each other, after all."

Once Adam got April into the car, he didn't know what to do with her. It had been a long while since he'd had a conversation with a girl that didn't involve lecture notes or a store counter between them. Come to think of it, Jay might be right about him needing to get out more.

"So can I drop you anywhere?" he asked.

"I don't really know," April replied. "I hadn't thought that far ahead. I just had to get out of that house. It's unbearable."

"Are you having trouble with your parents?"

"Stepfather." April said it in a tone that made it clear she didn't want to discuss him.

"You were at the bus stop. Which bus were you going to get on?"

April shrugged. "Whichever one came first, I guess. I figured if I was gone long enough... I just don't want to go home tonight."

"Doesn't seem like much of a plan."

"Nope. Not much for plans."

"Is there a friend I could take you to?"

"You're about as friendly as anyone has been to me all week."

Adam didn't like the idea of leaving her out on her own again. She'd already had one bad experience for the night. All she must've wanted was to curl up somewhere safe, and she didn't have that safe place. The more he thought about it, the more Adam felt obligated to offer her help. He couldn't rescue her and then desert her.

"If you want," he said, "I could take you back to my place. Just to give you a quiet place to sleep for the night. Things might not seem so bad in the morning. And I won't hassle you or anything. No strings."

April didn't respond for a long stretch of time, and Adam thought he must have said too much, or she thought he was asking too much. He glanced over at her and found that she was studying him. So not an offended silence but an assessing one. He must have passed whatever test she was running in her mind because when he caught her eye, she smiled and agreed to his plan.

OFFERING FOR APRIL to crash for the night had seemed like the decent thing to do at the time. Adam's good deed for the week. Unfortunately, Jay did not agree. He had dragged Adam over to the kitchen section of their flat to express his displeasure.

Adam was very conscious of April's presence over in the lounge section. These sections were not very far apart and were really only one not-very-large room. She was probably hearing every word they were saying, even though they were both trying to keep their voices down.

"You don't know anything about this girl," Jay said. "Or why she really decided to latch onto you like that. What possessed you to bring her back here?"

"She told me—" Adam started.

"She told you whatever she thought would get her what she wanted. Come on, Adam."

"It's not like you know so much about the girls you bring home. All the time."

"A hell of a lot more than 'she clung to me on a dark street and asked for help'."

"It's one night, Jay. And she had nowhere else to go. What was I supposed to do? Leave her on some random street corner?"

"Duh. Of course you were supposed to leave her. What kind of person throws themselves at strangers like that? Literally throws themselves. She could be some kind of psycho serial killer for all you know. And you've let her into our home."

"Exactly. *Our* home. I have just as much right to bring someone back here as you do."

"Sure. But could you assess their sanity first next time?"

"Oh, absolutely. I'll definitely do that next time."

Adam turned his back on Jay and walked over to April in the lounge section, an apologetic expression on his face.

"April," Adam called.

He could feel Jay glowering behind him, but Adam did his best to ignore it. He resented the way Jay assumed he couldn't think shit through on his own. He was perfectly capable of forming sound judgements of people. Why couldn't Jay trust him?

Adam never complained about all the women that Jay brought home. And there were a lot. Girls had been throwing themselves at Jay since they were in high school. Jay and his stupid, effortless, just-run-a-hand-through-my-hair-and-I'm-perfect good looks. Any other guy would be annoyed by it. But Adam never complained. Never felt sorry for himself, sitting at home while Jay was out with whoever was flavour-of-the-minute.

Jay was hardly ever even nice to these girls, and yet they still kept coming. Adam didn't know why they... actually, he did have some idea of why they might come back. Jay could be a self-centred asshole at times but never in the bedroom.

"You can sleep in my bed tonight," he told April. He never slept in the thing anyway. But that was probably more information than she needed to know.

"You don't have to do that, Adam. I don't want to be any trouble." April looked up at him with wide blue eyes, and any lingering doubt Adam had vanished. She was a nice, ordinary girl, not the crazy serial killer Jay was making her out to be.

"It isn't trouble," he said. "If you really haven't got anywhere else to go..."

Adam heard Jay snort and stomp off.

"But where will you sleep?" April asked.

"Where you are. On the futon, I mean, not in the, um... I'll show you where my room is."

Adam led April into his bedroom. His computer desk and chair, bed, wardrobe, and bookcase (which was overflowing with books) were crammed into the tiny space, and from his feet onwards, there were half-opened books and scribbled on papers lying everywhere: floor, bed, desk, everywhere. He knew exactly where to step to make it to the bed, and he began to stack the papers there into piles so that April could actually lie down.

"Sorry about the mess. There's not really that much room and... well..." he placed the pile in his hand on top of a bigger pile on his desk. "I guess I'm kind of obsessive about studying. That's what Jay says anyway."

"Your flatmate?"

"Um, yeah." There was a pause as he started on the floor piles.

"So, you're a student? At the uni in town?" April asked.

"No, Magill. Information studies."

"You study information?"

"Yeah, it's kind of a dumb course name. I don't know..." He finally stopped fiddling and headed for the door. "Well, um, the bathroom's at the end of this hall here. The door opposite is Jay's room. You saw the kitchen, right? So, I guess that's about it."

"Adam? Sweet dreams."

Adam smiled and closed the door on her. He took a few steps towards Jay's room and stopped. Probably better if he spent the night on the futon. It was only for one night. That's what she said. It wasn't like he was ever going to see her again anyway.

OR AT LEAST that's what he thought until he came home the next day and found her sitting on their doorstep.

"Hi, Adam."

"April. I didn't think I'd ever see you again."

"That crossed my mind too. And the thought made me so sad that I had to come back and make sure it didn't come true. Aren't you glad?"

"Uh... yeah, sure... Um, why don't you come in and sit down? I have to get rid of this stuff... Put it in the fridge." Adam held up the shopping bags in his hands.

He let April into the flat and carried the shopping over to the kitchen benches. After dumping the bags, he leant his arms on the kitchen sink and took a few deep breaths. Okay, so maybe her just sitting there was a little odd, but it didn't make her a crazy serial killer.

"I thought you were going to put it away?"

Adam jumped as April appeared at his elbow.

"Huh? Oh, yeah. Just a headache." Adam shook his head. "I've got a headache, so I was just... yeah I've got to put it away." He moved to the bags he'd left on the counter.

"I'll help," April said. "Frozen dinners? You guys really do live the bachelor life, hey?"

"Well... um... Jay, he's more of the cook, you know, than I am."

"Oh. I'll cook for you. I know I saw some pasta in that cupboard."

April started rummaging through their cupboards as Adam looked on. She'd seen pasta in their cupboards? When had she been in their cupboards? Had she come out in the middle of the night when he was sleeping and searched their place?

Shit. Shit. Shit. Where was Jay?

"See, right here next to the cereal," April said, pulling out a packet of pasta. "I saw it at breakfast this morning."

Breakfast. Right. That sounded much less concerning.

While April prepared dinner, she told Adam more about how bad the situation was at home. She was obviously having a hard time getting along with her stepfather.

"He's just on at me all the time. Like nothing I ever do is okay," she said, ending the ten-minute outpouring of complaints. "That's why I was so glad you let me crash here last night. I couldn't take it anymore. I just had to get away. I wish I didn't have to go back. It's just ... ugh."

"But where would you go?" Adam asked. He got the feeling that April was being a little overdramatic. Her story sounded like every other teenager complaining about their parents. Nothing there to make him really worry about her. If she'd told him the stepfather stories the previous night, he might not have been so quick to assume she really needed a place to crash. Maybe Jay had a point when he'd said Adam should've questioned her a bit more. She certainly didn't seem as reluctant to talk about it as he'd assumed.

"I'm not sure," April replied. "There's not really anywhere else to go."

She lowered her eyes to the sauce she was stirring, and her hair fell over her face. God, she wasn't crying, was she? And Adam was supposed to do what with that exactly?

"I'll work something out," she said.

"Isn't there anything...?" He paused, trying to think of something that would help in her situation. He hadn't clashed much with his parents as a teenager. "Well, you could try..."

"Staying here? Adam, I don't know what to say. You've been so great, I can't believe that you'd offer for me to stay like that."

"Neither can I," Jay said from the door. Adam had not heard him come in.

"Jay. Where've you been? You want something to eat?" Adam wasn't entirely sure what had just happened, but it was obvious that Jay was severely pissed.

"There's plenty," April added. Jay didn't even turn as April said this, just glared at Adam and left. Adam trailed behind him into Jay's room.

"You're home late," Adam said.

"Terry's car broke down." Jay unbuttoned his shirt and threw it on the floor. Next, he started to undo his jeans. When he was down to just boxers, he looked up and saw that Adam was still watching him from the doorway. "I'm going to go to sleep, do you mind?" he said. Adam remained silent. "Could you at least close the fucking door?"

Adam stepped into the room and closed the door. Jay then took off the boxers and headed towards the bed.

"Would you say something, please?" Adam said quietly. Jay turned to glare at him again.

"What? What do you want me to say?" Jay asked. "I thought I made my feelings clear last night. Then I come home to find you asking her to move in with us?"

"I didn't mean to..."

"I don't care how it happened, Adam. Just get rid of her before she knifes one of us in our sleep."

"She's probably harmless," Adam said, automatically going back to defending her.

Jay stared, with his mouth open in disbelief at what he obviously thought was his friend's stupidity, then turned his back in disgust.

"Jay." Adam went over and put one hand on Jay's shoulder and one hand on his hip. "Jay..." He breathed into Jay's neck.

Jay sighed. "Just fix it, you idiot."

Adam was tempted to keep arguing his point. But then, he hadn't actually wanted April to stay any longer either so he wasn't sure what was left to argue about. Better to go kick her out like Jay wanted.

April was calmly dishing up the pasta when Adam came back into the kitchen.

"April, look, I'm not sure what—"

"Is he okay?" April interrupted.

"Huh? He has to work the night shift that's all, so he has to sleep, you know, for tonight. April, listen—"

"Did he say why he was late? I mean, you were waiting for him, right?"

"Yeah. But his ex-girlfriend..." It was then that Adam realised Jay had never told him he was going somewhere with Teresa that day. Adam hadn't thought the two of them were still friendly. Jay didn't usually stay friends with his exes. But then Jay had never stayed with any girl as long as he had with Teresa.

Adam looked out of the window and noticed his neighbour arriving home. "There goes Dan," he said.

"Who's Dan?" April asked.

"Hmm?" Adam hadn't realised he'd spoken out loud. "Oh, our neighbour. Dan. Dan, the man with the van, out for another night of passion and heartbreaking."

"What's he like?"

"I don't know. I've never talked to him. Never met him, really."

"Then how do you know where he's going?"

"Well, he's always staying out all night, and with the van..." He shrugged. "We just..."

"Made it up?"

"Yeah."

"Oh." April all but rolled her eyes. Maybe he could get rid of her by convincing her of how boring and immature he was. That would probably take a while, though, and considering Jay's already high irritability on the subject of her being there, a more direct approach would probably be better. Besides, she did seem to take any slight opening he gave her. He'd have to be clear about this.

"I'm sorry, but you can't stay here," he said. "I mean, I'm sure you'll work things out at home if you try. I think it's better that you just go ... now. Sorry."

April wasn't happy about it, but she left, so... success? He should have been glad that she accepted it without any kind of scene, yet Adam felt conflicted about sending her away. Sure, he hadn't wanted a new flatmate. What he had done, though, felt more like appeasing Jay than asserting his own wishes. He'd kind of liked April. Even if she had been a little overdramatic.

Three

JAY COULDN'T BELIEVE it when the girl showed up again the next weekend looking forlorn and friendless, asking if she could hang out with them. Then Adam actually agreed. The idiot had been feeling guilty all week about how he had treated her, like he had been too harsh on her. Jay figured it was her due. What did she expect from some guy she barely knew?

This girl was the first that Adam had brought back to the flat since they'd moved there. Jay watched her out of the corner of his eye as she sat down on the floor with her head resting on the futon between him and Adam. He was trying to figure out what Adam found so irresistible that he had to help. There was nothing remarkable about her.

But then, if the previous weekend was anything to go by, she was perfectly comfortable in pushing Adam into doing what she wanted him to, and Adam had past history with following around girls like that. He'd dated one back in Ashdon Harbor. Gabby. Ugh. Even the thought of her made Jay inwardly shudder. How he'd hated that girl and the level to which Adam had fawned over her.

"So, what are we doing tonight?" April said.

Jay bristled at the way she said "we". It was unnatural how she had latched herself on to Adam so quickly. He had helped her out once and that made him her boyfriend? Shit only worked like that for people with wiring issues in the brain.

"What do you want to do?" Adam said, like her instant clinginess was perfectly normal.

"Let's go somewhere," April replied.

"Where?"

"Anywhere... Let's go for a drive," she said. "What about you, Jay? You wanna come?"

"It's Jason. And I got plans," he replied, keeping his eyes fixed on the screen in front of him.

"You didn't say anything this afternoon," Adam said. Jay just shrugged.

"Is it with Teresa?" Adam asked.

"Why would it be with Terry?"

"I don't know. I just thought... you know, after the other day... it doesn't matter. I'll go get the car."

Jay turned back to the television until he was sure they had left, then he got up and went to the phone. He'd lied to the girl when he'd said he had plans, but he didn't like the idea of sitting around all night wondering what Adam was getting up to.

"Tam. It's Jason. You busy?"

"IT WAS JUST the prettiest little thing, wasn't it? Did you see the little book open on the little desk? And the little cake in the little oven? Jason?"

"Huh? Yeah, it was all real small."

Tammy had seen a dollhouse in a store window on the way back to the car and hadn't stopped yammering about it since. Thankfully, all the attention she needed was a vague syllable here and there because Jay's attention had not been on anything in that store window. In fact, it had not been on anything in his physical presence since he'd left he flat. He might have miscalculated in assuming that leaving the flat would distract him from thinking about Adam and his stalker.

"Oh, and the little rocking horse. Adorable."

"Last stop. Everybody out." Jay turned off the engine and opened his door.

"Oh, I was having so much fun, I didn't even realise we were almost here," she said.

Fun. It means different things to different people. In Tammy's case, it appeared to mean being with someone who just let her talk all night without interruption. He sure hadn't been giving her any more than that while his mind was elsewhere.

"Hey, your flatmate's just arriving back too," Tammy said. "Isn't that funny? Getting back at the same time?"

"Yeah."

"Is that his girlfriend? I didn't know he had a girlfriend."

"Yeah."

Jay wasn't even listening by then (he hadn't really been listening well all night). He was watching the scene unfold at his own front door. Adam had been saying something to April when she suddenly rose up onto her toes and pressed her lips to his. It had been a while since Jay had seen anyone do that. It felt weird. It shouldn't have felt weird. It hadn't felt weird when he had seen Gabby do it in high school. But then, April seemed pretty weird all by herself.

All this flashed through Jay's mind in the few seconds it took for Adam to pull away. When Adam saw Jay and Tammy approaching, the guy blushed. What was that about? Jay gave Adam a bright flash of teeth, quickly turned his key in the lock, and went inside. Tammy followed, and he shut the door firmly on the new lovebirds.

"Better hole up and hibernate before the timid creatures come in. Might disturb their mating ritual," he said.

Tammy laughed, and he led her down the hall to his room.

"That's more than you've said all night. Not much of a talker, are you?" Tammy said.

He could reply that she only allowed him space for one-word answers in between all her babbling, but it wouldn't be strictly true anyway, especially that night. It was entirely possible that she was just talking to fill the silence, and he had been offering even more silence that night than on their first date. He shouldn't have called her really, he already knew they weren't compatible, but if he convinced her to go home now, Jay would be left alone with Adam and his...girl stalker.

"Silence," he said. "We go cave. Hump nasty. Not emerge till morning."

And for the first time in Jay's life, a girl slept over.

IT WAS A new experience, waking up to a girl in his bed, and Jay wasn't sure it was one that he wanted to repeat. He was feeling restless and edgy, like he wanted to shake her awake and get her up and out of the flat as quickly as possible. This seemed kind of unfair, seeing as he'd asked her to stay so he resisted the urge and wandered out into the lounge. Adam was lying on the futon and stared up at him blearily as he went in.

"Good morning to you too," Adam grumbled as Jay pushed his feet off the futon to make room to sit.

Jay turned on the TV and started flicking through the channels, more out of a compulsion to be doing something than any real interest in the programming. This appeared to annoy Adam even more.

"Do you have to do that this early?" Adam said.

"Got something better to do?" Jay asked.

"Sleep."

"Did you sleep out here? What for?" Jay said suspiciously.

"Nothing. Just pick a channel, will you?"

"Grumpy, grumpy. Didn't Little Miss even give you a tug to ease the tension last night? Stingy."

"Piss off, Jay. It's none of your business."

"We are touchy this morning. Since when has—"

"I'll bet you were."

"What?" Jay was confused, and it wasn't often that Adam confused him.

"Morning, all," Tammy called as she drifted through into the kitchen.

"Adam, what—" Jay tried again, but Adam cut him off.

"Forget it. I'm getting some coffee." Adam got up and crossed to the kitchen. Baggy T-shirt, boxer shorts, white socks, and spiky bits of hair that stood out on only one side of his head—Adam definitely wasn't a pretty sight when woken.

Finding nothing on the telly to grab his attention and not having the energy to figure out what the hell Adam's problem was, Jay decided to have a shower. Things hadn't improved when he came back. For one thing, Tammy was still there. For another, she was talking to April. The two of them were lounging on the futon, gossiping about celebrities, looking as comfortable as if they owned the place. Jay went in, took Tammy by the arm, and led her outside away from April.

"Isn't it a bit early for the cave man routine?" she said to him.

"What were you doing?" he demanded.

"What?" she said blankly.

Jay tried to control his anger. He wasn't even sure what he was angry about, exactly, but there it was insistently bubbling under the surface.

"What were you doing?" he repeated.

"I don't know. Talking?"

"To who?"

"Your flatmate's girlfriend, April. She just came over and—"

"Why?"

"Why? I guess she wanted to see Adam."

"I meant, why the fuck were you talking to April?"

"Who was I supposed to talk to? The fridge?"

"Might have had more interesting things to say."

"Than April? She seemed—"

"Than you, that's for sure."

"Hey." Tammy's anger was starting to rise too. "I didn't hear you complaining last night."

"I wanted to fuck you last night. Probably wouldn't have made any difference if I had complained. The only time you ever shut your mouth is when I put something in it."

Tammy tried to slap him for that, but Jay caught her hand before she could. He'd never meant to say that out loud. To her. He let go of the wrist slowly, watching to see if she was going to have another go.

"Just don't talk to April again," he said, quietly.

"What the fuck is your problem? You're telling me what to do now? You're not my boyfriend," Tammy said.

Jay made a face at the term.

"You weren't even that great, for the record," Tammy continued. "After all that shit they say at work—total disappointment."

This was obviously the worst thing Tammy could think of to say. She hitched her bag on her shoulder and stomped off. Jay watched her walk down the block. He put his hand through his hair and realised it was shaking. What *was* the matter with him? He couldn't believe the way he had just flipped out at Tammy. And over what?

He took some deep breaths and went back inside. Adam was flicking through the same channels he had with the same disgust.

"Hey. Dan's van is parked in the same spot. Maybe his sleaze streak's over." Jay tried to gloss over the scene he had just made.

"Hmm. Maybe he met the girl of his dreams and is finished with his wicked ways," Adam replied.

"Maybe he met the girl of his nightmares and decided to remain celibate."

"Are you guys talking about Craig?" April said from the kitchen. "He's decided it's finally his sister's turn, now that she's back from Melbourne."

"Who's Craig?" Adam asked.

"And why would we care what he does with his sister?" Jay added.

"Your neighbour. The one with the van. I was talking with him last night, after I left. Nice guy. Goes and stays with his mum a few nights a week. She's pretty sick apparently. I reckon it must be tough to spend so much time looking after an old fogey, but he doesn't seem to mind. Although, like I said, he's sharing mum-sitting duties with his sister now. That's why he stayed home last night," April explained.

"You talked to Dan?" Jay said with horror.

"Craig."

Jay went back into his room and flopped face down onto his pillow. A pillow that smelled like Tammy. Jay groaned. It was early and already this was turning out to be a very bad day.

Jay ended up falling back to sleep. Blessed unconsciousness. All was quiet when he woke up.

He looked around warily for the girl-stalker as he walked out of his bedroom. He didn't see April anywhere, though, so he went into the kitchen for something to eat. Adam was sitting at the bench that served as their kitchen "wall" with about five textbooks propped up around him.

"So where's the little woman?" Jay asked.

"Don't know, she took off a while back," Adam replied without looking up.

"We should all be thankful for that."

Jay opened the fridge, mulling over the scarce options available. Before he could even make a sarcastic comment about Adam's shopping abilities, he found Adam pressed against his back. Jay melted into the embrace.

"You're making the mini man tired, Adam," he said.

"I wouldn't call him mini," Adam said.

"A grown man would hardly fit," Jay replied.

Adam's arms loosened around Jay's waist, and Jay turned to see the confused look on his friend's face. All this time and sometimes Jay still had to explain his jokes. But then, that was half the fun.

"Adam." Jay spoke gently as if he was explaining something to a five-year-old. "If the refrigerator had a big man to turn the light on and off, there wouldn't be any room for the food. Now move, so I can shut it before his poor mini hand drops off."

Adam rolled his eyes and stepped back, but not before grabbing onto Jay's waist, pulling the other man with him.

"Adam, I'm hungry," Jay whined.

"I'm sure I could supply something nourishing." Adam mock-leered, and Jay instantly forgave him for his grumpiness earlier. Life was so much more interesting when Adam was in a good mood.

Their lips crashed into each other, the intensity of the kiss surprising Jay a little. He had wondered if Adam's new stalker would have changed things. If she had been giving Adam this, there would be no need for Jay's attentions anymore. But the way Adam was tugging at Jay's belt showed an enthusiasm for this that Jay had not been expecting.

Maybe things hadn't gone as far between Adam and April as he'd assumed. That was a cheery thought. He started tugging at Adam's clothes as desperately as Adam was with his. Adam should be more naked. Like, immediately.

When Adam's chest was exposed, Jay ducked his head and bit Adam just low enough that any marks would be hidden by a T-shirt when he went to uni.

"Ow," Adam said. "I know I said I'd feed you, but try to leave some flesh on there."

"Want me to—"

"Do it again."

Jay grinned. Oh, yeah. He could do that. The man would be marked all over before he'd finished.

JAY HAD HIS legs up on the futon, with his feet in Adam's lap and the laptop at his fingertips. The cinema websites were not giving him any joy.

"How is it possible that there is nothing worth seeing? At all," he said.

"Maybe because you're always taking some checkout chick to grope in the dark," Adam replied.

"Aw. Would you prefer I take *you* to grope in the dark?"

"No. I would prefer to have a movie we could both agree to watch without you having already seen it."

"I could watch one of them again. It's not like I would have seen all of it anyway. You know, being distracted by—"

"I know what you were distracted by. And I know what you're like when you've already seen a movie. I'd rather listen to the movie I'm watching without your commentary track, at least the first time."

"Pfft. What do you want to do then?"

"We could stay here."

"Again."

"We could go somewhere else, like a bar or something. When was the last time we did that?"

"I don't know. A few months ago."

"Nah. I reckon it was longer. Before Teresa. What is it with you two anyway? Are you back together?"

Jay shook his head. "Terry's living in Butcherville."

"She's dating a butcher?" Adam grinned. "You'd love that."

"Any guy that plays around with his meat as much as those guys do gives us all a bad name. He probably doesn't even remember where to put it when he does get a girl. Poor thing."

"Mmm," Adam agreed, shaking his head. "Tragedy."

Jay knew Adam was laughing at him, but he didn't care. Butcher/baker rivalry was an important aspect of his working life. Shit, they had to fill their day with something at work.

"So... a bar, huh?" Jay asked. "I guess it has been a while. Why is that?"

Jay put on a pondering face, as if he couldn't quite recall. He did actually remember why they hadn't, but Adam seemed to have forgotten, which was interesting.

"Probably because you're too lazy to go out and look for women," Adam said.

"Ah, Woolworths variety," Jay said.

"You always complain about Woolworths quality." Adam nudged Jay with an elbow.

Jay grinned. "All right. I'm in. As long as you don't throw up in some chick's lap again."

Adam's face paled, and Jay could tell that now he remembered why they had sworn off bars the last time.

"Come on," Jay said. "It's about time we got out of the flat. And who knows when I'll see you with your nose out of a book again? I better take advantage of it."

"You're the one who's always working ridiculous hours," Adam replied.

"Maybe you better take advantage of me then," Jay shot back.

Jay got up and stretched, waiting for Adam to decide if he was coming or not. Well, waiting for Adam to concede to coming. Adam rarely bowed out of anything, unless he was in freak-out study mode, so Jay didn't doubt the guy would follow wherever Jay decided to go. Before Adam could reach the point of concession, though, there was a knock on the door.

Jay frowned. Not again. The stalker was back. Jay started to feel like throwing up in a girl's lap himself.

"Adam. Hi. What are you up to?" April asked.

"Jay and I were just talking about going out for a drink," Adam said.

"Oh, like a bar? That sounds like fun."

"Um, yeah."

"I'm not eighteen yet, though."

"So?" Jay said.

April looked up at Adam with one of those wide-eyed looks. Probably batted her eyelashes at him.

"Well. Maybe we could go to the movies or something," Adam said. "Jay?"

Jay snorted and turned his back on the whole scene, disappearing into his room. He wanted no part of it.

"WE'VE REALLY GOTTA stop meeting like this," April said, as she breezed into the kitchen the next morning.

Jay just kept shovelling in his cereal.

"So, how's it going?" April asked.

Jay wondered if she was always so bright and cheerful in the morning. It was nauseating.

"Good night? Peaceful?" she continued.

Jay got up to leave.

"Why don't you like me, Jay? I'm a likeable girl when you get to know me."

"It'll be over in a week," he said.

"Okay. I mean, everyone knows that high school friendships don't last forever. I'm sure you'll find someone else when Adam realises what a loser you are."

"Watch your mouth, April."

April just laughed. It grated against Jay's already tense nerves. This chick pushed all the wrong buttons for him. And she didn't seem to care in the slightest.

Jay clenched his jaw shut to avoid saying anything that would upset Adam later. Then he turned and stomped back to his room. He needed to be away from this girl. He needed her to be far away.

"Been a pleasure talking to you too," April said to his back as he left.

Four

THE FLAT ALWAYS seemed really quiet when Jay was out. He somehow filled the space much more than Adam did, even with Adam's excessive amounts of clutter. On nights when Jay was working, the place was not only empty but also cold, impersonal. Adam spent a lot of nights just waiting around for Jay.

When April turned up the next Friday night, Adam was close to delighted. Spending time with April would be way better than spending another quiet night alone. It was a guilty pleasure, though, because he knew that if Jay was there, the guy would instantly start glowering. Adam opened the door with a wide smile anyway.

"April. Hey. Come in. I just got some takeout if you want some... if you're hungry... or you want to eat..." Adam ushered April into the flat. "How're things at home?"

"Fine. So where's Jay?"

"Work, you know..." Adam shrugged. It was then that he noticed her eye. She had a nasty shiner. "April. What happened? I thought you said things were okay."

Adam moved closer, and April used the opportunity to lay her head on his chest. She started shaking slightly, as if she was crying but trying not to show it. Adam put his arms around her and awkwardly patted her back.

"April, what happened?" he asked again.

"It's so awful there. I can't stand it. It's like I'm under surveillance twenty-four hours a day. And nothing I ever do is okay with him." She sobbed, clutching at his shirt.

"Your stepfather did this?"

April nodded.

"It's all right, April. You're here now. No one's going to hurt you."

God, that was a stupid thing to say. What could he do to protect her? But it felt like the right thing and she seemed to appreciate it. Adam wished he could do more for her.

"Do you want to stay here tonight?" he asked.

"No. It's okay. I just had to get out of there for a while. Let him calm down. Hell, let me calm down." She tried to laugh, but it came out shaky.

"Really, April. I think you should stay. I'll even sleep out here on the futon again if that will make you feel more comfortable."

"What about Jay?"

"He'll have to deal with it."

THE FIRST SIGN that Jay was home was two hands roughly shaking Adam awake.

"She's here again, isn't she?" Jay hissed.

The arms holding Adam shook him some more, and he opened his eyes enough to see a blurry figure in the dimness.

"Jay? What the hell?" Adam said. "I was asleep."

He tried to rub his eyes, but Jay still had a hold of his arms and shook him one more time.

"She's here," Jay repeated, still in that hissing whisper.

"April? Yeah, she—"

"Goddammit, Adam. What's a matter with you? Are you so desperate for a girlfriend that anyone with the right genitalia will do? It's not even about you for her. You just happened to be the idiot that stumbled into her path. Can't you see that?"

Adam was still half-asleep and was having trouble following Jay's logic, if he had any. It had taken this long for him to realize that Jay was whispering so that April wouldn't hear them.

He lowered his voice as well. "What are you talking about?"

"She's using you. She's looking for a sucker, and you're perfect. You let everyone push you around," Jay whispered.

"No, I don't. April's really nice..."

"You hardly know the girl."

"She's going through some bad times. Give her a break."

"Bad times? We've all had bad times."

"It's not the same. You didn't see her eye. Did you know he actually hit her, the stepfather?" Adam said, trying to convey the enormity of the situation with his voice.

"She probably hit herself in the eye to make you feel sorry for her."

"That's ridiculous."

"Yeah, well... Forget it, I know the drill. You won't listen until it all blows up in your face anyway."

"What's that supposed to mean?" Adam asked.

"It means that I know the drill. You have poor concentration skills, Adam, so when you get a girlfriend it's 'bye, Jay, thanks for playing'."

"I don't do that."

"Yeah. You do. I spent almost a year as third wheel to you and Gabby. I know what it feels like."

"April's not my girlfriend anyway."

Jay shook his head. "She's sleeping in your bed, cooking you dinner, coming to you with her problems, and taking it for granted that you'll spend Saturday night with her. Sounds like a girlfriend to me."

"But..."

"It's gonna end badly, Adam. I give it a few months, tops."

Adam rolled his eyes and lay back down on the futon. It was no use talking to Jay when he got like that.

Five

IT HAD BEEN a few months since they'd met, and to Jay's eternal annoyance, Adam and April were still together. She often spent the night, and Adam found that he enjoyed having her around. Jay, on the other hand, couldn't stand to be in the same room with her. Usually he just disappeared when she showed up, but for some reason, Jay had decided to stick around that night. Adam wished he hadn't.

They were all sitting in the lounge watching some boring movie about a kid whose parents were getting a divorce. Adam had spent the entire time waiting for the comments to start. Jay was never good at keeping quiet during movies that he didn't like and anything to do with family break-ups was always a trigger-point for him, so this one should have been a bitch-fest from the beginning. When the snide remarks came, the only surprise was that it had taken so long. And when April took the opposite side, that was no surprise either. She grabbed any opportunity to disagree with Jay. In truth, she probably secretly hated the movie too. Adam sure did. It had been the only movie on TV that all three of them hadn't seen or he would never had put it on.

"Why doesn't he just get over himself already?" Jay said, referring to the main character in the film. "His father's never coming back."

"How do you know?" April replied.

"The dad was a jerk from the start. They'd be better off without him anyway."

"Maybe he loved them. You have heard of that, haven't you, Jason? Love."

"Yeah. I heard about it. Just like I heard of the Easter Bunny and Father Christmas."

"Somebody obviously got coal in their stocking."

"Why are we even watching this crap?"

"*We* never asked you to. And I like it."

"Why don't we just watch something else," Adam said.

"No, I want to see the end," April replied.

"Why, April? Because you're mad at your daddy too? Do we get to hear you go on and on about how he abandoned you when the movie ends?" Jay taunted.

"Way I hear it, I'm not the one who's mad at my daddy." April smiled as Jay shot a hurt look at Adam.

Awesome. No doubt Adam was going to get another lecture about not talking about Jay to anyone, especially his freak of a girlfriend. Jay's words, not his. He had heard them enough in the past few months to know them by heart. That's why he didn't get up when Jay stormed out of the room. It all just made him tired.

"April, you shouldn't have..." he attempted half-heartedly.

"What? My father left, and I don't get all sensitive about it. I don't have topics that aren't up for discussion."

"You never talk about your family. Not really."

"Shh. I want to hear this." April pretended to be absorbed in the movie, or maybe she did have an actual interest. Adam let the subject drop.

He sent her home not long after, though, saying he had an assignment to finish, which was true. He was also tired of the whole situation. He liked April. He really did. But her presence was making his home life pretty miserable.

ADAM WAS STILL editing his assignment when April got back to the flat the next day. She flipped through a magazine on the bed while he fiddled with last minute changes. He'd told her "ten more minutes". It might have been slightly longer.

"Ha," he declared, smiling and leaning back in his chair.

"What are you so happy about?" April asked.

"It's finally done. The last assignment."

"You've finished your degree?" April asked, surprised.

"No. The subject."

"One subject? How many do you have?"

"Don't laugh," Adam said. She was. "This one was really hard. Well, not hard exactly, just kind of time-consuming, with lots of little extra assignments and stuff."

"It's not like anything would be that hard for someone as clever as you," April said. "It wouldn't even be a challenge."

"Uni's mostly organisation, once you've got that..." Adam trailed off when he finally caught her tone and realised she was teasing him.

"Smart guys are sooo sexy," she breathed as she kissed him. He was the one to pull away first.

"Let's do something to celebrate. We'll go to footy training," April said with enthusiasm.

"Footy training? How is that celebrating?" he asked.

"You said you never missed a game at Ashdon Harbor." She gave him a pleading look. "It'll be fun. Promise."

"All right. Just let me upload the document and turn everything off."

Adam wasn't sure why April was so excited about football training—if she was just glad to get out of the house, glad to get him out of the house, or anxious to see a bunch of guys running around in their shorts. He also wondered if she would have been less enthusiastic if she had known he'd gone to every game in Ash because Jay was on the team. He had been to a lot of practices back then.

After sending through his assignment, Adam discovered that April had wandered off on him. He shut the computer down and went to search for her. Instead, he found Jay in front of the television.

There had been tension between them ever since he'd started dating April, and it was beginning to wear him down. Adam hated arguments. Especially the we'll-just-be-quiet-and-pretend-it-never-happened kind. His parents used that one all the time. As a kid, he'd always been fearful about triggering one of their not-an-argument arguments.

"What are you watching?" he asked.

Jay shrugged and mumbled something uninformative.

"I was reading this article the other day. It said that Australians tend to mumble a lot."

"No kidding. Must have been some article," Jay said.

"So, what are you watching?" Adam asked again.

"Didn't we have this conversation already?"

"Yeah, but you mumbled and I—"

"Jesus, I don't know."

"Don't know what?"

"What this crap is." Jay gestured towards the television. "That's what I 'mumbled'. I don't know."

"Might help if you had the sound up a bit."

"No, I don't think it would."

"You wanna come with us to—"

"No."

"I didn't say where we were—"

"No."

"Well, maybe we could do something together tomorrow, just you and me."

"Don't put yourself out."

"Look, Jay, in case it wasn't immediately obvious, this situation has been—"

"What situation?"

"Us. How we've been. Barely speaking half the time and sniping at each other when we do. I don't... I don't like it. I want to make things right."

"You're doing a shit job so far."

"Well, how should I be doing it?" Adam said, exasperated.

Jay turned. He studied Adam from head to toe, opened his mouth...

"What's holding you up, Braybrain?" April chose that moment to drag him out to the car, and Adam didn't get Jay's answer.

"YOU DIDN'T TELL me you knew the entire team," Adam said as yet another player waved and yelled, "Hey, April."

"Didn't you know all the players in Ashdon?"

"Yeah, but—"

"Hi, April. Come to watch practice?" A middle-aged woman sat down on the opposite side of April in the stand.

"No, Aunt Kay, freezing our butts off on hard benches is just great foreplay," April said. Adam was fairly sure that she'd said it only to make him blush.

"So, we finally get to meet one of your friends?" Aunt Kay leaned over and spoke to Adam. "Kay Williams. I work at the bar." She indicated over towards the clubrooms.

"Don't you have work to do?" April said.

"April..." Adam started, but Kay just laughed.

"I do, actually. Don't forget to come in and say hello before you take off. We can have a chat. Steve would love to see you," Kay said, then she got up and disappeared as quickly as she had appeared.

"Who's Steve?" Adam asked.

"Number twenty-three," April replied. "Look at him. Talk about pathetic. Don't know how he gets a game every week."

"What I meant was—"

"Who was the best player in Ashdon?"

"I don't know. Not really a sport expert."

"What are you an expert on, Adam Pearson?" She narrowed her eyes at him. "Where is all this study taking you?"

"Back to Ash."

"Back to where you started from? What kind of adventure is that?"

"That is the formula. You go out, have an adventure, then go back home."

April made a face. "When I get out of here, I'm never coming back."

"What's wrong with Adelaide?"

"Probably nothing to someone who prefers Ashdon Harbor to any other place in the world. Seriously, if you could go anywhere, live anywhere..."

"It'd be Ashdon. It's my home."

"That is so boring."

"Where would you go?"

"Anywhere. Everywhere. Sydney. New York. Paris. Somewhere big, and not here."

"Okay. If I could really go anywhere?"

"Anywhere at all." April waited expectantly.

"Canberra."

"Hopeless."

"No, really. The National Library's in Canberra. They have this program for graduates... I'd never get in anyway. But that's like the top place in Australia. The best of the best."

"You sound like you're recruiting for the army." April laughed. "You should apply, though. If it's your dream."

"It's not a dream. You said anywhere, that's all. Wow. Number twenty-three really is bad, huh?"

"Hopeless," April said, not taking her eyes off Adam.

BY THE TIME Adam and April got down out of the stands after practice and headed towards the clubrooms, one of the players was already there waiting for April. It was number twenty-three. Adam wouldn't have recognised him out of uniform except that April had been pointing him out constantly.

"April, hey. Haven't seen you at practice lately," number twenty-three said.

"Yeah. Busy," she said as they headed into the bar.

"Going to introduce me to your mystery boyfriend?"

April rolled her eyes. "Steve, this is Adam. Adam, this is Steve. Steve's my aunt's adopted son."

"Hi S—"

"You could have just said I was your cousin."

"But you're not."

"I saw you out on the field. You guys seemed—" Adam started.

"Don't encourage him." April cut him off as she reached her aunt at the bar. "Aunt Kay, can I get a Diet Coke?"

"Sure, hun. It's good to see you. Did I mention that before? You haven't come round much lately," the woman said.

"Busy."

"Obviously," she said, looking at Adam. "Can I get you anything, sport?"

"Um, no thanks," Adam said. The woman's attention had moved back to April before he'd even gotten the words out.

"I ran into Henry the other day," she said. "Sounds like your mum is having a hard time. Do you think—"

"What was that, Aunt Kay?" April said as the rest of the football players came in and started shouting. Soon they all surrounded April and were asking if she was coming to the game on Sunday.

Adam felt like a tenth wheel. He kept moving back to let someone else who wanted to talk to April get through until eventually he wound up alone in a corner. He'd just sat down at a table when Not-Cousin Steve found him.

"Beer?" Steve said.

"No. I don't really drink," Adam said.

"So what do you do? Apart from take advantage of school girls."

"I'm sorry...?"

"Look." Steve pointed to where April was talking to about five of his teammates. "She's like a sister to all of them. Do you know what that means?"

"Um..."

"Hurt her and we hurt you."

"Huh."

"Get it?"

"Yeah. Sure."

"Good," Steve said and strode over to another table.

Adam had only known the guy for two minutes and he was the drop-kick boyfriend already? Or did he say that to all April's boyfriends? Had April's other boyfriends been drop-kicks?

Adam was starting to get a headache. He wished he had brought a book with him. Then he could look at it instead of seeing the way the other men were looking at him. Or maybe he could have hidden behind it so they couldn't look at him. He did have that Info Sci chapter to read too. He really should have brought the book with him.

"What are you doing over here in the corner, sadsack?" April must have noticed that he wasn't with her.

"Getting daggers from your not-cousin."

"Don't worry about him. Warren has offered to buy you a drink. Haven't you, Warren?" April poked the young man standing next to her.

"Huh? Yeah. You want a beer or something?"

"That's okay. I'm not much of a drinker."

"I could get you a Coke maybe," Warren persisted.

"No, you can't. Adam, come on, live a little. Have a drink." April tried giving him puppy dog eyes.

"I have to drive, April."

"You can still have one drink. You would if you were with Jay."

"One."

Adam's memory started to get slightly blurry not long after that. He remembered Steve giving them a lift home. He also remembered throwing up in Steve's car, which shouldn't have given him as much satisfaction as it did. He hoped it had been after they'd dropped April off. He wasn't sure.

He remembered Jay laughing at him when he finally got home and Steve had to help him through the door. It was nice to see Jay laugh, though it would have been better if it hadn't been *at* him. He was pretty sure he hadn't been intentionally funny.

Jay had helped him get undressed and lie down. It felt good to have Jay's hands on him again. Oh shit. Adam jerked upright in bed, fully awake. Then yelped at the pain in his head. The noise caught the attention of Jay, who ambled into the room.

"Awake then? Not like you to sleep in," Jay said.

"It was you last night, right?" Adam managed to croak.

"What was?" Jay asked. Adam gestured to himself and the bed. "Have my wicked way with you? Nah, wasn't me. You should really stop bringing strange guys home if you're not gonna remember it in the morning. Seems like a waste."

Adam glowered at him.

"Yeah, Adam, I put you to bed. That guy was disgusted just having to get you through the door. Who was he anyway?"

"April's not-cousin."

"Not…" Jay shook his head. "Never mind, I don't want to know." Then he left Adam to his hangover.

Definitely not the best idea, going to training.

Six

JAY SWORE AND pulled his scorched hand away from the hot tray. It had been one of those mornings.

"What's wrong with you? You've burned yourself more times this week than I have the whole time I've been here." Terry came over to look at his hand. "Run some water over it."

"I'm all right."

"Stop being such a male."

She jammed his hand under the cold tap and held him still. The sting in his hand subsided, but Jay knew it would come back when he took it away from the water. He should have been more careful. He usually *was* more careful.

"It's almost break time anyway," Terry said.

"No it's not."

"Be a rebel."

She took his hand out from under the tap and led him outside. Jay didn't offer any resistance. She was leading him away from work, after all.

When they got outside, Terry let go of his hand. Jay sat down on a crate, staring at the ground and ignoring the sting that was coming back. Out of the corner of his eye, he watched Terry as she paced a semicircle in front of him.

"Come on, out with it," she said.

"What?" Jay didn't bother looking up.

"Don't try and act innocent, Porter. I know you, you don't do innocent. There's something wrong. I've seen more of you the last few weeks than I did when we were going out, you've been totally distracted at work—well, more than usual—and no one knows who you're dating. So what is it? Some rare form of cancer eating at you? You actually dating someone outside of Woolworths? Don't tell me that girl from the checkouts broke your heart. I gotta say, I didn't think she'd be the one to do it."

"No. No. And no," Jay said.

"She sure does seem to hate you. It's not all those stories she's been trying to tell people that's bothering you, is it? No one believes them."

Jay shook his head. Tammy had been pissed, justifiably so. His behaviour towards her on their last date had been shameful. When she'd started telling the stories of what a jerk he was, Jay hadn't defended himself. Telling the truth obviously hadn't been getting her the sympathy that she'd wanted, though, because the more time that passed, the less any of the stories resembled anything that actually happened. As Terry said, no one believed them, so if it made her feel better, Tammy could say whatever the hell she wanted.

Terry squatted down in front of him and placed her hands on his knees.

"Are you really sick?" she asked.

"No. I'm fine. Little tired."

"Run-down." She tilted his head up and felt his forehead. "Maybe you should see a doctor."

"I'm fine. It's not physical."

"Then what is it? Talk to me. Maybe I can help. You've spent enough time listening to my troubles lately."

"Not that the butcher-related soap opera isn't interesting in itself," Jay said. Terry kept staring at him with a concerned look on her face, like he'd been mauled by a koala or something. "It's just... I feel... I feel like I really don't want to talk about it."

"Well, whatever it is, you're going to have to do something about it soon, sweetie, because you really look like shit."

"Thanks." Jay rolled his eyes. Terry just smiled and stood to go back inside. "Terry?"

"Yeah?"

"Why did we break up?"

"Seriously?"

"Seriously."

"Wow. She must have broken your heart..." She shrugged. "The relationship just wasn't going anywhere."

"And it is with butcher-boy?"

"I don't know. Maybe. At least there's hope it might."

"Meaning what? What did he say? In a couple of years, I'll weigh up our options, and if I can't find anything better, I'll marry you?"

"You're such a prick, you know that. At least he didn't say he never wanted a relationship. What did you think we were in, Jason?"

"I was honest. You know that's all he wants from you. If he thought he could get it without the relationship, he'd try. He's just too fucking ugly. So he lies and says he loves cuddles and long walks on the beach, really wondering how long it's gonna take to get laid."

"So?"

"So? You'd rather have an obvious lie than the truth."

"Sometimes the truth is too painful," Terry said.

There was silence, then their boss, Gary, stuck his head out the door next to them.

"You two have already had your break. Back inside. You can argue on your own time," he said.

He didn't wait for them to act on his order, just dropped it and went back inside. He knew they'd follow him. Not with any enthusiasm and certainly not with any urgency, but they would.

"Terry?"

"Mmm?"

"Just so you know... with you, it was the closest I've come to actually wanting it to work."

She smiled and looked even more worried. Jay briefly considered taking off, going home. Then he sighed and got up. He had a shift to finish.

"HI, JULES. MUM home?" Jay said into the phone.

"Nah. I'll tell her you called."

"How're things there?" Jay waited as his sister considered the motives for his sudden interest.

"Same as. How's the Big?" she said.

"Yeah. Fine."

"Jase, you okay?"

Great. He was starting to get the worried tone from his sister as well.

"Yeah," he replied. "I was just wondering whether you guys would be home on Sunday. Thought I might come up."

"Why?"

"To see my family. Is that a crime?" Jay asked. There was another pause as Julie considered her words.

"Mum'll be happy to see you," she said.

"Yeah."

"Jase..."

"What?"

"I guess I'll see you on Sunday."

"Yeah."

Jay disconnected the call and sat looking at the phone in his hand, no energy to do anything else. He was twenty years old and he wanted his mummy. What a loser. But he'd been so miserable lately. He didn't know why he thought seeing their faces would help, but somehow he knew it would. It's not like he had to get all mushy on them once he got up there.

"Hey," Adam said, walking into the room. "Whatta you doin'?"

"Nothing."

"Okay. Well, while you're doing nothing..." Adam trailed off as he sat on the futon next to Jay.

"What?"

"I don't know. I just wanted to say... I'm sorry if I haven't been around much."

"You apologise too much."

"That's what April says."

"How observant of her." Jay closed his eyes and leaned his head back on the futon.

"Come on, Jay. Do we really have to have this fight all the time?"

"Is it Tuesday already? You usually remember my existence around Tuesday."

"Don't be a dick. I just wanted to hang out. You're my best friend, and we hardly spend any time together anymore. It shouldn't be like that."

"Maybe if you didn't spend every waking moment with Little Miss Obnoxious..." Jay lost track of what he was saying as Adam ran a hand down his chest.

"She's not here now," Adam said.

Jay could hear the suggestion in the other man's voice, but he didn't open his eyes or move away as Adam's lips met his. And Jay tried very hard not to think about what Adam had been doing the last few days, or more precisely, who. Everything would be back to normal as soon as Adam got bored with his new toy. That's what Jay kept telling himself.

Yet, that constant annoyance at her existence wouldn't go away, even with Adam's tongue in his mouth. The guy wanted to play, and Jay would normally be more than willing. Hell, Jay was normally the one initiating. But this time, he couldn't muster up any enthusiasm. And it pissed him off. Why should he let her affect his life at all? She was nothing to him.

Jay shoved Adam off the futon and onto the floor, pushing any lingering thoughts of the girl-stalker out as well. She was not there. But Adam was. And it wasn't like she had contaminated him or anything. Adam was still Adam, same as always.

At that moment, Adam was sprawled out across the floor, looking confused, unsure if Jay had just pushed him away or if it was part of the game. Jay followed him down and resumed the kiss with determined vigour. Trying to convince Adam that things were still okay with them. That this was still okay. It was going to happen because he wanted it to happen and Adam wanted it to happen and fuck anyone else.

Jay couldn't relax into it, though. No matter what Adam gave him, he felt frustrated and impatient and it all came through in his reactions. There was none of the usual playfulness that had characterised these encounters in the past. Touches became grabs, kisses became scrapes of teeth against flesh, teasing became tight-fisted grips. Adam soon caught the mood too. Everything between them became hard and fast and rough.

It wasn't about getting off. Jay was just proving... he wasn't even sure what he was trying to prove. Or who he was trying to prove it to. But whatever it was, it wasn't working.

Seven

JAY WAS HUMMING along to the radio. Some silly, catchy pop tune. Adam could always tell Jay's mood by the kind of song he was listening to. Death metal meant time to take a long walk away from the flat.

When Jay noticed Adam standing there, he grinned.

"You'll be happy to know that I've finally given in to all your pleading," Jay said.

"Hmm?"

"That means I'm coming with you today."

"Oh."

Adam had been asking Jay to come with him to Ashdon Harbor for months. Any other week, he would have grinned along and joked that it was about time Jay went. Not that day, though.

"What's the deal? I thought you wanted me to go," Jay said.

"I do. It's just that..."

Jay tilted his head, waiting for Adam to explain his sudden reluctance.

"I kind of already have someone coming with me today. April," Adam explained.

"April's going? Why would you take her to Ashdon?"

"Company? It's not like you've been jumping up and down about going lately."

"I'm going today."

"Which you told me about five seconds ago. What do you want me to do, Jay, call her and tell her I've changed my mind, she can't come?"

"Yeah." Jay pronounced it like *duh*.

Adam just rolled his eyes and turned away.

"She asked to come, didn't she?" Jay said.

"So?"

"Typical."

Adam turned back.

"What's that supposed to mean?" he asked.

"You do every little thing she asks you to do. It's pitiful. Are you really that whipped?"

"It's not like that. She's my girlfriend. Why wouldn't I want to do stuff with her?"

"Your girlfriend," Jay said, voice dripping with contempt. "Some girl bats her eyelashes at you and you're following her around like a damn puppy."

"I don't do that."

"Yes, you do. Hello. Gabby. It was exactly the same."

"It was not the same."

"It feels the same."

Adam sighed. He didn't know how many more times he could have the same argument with Jay. "Are you really coming this time?" he asked.

Jay shrugged. "I told Julie I would."

"Then come. How bad do you think a few hours in a car with April will be?"

Jay raised his eyebrows.

"You'll survive," Adam said.

There was a knock on the front door. April. Brilliant timing. Adam went over and opened the door, one eye on Jay to check how he was coping with the news of April's presence.

"Hey, April. Jay's coming with us today," Adam said before Jay could slink off to his room to sulk and get out of it.

"Why?" she asked, screwing her nose up at the idea.

"Purely to irritate you, April," Jay said.

"Jay didn't know you were coming until now," Adam clarified. "He's going to visit his family in Ashdon."

"He's got his own car. Why can't he just go on his own?" April whined.

"We have to go right past his mum's place anyway. It's not a big thing to drop him off," Adam said. "It wouldn't make sense to take two cars and waste the petrol."

"Guess you're stuck with me, Little Miss," Jay said as if he hadn't just been arguing with Adam about the exact same damn thing. Adam clenched his jaw shut to avoid pointing this out.

"Little Miss? What's that supposed to mean?" April asked Adam.

"Who knows?" Adam hesitated, then said it anyway. "It's a long drive and a small car. I'd rather not have you two sniping at each other all the way up there. Could you both reel it in a bit?"

"Just on the way up? What about on the way back? We can hate each other all we want on the way back, right?" Jay said.

"That's not helpful," Adam replied.

Jay grinned. Adam could never stay mad at Jay when he flashed that goofy grin. And he sure deserved it sometimes. When Adam turned back to April, the ghost of a smile was starting to play around the edges of his mouth. Her scowl quickly wiped that almost-smile off his face, though.

"April, would it hurt you to be polite, at least?" he said. "For me?"

"Whatever," April said.

Adam was going to take that as a win. It was probably as good as he was going to get out of either of them.

APRIL SCOWLED AT the fuzz that had been the radio a few seconds before.

"The signal's too weak to get this far, that's all," Adam reassured her. "Happens every time." This comment didn't seem to lessen April's displeasure.

"Can't we get anything else?" she whined.

"Our company not good enough for you, Little Miss?" Jay said.

"As a matter of fact—"

"What do you think so far, April?" Adam interrupted. "I love it out here, away from the city. The drive always makes me feel better."

April looked out her window.

"Quiet," she said.

"Exactly." Adam smiled at her.

A few minutes later, April sighed.

"I'm sorry," Adam said. "I'm not real good company, I guess, am I? Used to making the trip alone. Sometimes Jay would come, but not so much now."

"How about a car game?" Jay said.

April rolled her eyes, but Adam responded with enthusiasm. He would take anything to keep the two of them distracted.

"A car game?" April said. "Like what?"

"I don't know." Adam went quiet, thinking. "What about cloud shapes?"

"That's not a car game," Jay said.

"Doesn't matter."

"What's cloud shapes?" April asked.

"You know, where you look at the clouds and tell what shapes you can see in them," Adam said. "I can see a hippo. You see it? In front."

"Sure," April said, without looking.

"What can you see, April?" Adam asked.

She looked around but said nothing.

"I got one. Over this side," Jay said, pointing. "I see a skinny guy puking his guts out after a night out."

"Gross," April said.

Adam looked where Jay had pointed and saw a cloud that did look a little like a face if you squinted the right way. Next to it was a smaller, pink-tinged cloud.

He pressed a button on the radio and waited, gripping the wheel, as it skipped through the stations trying to find a signal, any signal. It eventually landed on a classical music station. He listened for a few seconds, then grinned.

"Jay, do you remember this?" he said. "It was in that movie. Remember? We saw it at TTP, and those stupid girls behind us were giggling the whole time because we were..." He stopped in mid-sentence.

"I don't remember," Jay said blandly.

Adam leaned over and changed the station again. Silence descended as he searched.

"AHH. HOME, SWEET home," Jay said finally.

They had reached Jay's mother's house. It was a small well-worn blocky structure, but it felt more like home to Adam than where he would be taking April later. Jay's teenage sister, Julie, came out to greet them.

"Hey, Adam. I guess this is April," Julie said.

"Yeah," Adam replied. "April, this is Julie, Jay's sister."

"I didn't know Jason had a sister," April said.

"That's okay, I don't usually tell people he's my brother either," Julie said.

"They already know, Sis," Jay said. His sister peered at him.

"Jase?" she said in mock surprise. "I'd almost forgotten what you looked like. Lucky you came with Adam, or I wouldn't have let you in the house."

"It hasn't been that long," Jay said. "I'm going inside—maybe someone in there will appreciate me."

"I doubt it. I don't think that Joe's the appreciative type, even of prodigal sons."

"Joe? I thought it was Stan."

"God, Stan was like, February. Keep up, Jase." His sister grinned as Jay put his arm around her and they both went inside. "You coming?" Julie called over her shoulder.

Adam looked questioningly at April. She shrugged, and they followed. The front door opened into a lounge room containing a grubby man in an armchair, holding a beer and snoring in front of a television. He did not look up as they walked through to the kitchen.

"Well. Where the hell is she?" Jay asked. Julie rolled her eyes and stuck her head out the screen door at the back of the room.

"Mum, your idiot son is here," she called.

"You're sharp today, kiddo. Been practicing on the comatose?" Jay indicated the lounge room.

"Not as much fun when they have an IQ of a snail."

"Must make you miss Patrick. He was almost a slug."

Jay's mother walked in at that point. She was wiping her hands on the front of her shirt, which didn't make them any cleaner as the shirt was already about 90 percent dirt where she must have done it before. Then she hugged her son like she hadn't seen him in years. It hadn't quite been that long. More like months.

"Jason. Let me look at you. Have you been eating?" she asked.

"Better than I did here." Jay grinned as his mother pretended to slap him on the arm.

"And what about you, Adam? Keeping my boy out of trouble?"

"As much as I can, Mrs Porter," Adam replied.

She rolled her eyes and looked at her son. "Twenty years old and still calling me Mrs Porter. I swear this boy will be calling me that at eighty."

"If we're still friends by then," Jay muttered. Everyone stared at him.

"This is Adam's girlfriend," Julie said awkwardly, pointing to April.

"Well, hello, Adam's girlfriend." Jay's mother gave April a bright smile and went to shake her hand. April hesitated, looking down at the dirt caked on the woman's hands. Mrs Porter wiped them on the back of her jeans and took both of April's hands in hers. "It's a pleasure to meet you..."

"April."

"Oh, that's pretty. How long have you known these two hoodlums?"

"Almost four months."

"And off to meet the Pearsons? Must be getting serious." She winked at Adam and he blushed. Jay chose that moment to knock the water jug off the table.

"Shit," he said, and that time his mother did gently slap him.

"Mind your language and clean it up," she said. "And where are my manners? You kids want a drink?" She took a dusty glass off the cupboard, looked inside, and absently rubbed the inside with the aforementioned dirt-shirt, all the while still talking. "What would you like? We got juice. We got milk. We got lemonade."

"I'm fine," April said, eyeing the glass.

"Anything you want. Except water." Mrs Porter laughed.

"Juice would be nice," Adam said.

"But Adam, we don't want to be late," April said.

"We won't—"

"That's okay. Go on. First impressions count," Jay's mother said.

"Thanks, Mrs Porter. I guess we'll see you later then."

"Of course. You've never been a stranger. Not like some." She turned to Jay. "No, don't use that to wipe it up."

Mrs Porter was distracted by Jay's inefficient attempt to mop up all the water he'd knocked over. April used the opportunity to chirp a quick "bye" and drag Adam out. Julie followed them and snagged Adam's wrist before they got to the front door, extricating him from April's grasp. He paused in the doorway, letting April go on ahead to the car.

"What's with Jase?" Julie whispered.

"What do you mean?" Adam said.

"He seemed really weird on the phone. Has something happened?"

"No. I don't think so. He has been pretty quiet lately, but he was in a good mood this morning. Looking forward to seeing you."

"See, that right there. Since when does Jase look forward to coming up here?"

Adam shrugged. April was leaning on the car, looking at him meaningfully, so he had to go.

"If there is something wrong, maybe he'll tell you today," he said and hurried out.

"What was that all about?" April asked when Adam caught up with her.

"I could ask you the same thing. We wouldn't have been late."

April just shrugged and got in the car. Adam got in the other side and started it up, but he couldn't let her behaviour go.

"The Porters are good people," he said. "They've always been good to me. This was my second home growing up."

"They seemed nice," April said.

"They are nice."

"Kind of makes you wonder where Jay gets all his moodiness from."

"God, April, will you give it a rest? Jay is the most loyal and generous friend I've ever had. You just don't know him like I do."

"Whose fault is that?"

Adam didn't answer, just pulled the car away from the Porter house. It was true that Jay had been at his most prickly of late. Ever since April had shown up. Adam sometimes missed the light-hearted Jay who would joke him out of his moods.

"COULD YOU PASS the gravy please, Adam?"

That was pretty much as far as the conversation had gone through lunch. Adam was used to it, but he wasn't sure how April was coping. Sitting down in the living room afterwards, conversation would be more necessary. Without the excuse of eating, Adam figured his parents would have to fill the silence with something. It's not like he came down here every weekend to be ignored. Although, often all he got was a one-sided news swapping where he stumbled to find things that he'd done that week. Then he usually made his way over to the Porters. He didn't think the Porters would be an option that day.

"Do you go to the university, April?" Adam's mother asked.

"No, I... um... I don't go to uni. University," April stammered. It amused Adam to see the confident girl so nervous around his parents.

"April's still in high school," he said.

"Finishing up this year," April added.

"What are your plans for next year?" asked Adam's father.

"Well … I'm not sure." April looked over at Adam. He guessed she was looking for help, but he wasn't sure what she wanted him to do. They'd never discussed her future. They'd never really discussed anything important.

"She's still considering her options," he said. "Whatever she chooses, she'll be studying for at least three years so she wants to get it right."

"Adam's done very well at his university. Maybe he could help you decide," said his mother.

"Maybe. But I don't think I'm going to apply to that university. I've been looking into some interstate. Sydney mostly. Although I did look up one in Canberra the other day." April smiled at Adam, but he just gaped. Interstate? This was the first he'd heard of it.

"But I thought…" Adam's mother started. "Well, Adam's never brought anyone here since he went to the city. I thought things were…"

"Bringing her doesn't mean we're getting married or anything, Ma," Adam said.

"It seems strange to bring her all this way if you knew she'd be leaving in a few months," his father said.

"She wanted to come," Adam said.

"I figured Adam might want to come with me actually." April had no idea what she had just done.

"To Sydney?" Adam's mother seemed aghast.

"Or Canberra. Well, it's not like Adelaide's the centre of excitement, is it? I figured I might be able to convince him. Especially if he gets the position in Canberra."

"Canberra?" Adam's father said it like he had never heard of the place.

"Yeah. The National Library. The Dream Job. You know."

There was total silence. They didn't know.

"I'll go and get the cake," Adam's mother said absently, wandering out of the room. Adam got up and followed her, leaving April with his father, for once not even considering her feelings.

"Ma…"

"It's all right, Adam."

"No, it's not."

"You know we love you. We'd never hold you back. If it's your dream to—"

"It's not. The plan has always been to come back to Ashdon."

"But there's nothing here for young people. If Adelaide isn't exciting, well, Ashdon..."

"You should follow your heart," his father said behind them, surprising Adam, who'd thought he was still with April.

"My heart's not in Canberra. It's here, where it's always been." Adam put his arms around his mother. "I've never been a city boy anyway, that's what you always said. April just doesn't understand."

He sighed, because he didn't know if he could make her understand. A part of him thought if April wanted to go, his life would probably be simpler without her.

HALFWAY THROUGH THE drive to the Porters' from his parents' house, Adam pulled over and stopped the car. The afternoon really hadn't gotten any better after April's little announcement. His parents didn't seem to like April very much, and at that moment, Adam wasn't sure he did either.

"I guess this is where you yell at me," April said.

"What makes you think I'm going to yell at you?" Adam asked quietly.

"Let's see. There were the angry glares at your parents' place, the frowning silence in the car, and, oh yeah, the fact that you pulled over in the middle of friggin' nowhere. What did I do to upset you so much?"

Adam turned to face her. "What did you do? April, you never even told me you were considering going interstate next year. Why would you start talking about it today? To my parents?"

"I did tell you. I told you that I'm not sticking around any longer than I have to. And why does the word 'interstate' make everyone gasp in horror? You said you wanted to go to Canberra—"

"That is not what I said. I could never live there."

"Sure you could. You just need to have some confidence—"

"You don't get it. You have no idea what you just did."

"What? Adam, that's what I'm asking. What's the big deal? I was just talking."

"My parents, they never thought they could have kids. I'm like their miracle. You just told them that you want to take that away. It was hard enough on my mum when I moved to Adelaide. How often would I see her from Canberra?"

"So you were seriously just going to come back here to—"

"Yes, I am."

"But you could do so much better than that. You shouldn't let them stop you from doing what you want."

"Ashdon *is* what I want, April."

"It's not what I want."

Adam had nothing to say to that.

Eight

"I WAS JUST pulling up some weeds. Don't suppose you'd want to help?"

"Don't suppose," Jay told his mother.

"All right. I haven't got lunch ready yet so why don't you... Have you met Joe?"

"Passed him. Passed out."

"Oh, well, Julia will have to entertain you for a while." She pulled him into another embrace. "I am glad to see you, Jason."

She smiled and went to the bathroom to wash up before she got too emotional. They weren't that kind of family.

Julie had wandered off to say goodbye to Adam, so Jay went and sat on her bed to wait for her. For all their talk of his absence, nothing had changed all that much since he'd been gone. Julie changed the posters on her walls as often as their mum changed the man in the living room. But, just like the man in the living room, the men in the posters all looked the same to Jay.

Julie must have been doing homework when he'd arrived because her books were open on the floor with a pen lying on top. Jay started flipping through one of the books, grimacing at the contents. It all seemed way too familiar, even after four years.

"Didn't anyone ever tell you that snooping is rude, dangerous, and just plain wrong?" Julie said as she came in.

"No," Jay replied.

"Me neither. So spit."

"What?"

"No, that would be my question."

"Sorry, but your logic stumps even me."

"I'm asking what's wrong. And don't say nothing."

"Okay. Not a thing is wrong." He got hit for that.

"Adam says you've been real quiet lately. But happy today."

"Happy to see you guys."

"So what's with the quiet?"

"I don't know. Not. He's probably just busy."

"With April?"

Jay flinched at her mention of April's name.

"Yeah," he mumbled, hoping that Julie hadn't noticed the flinch. The girl could make a thing out of any situation, and when she did, she never let it go.

"You don't like her much, huh?" Julie asked.

"Don't know her much," Jay replied.

"Well, I don't like her. Did you bring me something?" Julie started rummaging through her brother's bag. Privacy was never really encouraged in their family.

"What are you, ten?" Jay said, not moving to stop her.

His sister found the CD he'd brought her and put it straight in her CD player. It seemed like she was going to drop the subject of April after all. That was good. It wasn't like Jay had any desire to talk about April.

And yet, before even one whole song played, he found himself asking, "So, why don't you like her?"

"Why don't you?" Julie replied. Jay just looked at her.

"Fine," Julie said. "I don't like her because she seemed kind of snooty. And she was wearing the ugliest pair of shoes I've ever seen in my life. You don't like her because you're in love with Adam."

Some more of the song played before Jay replied.

"I'm not in love with Adam," he said.

"Are too."

"Am not."

"Are too."

"Am not!"

"Are too."

"Am not!!"

"Are too."

"Am... oh, fuck it." Jay sighed and almost an entire song played before either of them spoke again. "I don't want to be, Jules."

"I don't think you get much of a choice, big brother. The question is, what are you gonna do about it?"

"Nothing."

"It's not gonna go away if you ignore it."

"Everything goes away if you ignore it long enough."

"That doesn't even... Hey, if he marries the fashion victim, can I have his room?" Julie asked excitedly. Jay pretended to throw her pillow at her.

"Seriously, though," she continued. "This town is starting to peel away my sanity."

"You had any?"

"Jason, George Martin tried to feel me up the other day. Do you have any idea what that's like? George Martin. If he'd succeeded, I would have had to burn it off."

"His hand or your tit?"

"My tit. I would have done worse to his hand."

"Well, you can have Adam's room soon anyway. He's moving back to this sanity sapper next year, remember?"

"You won't be coming back?"

"Please. It's taken me this long to build my sanity back up."

"You mean it, Jase?"

"Don't I look sane?"

"Actually no, you look like crap, but I meant the room." Julie's tone remained light, but Jay saw real hope in her eyes.

"Yeah. Why not?" he said. His sister hugged him. "'Bout time. Where was my hug when I got here?"

"Reunion hugs are reserved for people who have legitimate reasons for absence. Not people who are too lazy to get their fat arses up here."

"You really think it's fat?" Jay asked in mock anxiety. He stood and started turning around, trying to look at his own butt, and fell over, leaving them both laughing hysterically.

"Lunch," their mother said, popping her head in the door. She smiled as she saw them laughing together and went back into the kitchen.

"This ought to be fun," Jay said to his sister.

"Lots," she agreed.

The two of them filed out to the kitchen and sat with their mother at the table. She had made a sandwich for each of them and one for herself.

"So what have you two been talking about?" their mother asked as they all started eating.

"Love," Julie said.

"Speaking of which, shouldn't John be joining us?" Jay asked.

"*Joe's* still sleeping. Don't worry about him," Mrs Porter said. "So who's in love?"

"Hmm?" Jay said.

"Julia said you two were talking about love. So which of you is in love?"

"Neither," Jay said as Julie said, "Jase."

"Jason? Really? How wonderful. When do we meet her? What's she like?"

"You have met," Julie chimed in.

Their mother's face darkened.

"Don't tell me you've gotten yourself in a love triangle with your best friend," she said. Jay choked, Julie snorted, and Joe chose that moment to wake up.

"What's for lunch, woman?" he called from the lounge.

"Whatever you come and make," their mother replied, still looking at Jay. "I mean, she's pretty enough, I suppose, but surely it's not worth losing—"

"I am not in love with April," Jay said emphatically.

"Glad to hear it," Joe said as he entered. "Who's April?"

"His best friend's girlfriend," Julie replied.

"You wanna stay away from that. Not worth losing a mate over, even if she is a fine lookin' sheila," Joe said.

"I thought her eyes were too close together actually. And she had on the ugliest pair of shoes..." Julie said.

"Julia," their mother admonished, then leaned over towards Jay. "Jason, honey, if you feel—"

"I don't feel anything for the freak, okay. I don't even like her." Jay was starting to get irritated by the conversation.

"Huh. You admitted it. I knew you didn't like her." Julie smirked.

"Bite me."

"Children." Their mother gave them both a warning look. "Can't you act civilised for a few hours? What I was going to say was that love is a beautiful thing and you shouldn't be afraid of it. It's wondrous like... like a bubble. It lifts you up so high that the cares of the world are tiny, irrelevant dots. But it's a fragile thing and you shouldn't prod it or you'll come crashing down mighty fast. So, we won't ask. You just cherish it while it's there." She gazed off into the distance for a few moments, then excused herself and wandered out.

The two siblings were left watching Joe as he ate a corned beef sandwich. That got boring quick, though, so they got up and went to the sink.

"Love is like a bubble?" Jay said softly to his sister.

His mother often said weird things like that. Love is a bubble. Love is a flower. Love is a stuffed animal that was too old and had lost an eye and half its stuffing. It had been twelve years since their father left, and their mother still wasn't over it. Jay wasn't sure he was over it either. Every time his mother got teary, he hated his father more than... well, even more than April.

"I think it's a great metaphor," Julie said as she filled the sink with water. "Love is a bubble, all it takes is one prick to burst it."

"Who's the prick to burst your bubble?" Jay took out a tea towel. It really was starting to feel like old times.

"Personal experience or observation? 'Cause you all seem like pigs to me." She handed her brother a dish. "Well then, oh wise one, what is love like?"

Jay put on a serious face, thinking. "Love. Love is like my arse. It looks nice from the outside, but when you get right down to it, it's full of shit."

Julie put on her serious face as she seemed to consider the statement. "Love is like your arse, or love is often in your arse?"

Much tea towel flicking and water tossing ensued. By the time they paused to catch their breath, Joe had left the room.

Jay had to ask. "How did you know?"

"What, about you and Adam? Shit, Jase, I saw his room. No way anyone was sleeping in there. Are you gonna tell him?"

"That he's not sleeping in his room? 'Cause I'm pretty sure he is."

"That you love him, stupid."

Jay just silently shook his head.

"He'd probably dump her if you did."

"And what?" Jay asked.

"And you'd both live happily ever after?"

"Right. I'm not in love with Adam."

"Okay."

"It's not like I'm gay."

"Of course not, Mr Love is in my Arse."

Nine

ADAM WAS A little preoccupied when the phone rang so he didn't hear it on the first ring. When he did hear it, he moved to extricate himself from Jay's lap.

"Just let it go," Jay murmured and went back to sucking on Adam's lower lip.

"I can't," Adam said. But he kissed Jay back anyway.

The phone rang for a few more rings and stopped.

"Problem solved." Jay pulled Adam back onto his lap.

Adam instantly forgot all about whoever might be trying to reach him. Jay was right there. Beneath him. Growing excited by Adam's presence. That was the only thing filling Adam's mind. Well, truthfully, the only thing that was on Adam's mind was getting rid of all these damn clothes. Why did people wear so many of them? That was easily fixed, though. He just had to move off Jay enough to get them both naked.

He tried. He really did. But maybe not that hard. It was difficult with Jay's hands in a vise grip on his hips. And boy could that man kiss. Adam didn't want to stop what they were doing. On the other hand, it would be so much better with less clothes. Ugh. Why was life so complicated?

He tugged at Jay's T-shirt half-heartedly. Jay paused long enough to murmur a question. *Off?* Adam believed it was. He nodded. Whatever it was that Jay had said, Adam would have assented to. The guy never had a bad idea. Not when it came to this.

Jay pulled the offending item of clothing over his head and chucked it across the room. Then he grinned at Adam. God, how that smile did something to Adam's insides. And he had to get up. His own clothes were just way too restrictive.

They were gone almost as quickly as Jay had tossed the T-shirt. Adam kicked them away and knelt, naked, between Jay's thighs. He could see Jay's cock straining to get through the zipper on his jeans. It was only right that one friend should help another out, and that cock sure needed the help so Adam obliged.

He had meant to remove the jeans altogether, Jay even raised his hips for the procedure, but once the cock was free, Adam couldn't resist tasting it. It had been a while, but this was all instinct anyway. Just taste and texture, and Jay.

The tension that had begun to come between them over the last few months was gone, and it was just them again. Life was back to the way it was meant to be.

A KNOCK ON the door interrupted Adam's thoughts about starting another round. He and Jay were both still naked, and the flat reeked of their recent sex.

"Be very, very quiet and they'll go away," Jay whispered.

That sounded like a brilliant idea. Adam's mind wandered to what he could do to Jay that would still have Jay staying "quiet". Hmm. Not much. He was a bit of a groaner. Would that carry through the door?

"Adam," April called. Oh, shit. Shit. Shit. Shit.

"Or not," Jay said.

Adam frantically started to get dressed. Then he glared at Jay.

"Get dressed," he hissed.

Jay just stared for a few beats. Then he gathered up his clothes and disappeared into his room. Adam took some deep breaths and opened the door.

"April, I thought you were going out with your aunt tonight."

"So did I. But then I realised it was gone. Adam, I can't have lost it. Please tell me you've seen it."

"What?"

"The brooch. The one I was talking about on the phone."

Adam looked blankly at her.

"I left you a message. You didn't get it?"

"Um... no. I just um... I just came back from... jogging... I haven't had a chance. I was going to take a shower when you knocked... I'm all sweaty, you know... um... so you stay here, and I'll be, like, five minutes, okay?"

"Adam, you don't—" April looked really miserable, but all Adam could think of was washing Jay's scent off his skin before she smelt it.

"Five minutes," he said again, guiding her down onto the futon. "Just sit down. I'll have a shower, and then you can explain it all to me, okay?"

He bolted for the bathroom before April had a chance to reply. Inside, he locked the door and took some more deep breaths, leaning over the sink. When he looked up, he caught his own eyes in the mirror.

"Jogging?" God, he was such a dick. What was he doing?

He tried to shower as quickly as he could and made his way back to the lounge room, still a little damp. Jay's room sounded awfully quiet as he walked past. After the piercing laser glare Jay had shot at Adam before going in there, Adam had assumed that Jay would play his death metal at a high volume. Adam had never been sure whether the music was supposed to help Jay get his feelings out or to punish Adam for pissing him off.

April was still sitting on their futon, staring at the wall, when Adam got back.

"Sorry about that," Adam said, intending to sit down, put his arm around her, and hear all about whatever drama she had going. Before he had a chance, April jumped up at him again.

"So what's the problem?" he asked.

"My mother's brooch. I can't find it. I remember having it the last time I was here, when we went up to Ashdon Harbor. I was fiddling with it in the car on the way back. That's why I called. Have you seen it? Did I drop it in the car?"

April's eyes were wide with panic, and her words were coming fast, like she thought the whole mess would be over more quickly that way. Adam hadn't thought much about how upset she was when she'd arrived. She was always either way up or way down.

"What does it look like?" he asked.

"It's a tiny blue butterfly with a clasp at the back. Oh, Adam, I can't lose it, I can't. Not that."

"I haven't seen it, but I'll go out to the car now and check, okay?"

Adam tried to push her back down onto the futon, but April would have none of it. She followed him over to the counter as he grabbed his keys and then followed him outside. She stayed so close, Adam was a little concerned about tripping over her feet.

They'd barely made it out the door when they ran into Jay. Adam hadn't realised Jay had left the flat.

"I saw this on the ground on the way to the car. Is this it?" Jay said, holding his hand out. In the middle of his palm sat a metal butterfly.

"Oh, my God. Yes." April snatched the butterfly and grabbed Jay in a tight bear hug. "Thank you."

Jay looked shocked and quickly pushed April back at Adam.

"It was no big deal. It was just sitting there on the ground." With that, he disappeared back towards the car park again.

April went back inside, grinning stupidly at the butterfly in her hand.

"I can't believe he found it," she said.

"Yeah. Jay's good like that."

April just smiled. He probably should have left it at that, but Adam saw it as an opening for bringing harmony to his life. He never was too smart about women.

"You have to admit, now, he is good for something," he said.

"I suppose," April said, putting the brooch in her pocket and collapsing onto the futon. She made a face. "What does he do in that room of his anyway? He was half-undressed and all sweaty and mussed up like he'd been screwing around, but there was no one else in there."

"You were in Jay's room?"

"I wanted to ask him if he'd seen the brooch."

Wow. She must have really wanted it back.

"Lucky you did," Adam said.

"Mmm." April laid her head on his shoulder, contentedly. After a moment, when Adam didn't snuggle down with her, she sat back up and looked at him. "Are you still mad at me?"

"Mad at you?"

"For what happened at Ashdon. With your parents."

"No... I'm not mad anymore. I just wish you were a little less impulsive sometimes. If you'd mentioned going away to uni beforehand, I would have warned you not to bring it up with my parents."

"You still love me, don't you?"

"Yes," he replied automatically.

They had not used the L-word yet, and Adam was a little surprised that she'd brought it up so casually. But his answer had felt right; he did care for her. Maybe they could handle the differences between them. Maybe Jay could get used to her being around. Maybe he should just stop putting himself in situations like the one he had that night.

Adam pulled the girl close and stroked her hair, enjoying the intimacy.

"You'll always be here for me, won't you, Adam?" she whispered in his ear.

"Of course."

"Forever?"

"Yeah."

"MUM, YOU REALLY didn't have to go to all this trouble," Adam said as his mother wrestled the tea towel out of his hand. She always washed and wiped the dishes herself, but Adam felt like he had to at least make an effort to appear like he wanted to help.

"It was no trouble," she replied. "And how often do we get our son for a whole night anymore?"

"It's good to get out of the city," Adam said.

His mother had no idea how much of a relief it was to get away from Adelaide. The situation at home was getting complicated, and Adam could sure use a breather from it all.

"And how is April?" Mrs Pearson asked as she wiped the dishes.

Adam didn't answer straight away, considering if it was a loaded question. He knew that his parents didn't like April very much.

"She's good."

"And things are going well with you two?"

"Yeah. Fine. Great."

"And Jason?"

"What about Jason?" Adam said, his voice level skipping up a notch. Since when did his mother ask about Jay, and in the same breath as asking about Adam's girlfriend?

"Is he well? You didn't say anything about him at teatime. Usually it's Jay this and Jay that."

"Oh, yeah. He's okay. You know Jay, working, sleeping, being annoying."

"Do he and April get along?"

"Why wouldn't they?" Adam snapped.

His mother started at the tone in his voice.

"I just remembered how jealous he was about Gabby when you were at school," she said.

"Why would he have been jealous of Gabby?"

"Because you were spending a lot more time with her than with him. Honestly, Adam... friendships are important. Just be careful, that's all. It never hurts to have someone that will always stand by you."

"Isn't that what relationships are for? What marriage is for? To have someone to stick by you. Forever."

"Relationships end and when they do..."

"What are you trying to say? You think April's going to dump me like Gabby did? Well, what if she doesn't? What if we get married and have lots of kids and live happily ever after? What about that?"

"I just want you to be happy. If that—"

"Ugh," Adam spat out. "'I just want you to be happy'. That's what you always say when what you mean is: 'I think what you're saying is stupid'. God, can't we ever just say what we mean in this family?"

She stared at him, shocked at his outburst. Pearsons did not have arguments. Pearsons did not yell. They bottled things up and went around cursing each other under their breath.

"What do you want to say, Adam?"

"Nothing," Adam said, shaking his head and backing out of the room.

Adam's father was watching some reality show in the lounge room. This was an enigma in itself. His parents did not like reality television. It seemed that everyone was acting out of character that day: Adam's outburst, his mother caring about Jay, and now his father watching television garbage.

"What's this?" he asked, sitting on the chair next to his dad's.

"I don't know. All this rubbish looks the same. It was meant to finish fifteen minutes ago," his father grumped. "Look at that, it doesn't even look like it's ending. How can people watch this nonsense anyway? You can't even hear what they're saying."

"They're beeping out the swearing." Adam thought he'd explain, but his father still didn't look impressed. "Anyone interesting on it?"

"Humph. It always comes back to the same thing. Idiots talking about sex or money or insulting each other."

"Well at least they don't have that man anymore," Adam's mother said, coming in from the kitchen.

"What man?" Adam asked.

"The poofter," his father answered. "You know that television is going to hell when they let that lot on. As if anyone wants to hear about shirt lifting."

"Mmm." Adam wished he hadn't asked.

Ten

SINCE WHEN DID sitting outside at a café mean that you were public property for any passing lowlife to latch onto? Jay frowned with considerable effort, but it didn't stop the idiot from sitting down across from him and yammering a mile a minute.

"People always said Adelaide was like a small town, and I never knew what they meant, it always seemed so big as a kid. But then here you are, and what are the odds of that?" she said. "I'm only here for a few days, then I've got to get back. But how are you, what have you been up to? Ash still the same? Well, it always is, isn't it? What are you doing? Cooking or something, I think I heard. How's that going? I've been meaning to look everybody up while I'm here. You're in the phonebook, right?"

"Hey." Terry sat in the other chair at the table, and Jay pushed his sunglasses to the top of his head.

"You okay?" he asked Terry. "You sounded upset?"

"Do we have to talk in front of your latest conquest?" Terry indicated the girl in the other chair.

"I'm not his anything," she said.

"Never seen her before in my life," Jay said at the same time.

"You haven't changed at all, Jason." The girl held her hand out to Terry. "Gabrielle," she said. Terry just looked at her. "Jason and I went to the same high school."

"Where she tore Adam's heart out, played around with it for kicks, and then tossed it on the highway to watch it be run over."

"God, you're so melodramatic. It was high school—"

"Yeah. High school. We never liked each other then. I don't see why a few years means we should catch up like old buddies. I thought you were a waste of space then, and I'm sure I'll find you a waste of space now."

"And I always thought you were a heartless bastard. I'm sure that hasn't changed either."

At this slur, she stormed off. Jay was not sorry to see her go.

"She sits down and pretends to be my best friend without mentioning Adam once, like he doesn't exist, and I'm the heartless bastard?" Jay said.

"Apparently," Terry replied. Jay shook his head. "Feel better after pissing off a girl you hated three years ago?"

"Yeah. You?" Jay asked. He made Terry smile, in spite of herself. "So, tell me. Why was I summoned?"

Terry looked at him and sighed. "You're going to say I told you so."

"Okay. I told you so. What's wrong?"

"David—"

"Ah, butcher-boy," Jay interrupted. Terry gave him a dirty look.

"David cheated on me. Kind of."

"Kind of? How can you kind of cheat?"

"He kissed someone else. But he confessed, and he was drunk, and he seemed really sorry..."

"And he said he'd never do it again," Jay finished for her. "And he won't... until the next blonde Swedish model, wet T-shirt contest."

Terry looked hurt.

"Terry, you know I care about you, but at the risk of sounding like a heartless bastard, why are you telling me this? When did we become girlfriends?"

"My 'girl friends', they all say the same thing: that I should drop him because if he does it once, he'll do it again. I thought maybe... Jason, what was he thinking, I mean—"

"Wait. You called me to explain the male psyche?" Jay was almost laughing. "What you really want is someone to say he won't do it again and you can live happily ever after. Ask him. He'll say it."

"Do you think he'll do it again?"

Jay sighed. "Hell yeah, he'll do it again. He's a guy, Terry. If you let him get away with it, he'll do it again. It's what guys do. There is no such thing as a good guy."

"Great. Thanks. So, he is crappy and he'll do it again, but hey, what the hell, it's not like there's anything better anyway."

"Exactly."

"You're a real ray of sunshine."

"I could call you a waste of space too if that would cheer you up."

"Immensely."

"Waste of space." Jay grinned and Terry smiled.

"Why do I like you at all, Porter?"

"It's a mystery."

BY THE TIME Jay got back to the flat, Adam was already home. He appeared to be doing nothing more than staring into space. And it looked like he had been doing it for a good while.

"Have fun in Ash?" Jay asked as he walked in. The other man just sighed. "God, what is with everybody today?"

"Everybody?" Adam asked.

"Terry. Butcher. Don't ask. So, what's with you?"

Adam sighed again. "Have you ever felt like no matter what you do, you're screwed?"

"Wow. I always knew that if you thought long enough you'd come up with the meaning of life."

"Ha." Adam barely even glanced up. Jay went to put his arm around his friend, but Adam pushed him away. "Don't. I just... I'm gonna go get some sleep."

"Adam, it's eight thirty," Jay said.

"Huh."

"What happened at your parents' place?"

Adam turned to Jay. "Do you know that my mother thinks that April will break up with me?"

"I always thought she was an optimist."

"She likes you better. How funny is that?"

"So she has good taste..."

"She shouldn't like you at all."

"Wow. Thanks."

"I didn't..."

"Didn't what?"

"I don't know. I just don't know anymore."

ADAM CONTINUED TO be in a weird mood for weeks after that, and Jay couldn't figure out what the deal was. It felt like he was living with a ghost. He'd see Adam going from room to room out of the corner of his eye, but any kind of communication only led to frustration, and if he tried to touch the other man, Adam would disappear like magic.

At one point, Adam said he was stressed about some job interview, like that explained things. To Jay, this was even more of a mystery. As far as he'd known, Adam already had a job lined up down near Ashdon. Adam had been talking about it for the past three years. Then, all of a sudden, he was stressed about a job interview in Canberra.

Jay stood in Adam's doorway that afternoon for what could easily have been a full five minutes without Adam acknowledging him. He tried clearing his throat a few times, but still nothing.

"You want a ride to the airport on the day or what?" Jay asked.

"Nah. I'll just get a taxi," Adam replied. He didn't bother to face Jay when he spoke. This was nothing new; Jay had been seeing a lot of Adam's back lately.

"It'll cost you fifty bucks for a taxi, Adam."

"It's a really early flight..." Adam shrugged.

"I'm used to being up early."

"I don't want to put you out."

"Since when?" Jay snapped.

"What is that supposed to mean?" Adam finally turned around to face him.

"What are you doing anyway?"

"Thinking about what to wear to the interview."

"What's there to think about?"

"God, Jay. This is important. Don't you know anything about making a good impression? About showing your professionalism and competence."

"Your competence in dressing yourself?" Jay asked.

"You wouldn't understand." Adam turned around again, effectively dismissing Jay.

"No, I don't understand. I don't understand why some stupid job in Canberra is so vitally important all of a sudden. So important that you stand there staring into your wardrobe for half an hour."

"It's not some stupid job. The National Library, it's..." Adam floundered, with his mouth open and his hands gesturing vaguely.

"A library for the nation?" Jay supplied.

"Why can't you ever take anything I do seriously?"

"What?"

"You always do this. Everything is a joke to you. High school, uni, getting a job. You don't take anything I do seriously."

"I don't take anything *I* do seriously."

"Exactly." Adam punctuated this by gesturing at Jay, as if his remark had absolutely proved Adam's point.

"So, Canberra is seriously where you want to be?"

"Yes."

"Canberra?"

"What's wrong with Canberra?"

"It's full of politicians and porn."

"And the National Library."

"Huh... What about Ashdon?"

"What about it?"

Jay just stared at Adam.

"We'll leave about five thirty," Jay said as he walked out.

Adam had always been the one with the plans, the one who knew exactly where he was headed and why. Sure, he had been useless with day-to-day organisation, but that was Jay's area. Jay never cared where he would be in ten years. As long as he had this month's rent and expenses, he was happy. Now Adam was acting like all the plans he had made didn't matter, like the last three years didn't matter. Jay wasn't sure what to do with that.

Eleven

"WHAT'S THE WORST that can happen? You'll fail? So what? You'll come back and do it again next year. It's no big deal."

These were the words Jay had given Adam when he was freaking out about Year 12 exams. Adam repeated them to himself again. *What's the worst that can happen? You'll look like a complete idiot and they won't hire you? So what? You don't really want to move to Canberra anyway.*

Adam flipped through the newspaper without seeing any of the words. He'd read some of those "Interviews for Dummies" type books before coming out to Canberra, and they'd said a person makes an impression before even getting into the interview. How you treated a receptionist, what you read, basically anything you did reflected on you. That's why Adam had grabbed the newspaper from the newsagent that morning rather than a comic or paperback. He wanted to look smart, up to the minute, capable—none of which he felt at that moment, sitting in the National Library.

Adam was starting to wonder why he was even there. It was all so big, so important looking, and he was just some dumb kid from Ashdon Harbor. What made him think he could do this? Move to Canberra. On his own. He couldn't even manage to pay the rent on time. He would have gotten kicked out about six times back in Adelaide if Jay wasn't so anal about money and bills. Adam didn't even know where to start in counting the number of times Jay had bailed him out.

When they were in school, Jay used to have to remind him to get money from his parents for excursions. One year he still forgot, even though Jay had been reminding him every day for a month. Jay just laughed at him, forged his dad's signature on the permission slip, and somehow convinced some of the kids to lend him money. Jay paid it all back too, eventually, even to those who'd forgotten they'd given any.

Jay never forgot anything, not like Adam who had Post-it notes all over his bedroom reminding him of deadlines. Jay reminded him of everything else. What was he going to do without Jay?

He'd have to get a diary.

"TAKE A SEAT, Adam."

There were two interviewers, a man and a woman. Adam sat across from them and took a sip from the glass of water they placed in front of him.

"First, Christina is going to ask you about your skills, then I'd like to see how much you already know about the library and the Graduate program. Don't be nervous—you've already done extremely well to get to this stage." The man smiled. Adam tried to smile back, but he wasn't entirely sure his face muscles were working adequately.

"Why don't you start by telling us something about yourself?" the woman said.

"Uh, okay. Well, um, I'm about to graduate from the University of South Australia—the information studies degree. Originally, I'm from a town called Ashdon Harbor. It's about a three-hour drive from Adelaide. We have a little library there. The librarian is the nicest person I ever met. She worked really hard to try and catch the interest of us kids, and she was always trying something new. She was like a surrogate mother, you know, making us all believe we could do anything. A friend is at university studying veterinary science because Mrs Porter encouraged her. Anyway, a few of us did work experience at the library, and I found I just loved it. I was really helping people—whether that was giving them the information they needed or just an escape from reality. I guess I just wanted to give the next generation of kids what I had. So I went to university and here I am."

"You planned to work in a rural situation, helping kids 'like you were'?" the woman asked.

"That was the plan, yeah. There's a library a couple of towns over, and their librarian has been thinking of retiring. Mrs Porter convinced her to hang in until I graduated."

"So why did you apply to the National Library? Why do you want to work here rather than in the position that's waiting for you?"

"After hearing so much about this place at uni..." Adam shrugged. "It's the best."

Then Adam finally remembered all the answers he'd prepared earlier, with the help of his trusty Dummy books. "The NLA is at the forefront of library innovation, and it holds a collection of importance for the entire country. It has no equal. The graduate program itself is a wonderful opportunity for new graduates. It offers so many chances to learn and across lots of different areas. I couldn't imagine a better opportunity."

Adam felt a twinge of guilt at this as he remembered telling Mrs Porter that her library was the best place he could ever imagine working.

"What about the job waiting for you?"

"Three years ago, I considered it the only choice. Ashdon Harbor was my life, my world. But then I moved to Adelaide, and I discovered that there is so much more out there. I've done a lot of growing up since I left Ashdon, and I think that it has made me a more mature, reliable adult."

"And what do you think are your strengths and weaknesses, Adam?" This question was from the man. The lady had seemed a bit ticked off that he had made arrangements to go back to Ash and was now changing his mind. Adam figured he'd better not say his best quality was loyalty.

"I would say that I'm a hard worker, I'm thorough, and I take problems seriously. For example, during study I..."

At this point, Adam's mind shut off a little as all the things he'd rehearsed came out of his mouth automatically. He gave smooth, coherent answers to all the questions and didn't stutter or pause. Not a lot anyway. All in all, the interview didn't go too badly. Still, the first thing Adam thought as he walked out was: *Thank God it's over.* And he immediately put the whole thing out of his mind.

EXCEPT IT WASN'T over. Adam found that out the next day, just before he was due to fly back to Adelaide. He put down the phone and just stared at it. This was it. No turning back. They'd offered him a position in the program. But the even more unbelievable thing was that he had accepted. He was moving to Canberra in February.

Had he lost his mind? What was he going to do in Canberra? Where would he live? Who would he talk to? How was he supposed to visit Ashdon every week from Canberra? Adam reached for the phone to tell them he'd made a mistake, couldn't take the job, family emergency, his pet turtle was on life support, anything.

Just before he unlocked the phone, he stopped. *Great, now I'm hysterical*, he thought. What could he tell them? Really? He'd only told them yes less than two minutes before. How stupid would that make him look?

Why did he even apply? He never wanted to move to Canberra. He'd never left his home state until two days before. He'd just been so stressed about the situation in Adelaide, with April and Jay. And April kept talking about her plans to leave. He'd just looked at the site out of curiosity. When they called about the interview, he figured he could go, tell April that he tried, and then she would see that the whole idea was ridiculous once he was rejected. And maybe she would decide to stay. It had never occurred to him that they might actually want him. Why the hell would they want *him*? Damn the internet and its ease in "sending" on a whim.

Adam reached for the phone again and swiped to his frequent contacts. The call rang through to MessageBank. Adam disconnected before the recorded message was finished.

He got up and paced. Where the hell was Jay anyway? He was having a panic attack, or an anxiety attack, or some kind of life-altering crisis and what was Jay doing? What could possibly be more important than his best friend's life? Selfish bastard.

Adam collapsed onto the bed and let out a breath that was half sigh and half moan. All he wanted to do was go home, but then where was home? Not Ashdon Harbor after all.

"DID YOU GET what you needed in Canberra?" Jay asked.

He had picked Adam up from the airport. Adam should be grateful, but he couldn't seem to muster up any gratitude. This Canberra thing had just proven that he really needed to do something about the home situation. It couldn't go on the way it was. It was stressing him out so much that he couldn't think straight.

"Well?" Jay looked across at Adam, expectantly.

"Oh, yeah. It went fine. I guess. I don't know," Adam replied.

"Little Miss isn't still pissed you went without her is she?"

"No. Probably. It's not her. At least..."

"You deserved some time to yourself. Let her bitch."

"It's not... I don't want to talk about Canberra."

"O-kay. Stuffy old libraries and museums are traumatic. Gotcha."

"Jay..." Adam's tone was serious.

"What?"

"There is kind of something I've been thinking about lately. And... Well, with current events, I kind of wanted to talk to you about it."

"Okay," Jay said warily.

Current events? What the hell? Adam should have rehearsed this speech, but Jay was waiting so he soldiered on.

"April and I have been together for a while, you know," he said, "and I just..."

"Maybe I'm not the one to talk to about this, Adam."

"Of course you are," Adam said, surprised. "Who else...? I just... I was thinking maybe I should tell her."

"So tell her. Why are you asking me about it?"

"I thought maybe you wouldn't want me to."

"What have I got to do with it?" Jay sounded genuinely confused. "Wait. What are you talking about?"

"You want to tell April you love her... right?"

"No. I mean we already... I was going to tell her about us."

"Us? You and me? What about us?"

"You know, what we do."

"Like watch TV?"

"No. That we..." Adam was getting frustrated. He was sure Jay was just acting dumb. He must know what Adam meant. Why was he making Adam say it? "You know... that we have sex."

"Why would you tell her that?"

"We've been going out for seven months. I thought it was only fair—"

"Fair for who? If you tell her something like that, it'll just put ideas in her head. Whenever we're together, she'll think of it. When you come back home alone, she'll wonder. It'll ruin the relationship. You shouldn't do it. Do you really want her to think that every time she leaves us together we'll be fucking?"

"We usually are."

"No, we're not."

This was true. Adam wasn't even sure when they'd last had sex.

That was a lie. He could remember it distinctly. The night April showed up straight afterwards.

"If you're feeling guilty, then don't do it anymore," Jay continued. "But don't make me a reason to break it off."

"I don't want to break up with April."

"What do you think she's going to do if you tell her? Pat you on the head and say 'gee, honey, that sounds like fun'? Grow up, Adam. Just leave it alone."

"Maybe."

"What brought this on anyway?"

"I've just been thinking about the future. About next year. And the future... I've just been thinking, that's all."

"You haven't been thinking about marrying her or anything, have you?"

"What? No. But moving in together maybe."

"Her move into the flat, you mean?" Jay asked. He looked thoroughly appalled at the idea so Adam put him out of his misery quickly.

"I won't be in the flat next year, remember."

"She won't move to Ashdon."

"I know."

The conversation had gotten away from Adam. Maybe he should wrap things up before he made things even worse between him and Jay.

"I was wondering," he said. "Would you come out with us this weekend? I know you don't like to, but this is important."

"What for?" Jay asked.

"Just please say you'll come."

"Yeah. Whatever."

"You don't have a date or anything..."

"It's not going to take all weekend, is it? Whatever mystery thing you have planned."

"No. Not all weekend."

"Then I'll be there," Jay growled.

The glare Jay shot Adam clearly meant the conversation was over. That suited Adam fine. He totally should have rehearsed for this. Made flashcards even.

JAY WAS PROBABLY right about not telling April about the two of them. He was usually right about everything. It was one of his more annoying traits. He was also probably right that it was time he and Adam stopped fooling around. It had just been a convenience thing when they both didn't have full-time girlfriends. Right? Adam had April now. So that part of his life was over. That seemed pretty clear. And if it was over, not telling April wasn't that big of a deal.

But he did still need to do something about the tension between Jay and April. He felt like he was being pulled in two different directions by them. It shouldn't be that hard to have a friend and a girlfriend. These things were done by millions of people every day. It wasn't like he wanted them to become great friends. He'd settle for stopping them from attacking each other every time they were in the same room.

So he took his girlfriend and his best friend to dinner. Adam told them, in no uncertain terms, that they had to learn to get along. They were the two most important people in his life; he was going to make them get along. That was the gist of his little speech as they entered the fancy café in North Adelaide where he proceeded to spill pasta sauce all over his new shirt. He didn't care, as long as the two of them came out of the restaurant friendlier than they went in. Unfortunately, it wasn't going well.

"Come on, there must be something the two of you have in common other than me," Adam said.

"I don't know. I guess we both have fathers that left," April said.

"Nah. My old man never left. He's around the house somewhere, we just can't seem to find him under all the dust and dirty laundry," Jay said.

"That wouldn't surprise me," April replied.

"Jay, do you have to? I mean, can't we all just have a real conversation?" Adam asked.

"You actually expect us to bond? Form the 'boo-hoo, my daddy left me' support group? Not likely."

"Let's talk about something else," Adam said.

"Of course not when you're off in a corner pretending it never happened. Like he never existed. It's sad," April said to Jay.

"So I'd be better off acting like he was coming back like you do? That's real denial," returned Jay.

"Obviously *your* father was never coming back. I'd never come home either if I was coming home to you. Even if it would make you into a miserable wreck."

"You think I ever missed my father? God, you've got your eyes shut so tight I'm surprised you can even see Adam's dick to suck it. I'm glad he's not here. If he was here, I'd spit in his face."

"You don't mean that. He's your father."

"You don't know anything about my father. Hell, you probably don't even know anything about your own. He's probably as much a prick as I am," Jay said.

"No one could ever be as much a prick as you are," April said quietly. Then she got up from the table.

"Wait, you can't go yet," Adam said.

"This is obviously not working, Adam."

"But I haven't told you my news yet. I wanted to tell the two of you together. This isn't exactly how I pictured telling you, but..." He should have known better.

"What news?"

"I was offered a position in the Graduate Program in Canberra." Adam smiled hopefully but only got one smile in return. "You know, the interviews—they offered me a place."

"And you accepted?" Jay looked almost offended.

"Of course he accepted." April looked delighted. Perhaps even more so because Jay didn't.

"But what about Ash? What about your parents?" Jay asked.

"They've always told me to follow my heart, my dream, so that's what I'm doing," Adam replied.

"Well, if that's what you really want... Congratulations, I guess," Jay said.

"It's great, Adam. Don't listen to him. He's just a Tafe loser anyway, what would he know?" April said.

Adam started to admonish her for dissing Jay (again!), but then she was hugging him and when he let her go, Jay had already left.

"April, this has really got to stop," Adam said, sitting back down and looking at her with resigned disappointment.

"What—"

"April, you know what. I told you why this was important." He took her hand. "I love you, but Jay has been my friend since we were kids. He's important to me too. Maybe it was too much to hope that the two of you could ever be friends. But do you really have to argue every time you see each other? Especially if we..."

"What?" April was starting to look sulky.

"It's just that you did talk about applying to uni in Canberra..."

"You want me to come with you?" April went from sulky to excited in two seconds.

"I was thinking about asking you."

"Until I argued with Jay?"

Adam nodded.

"If we're in Canberra, it's not like we'll ever see him again anyway."

"April."

She jumped into his lap and gave him a quick kiss. "I'll try. I promise I'll try to be nice." She batted her eyes at him and he laughed.

Twelve

JUST ANOTHER DULL morning at work for Jason Porter. He'd been through every task so many times by this point in his apprenticeship that he could probably bake all this stuff in his sleep. He was hoping to just get through the shift on autopilot. His coworkers seemed to have other ideas, though. They didn't need to concentrate either and wanted to talk.

"So, how was Courtney last night?" Kevin asked, wriggling his eyebrows.

"Leave him alone, Kevin," said Terry.

"She's pretty big." Kevin motioned outwards from his chest. "Are they real?"

"Who cares?"

"Stop being a spoilsport, Terry. Gotta get my kicks somewhere. So, Jason, my boy..."

"Oh... my... God," said Beverly as she flounced in. "You didn't?" This aimed at Jay. "Oh, my God."

"What?" Terry said.

"He didn't tell you? Oh, my God."

"Yeah. We got that, Bev, but what's behind it?"

"I just heard from Tracy, who talked to Sarah, who got it from Tammy..."

"What?"

"Tammy bumped into Courtney last night..."

"God, she didn't talk to Tammy?" Jay shook his head. "Poor girl. You're right. This is a tragedy."

"What's the news, Beverly?" Terry had already started to lose interest. She almost began to work.

"Jason stood her up. Courtney. Never showed."

"I think we all know what stood up means, Bev," Jay said, and all three stared at him. "What?"

"I know you've been acting weird lately, but... Courtney? Why?" Kevin shook his head sadly.

"Seriously, Jason, that's not like you." Terry had that concerned look again.

He was fine, dammit. "It's no biggie," Jay said. "I just had a shit night. I'll call and apologise."

"A blow-off and an apology. It is a day of firsts."

JAY DID ACTUALLY call and apologise. It wasn't like he was a total jerk. He knew he was in the wrong for standing Courtney up. He just hadn't been able to face anyone after finding out about Adam moving. Pathetic.

According to Courtney, making it up to her somehow involved sitting in her kitchen drinking coffee. Jay could probably imagine worse punishments. The kitchen was all shiny steel with black leather stools and fancy-looking equipment. Someone there obviously either liked cooking or liked buying shiny new things.

Courtney managed to look both out of place in it and right at home. She was wearing jeans that looked like they'd seen a lot of years of use, a baggy T-shirt that said "enjoy the little things" in faded lettering, bare feet, and no make-up. She appeared completely comfortable in the shiny and new around her, though. She'd always seemed completely comfortable at work too, so maybe that was her natural state.

"You know, when you said coffee, I thought you meant we'd go and buy some," Jay said to her.

"When you said date, I thought you'd be there," Courtney replied.

"Touché."

"It is good coffee, though."

"Yeah. About last night, I know it was a shitty thing to do—"

"Forget it. How come your friend's moving anyway?"

"Job."

"Good job?"

"I guess. Yeah, it is. I'm supposed to be happy for him, aren't I?"

"Probably." Courtney smiled. She was pretty when she smiled.

"It's just that it's in Canberra."

"Yeah. You said."

"That's really far."

"It's not as far as Alaska."

"He's never been out on his own. He moved from his parents' place to the flat with me. Who's going to look after him in Canberra?"

"Um. How old is he?"

"I didn't mean it like that... Well, I don't know, maybe I did. You don't know what he's like. We would have been kicked out of our flat about twelve times if he had to remember the rent himself. He forgets everything."

"Then he'll have to learn. If everybody always did stuff for him—"

"Yeah, but he's always been so hopeless. He's been following me around since kindergarten. He was like one of those stray puppies they say follow people home. It's not like I—"

"Is that what bothers you?"

"What?"

"That you won't have anyone to follow you around anymore? Must be kind of upsetting losing your shadow. Or your puppy. Who will look at you with those big brown puppy dog eyes, all loving and trusting?"

"I never said he had brown eyes."

"No, you didn't."

The two of them sipped their coffee. Courtney was right; it was pretty good. Jay would have to try and convince Adam to pitch in for a decent coffee machine. He'd have to do it pretty quick too, before the idiot disappeared.

"Courtney," Jay said. "I've got to tell you something. This is serious now."

"All right." Courtney put her cup down.

"Kevin seems to have some obsession with finding out if your breasts are fake." Jay gestured his utter disgust with this enquiry. "I just thought you should know."

"Who the fuck is Kevin?"

"I really have to repeat that." Jay laughed.

"Why would he think they were? They're not that big."

"Compared to what?"

"I don't know... Tammy's? I saw her last night."

"So I heard. I was amazed you agreed to see me after you spoke to her."

"She doesn't like you much, huh?"

"Not really."

"So is any of what she said true?"

"What did she say?" Jay heard the front door open as he said this.

"It must be my father. He doesn't usually get home this early," she said.

She went off to greet her father. When they both came back, Jay somehow found himself agreeing to stay for dinner. It might have had something to do with the guilt at standing her up. Or maybe he was starting to avoid the flat. He certainly didn't have any urgent need to go home.

AFTER DINNER, COURTNEY led him out onto their porch to say goodbye. The night had been enjoyable, and Jay had come to the conclusion that Adam's little announcement wasn't really the disaster he had imagined it to be. It was Adam's own life being wrecked, not Jay's. Adam would probably come home with his tail between his legs in a month anyway. And, in the meantime, there were other people to hang out with, like Courtney and Terry. Hanging out with Courtney could be fun.

"I never did tell you what Tammy said, did I?" Courtney asked. Jay shook his head. It wasn't something that had come up in conversation around her father. "I remember she tried to start some pretty out-there rumours when you two broke up."

"We only went on two dates," Jay said. "I wouldn't say that qualifies as a break-up."

"Well, they must have been some bad dates. When she got to that stuff about you and the dogs..."

"Yeah. I don't really know where that one came from."

"We all just figured she was getting more extreme seeing as no one believed what she was saying ..."

"But you actually believed the stuff about the dogs? 'Cause I don't really eat dogs."

"No. Not the dogs. But my dad has a pretty good gaydar—"

"I'm not gay," Jay said quickly.

"Fair enough. Just let him down gently then."

"Is that what she said last night?" Jay said, without really registering Courtney's last comment.

"Actually, she said you couldn't get it up."

"Well, that's not true."

Thirteen

CHRISTMASTIME. IT HAD always been Jay's favourite time of year. And despite all the shit that had been going on lately, Jay was determined to enjoy this one as much as he could.

"You going to tell them about Canberra?" Jay asked Adam as they were loading the car to go down to Ashdon Harbor.

"I don't know. I don't want to ruin Christmas," Adam replied.

"Mmm. Plus you want to leave it till the last possible moment."

"I just don't want to upset them."

"Mmmhmm." Jay rolled his eyes.

"Are you sure you don't want to be with your family for Christmas?" Adam asked April.

"Adam, how many times are you going to ask me? Every ten minutes on the way up?" April replied.

She was going up to Ashdon with Adam for some unfathomable reason. Jay had stopped questioning what she wanted to do.

"That's the thing, April," Adam said. "Once we're there, we're there, you know?"

"I know."

"So I'm just asking this one more time before we go. That's all."

"That's all?" she asked. He nodded. "Then for the last time, I want to spend our first Christmas together, together. I'll be able to see my family when we get back."

"It's just that—"

"I know, Adam."

"All right, as long as you're sure."

"I'm sure." April looked exasperated.

They were arguing already, and Jay couldn't help grinning.

"Hey, April, how come you aren't having Christmas at the Williams residence anyway?" he asked. It wasn't that he cared, but if the subject annoyed her, Jay was all for it.

"It's the Bradbury residence. My stepfather's name is Bradbury."

"Well, how come you're not having Christmas at the Bradbury residence, then? You met Adam's parents, but he's never met yours."

"I wouldn't want to deprive the Pearsons of their Christmas miracle. How come you're not going to your girlfriend's house? You've been spending a lot of time with her the last few weeks. Doesn't she deserve some quality festive love?"

"I don't think that Courtney and I have progressed to that stage of our relationship. Besides, I've already met her father. Nice guy." In the spirit of the season, Jay started to hum along with the carol on the radio as they pulled away from the flat.

"Why are you so chirpy anyway?" Adam asked.

Jay just smiled.

AFTER ADAM AND April dropped Jay off at his mum's place, it was only the three of them (Jay, Julie, and their mother). Christmas always was, no matter who Mrs Porter was dating. Christmas was for family.

That first Christmas after their father left, Jay had thought he could never enjoy the day again. How could he? It was a time for family and his family no longer existed. That's how it had felt anyway. But his mother had tried so hard to make it special for Jay and Julie. Pushing out the smiles and food and presents and just doing everything she could to make sure they knew they were loved and wanted. Jay didn't feel any Christmas cheer that year, but seeing how hard she was trying, he'd faked it. She deserved that. She'd stayed.

Jay had learned something that day. Family stuck together. And anyone who didn't, didn't deserve to be family. When he moved to Adelaide, he'd missed a lot of visits but never Christmas. He wouldn't dare stay away on the day of family togetherness. He'd never hear the end of it. Besides, they were his family, and he cared about them more than anything in the world. Christmas was just a yearly reminder of that.

"I won't leave it so long between visits anymore," he said at dinner that night.

"Sure you will," Julie countered.

He swatted her, but she just laughed.

"You say the same thing every year, you know."

"It's a nice sentiment, Jason," their mother added. "But we know that it's hard for you to find the time to get up here as often as you'd like."

"Hard to find the time?" Julie said. "More like hard to find the motivation."

"Julie."

"It wasn't an insult, just an observation. Jase isn't one to do anything he doesn't want to." She shrugged. "We love you anyway, for some reason. Dork."

"Aw, shucks, sis. All this sentiment. It must be Christmas," Jay said.

"Yeah. Don't get used to it."

"What about you, Jules? You gonna promise Mum that you'll come back and see her more often than the Wayward Son?"

"Uh, no! My New Year's resolution is to get the hell out of here and never look back."

"Cheers to that," Jay said and held his glass out to Julie. They clinked and drained their drinks.

"What do you reckon, Mum?" Jay turned to their mother. "If we're both down in Adelaide, you should come and visit *us*."

"Hmm." Their mother avoided meeting his eyes. "I'll think about it."

"You should," Julie contributed. "You've never even seen Jase's Den of Sin."

"And you make it sound like such an attractive tourist destination," Jay added.

"I said I'd think about it, Julia." Their mother used her tone of finality, and they dropped it. She had not been to Adelaide since their father had disappeared there with some floozy who had waited tables at the diner.

JULIE BOUNCED INTO Jay's room that night just as he was drifting off to sleep. She pretended that it was to talk over some details for the next year. Now that Adam was vacating the flat, Jay had officially offered Julie his room. She had seemed genuinely excited about moving to the city; she had gotten herself enrolled into school and everything. It had been a bit scary how quickly she became organised, but Jay was looking forward to the company. The flat would feel kind of empty without Adam.

Of course, there weren't any details left to talk over so it didn't take long before the real reason for Julie's visit came out.

"You gonna tell me what happened with Adam?" Julie asked, giving him an innocent look from the end of his bed.

"Nothing."

"Come on. You've been avoiding talking about him all day. And it seems like each time I've talked to you lately, you've been more and more down. Then today you're happy."

"It's Christmas, Jules."

"But what happened?"

"Nothing. I'm over it, okay?"

"You're over it? Just like that? After all..." Julie narrowed her eyes. "Who is it?"

"What?"

"If you're over it, there must be someone else. Who is it?"

"That isn't always the way it works you know."

"It does with you. You never seem to spend more than a fortnight on your own. Who is it?"

Jay just sighed.

"At least tell me if he's male or female," Julie persisted.

"*He*s usually are male."

"So it's a he?"

"I thought he was a he."

"What?" Julie appeared confused.

"You asked whether he was male. I said *he*s usually are."

"Jason." Julie rolled her eyes. "Is your lover a male or female?"

"Go back to bed, Jules."

She did go back to bed, but didn't let the subject drop. For the next two days, she persisted in trying to get him to say more about the sex of "his lover". Jay was finding it hard to come up with new and creative ways to tell her to shut up. Luckily, he was just about to head out the door and back to Adelaide. In fact, he was gathering up his stuff (in between throwing things at Julie) when his mum wandered in to say goodbye.

"All ready?" his mother asked.

"Yep. Pretty much," Jay replied.

"I suppose Adam's got most of his things packed for his move back up here."

"Hasn't he told you guys yet either?" Jay asked.

"Told us what?"

"He hardly ever comes here anymore," Julie told Jay.

"He's not coming back to Ash. He's moving to Canberra," he informed them.

"What? Why would he do that?" Julie said.

"Can you imagine her living here?" Jay said. "Not likely."

"He's going to Canberra for her?"

Jay shrugged. "He got a job there."

"If it's what will make him happy..." Jay's mother trailed off, shaking her head. "He just always said he was coming back."

"Things change, I guess."

"His parents won't like it," she said, meaning, of course, that she didn't like it. If Jay was honest, he didn't much like the sound of it either, but it wasn't Jay's decision, and he'd made his peace with it.

IT HAD BEEN a great Christmas, as always, and Jay's good mood was still in evidence when he went back to work that night and all throughout his shift. In fact, when Tammy planted herself in his way as he was about to go home, he actually smiled at her.

"Hey, Tam. How's it going?" he said.

"You seem happy," she said.

"Ecstatic. I'm going home." Jay waited for Tammy to move or say something. She did neither. "Well, I'll just be on my way, then." She still didn't move, and Jay's mood started to slip a little. "What do you want, Tammy?"

"You and Courtney okay?"

"Yeah. Fine."

"I heard she was out on her own last weekend." Tammy paused, waiting for a response. "That doesn't bother you?"

"Why would it?" Jay said.

The fact was, he had never actually been out with Courtney. Just had that coffee at her place. He'd seen her again, of course, but they'd never actually gone out.

"You're a possessive guy," Tammy said.

"Am I?" Jay was struggling to keep his voice sounding cheery.

"Too possessive."

"Are you getting to a point?" Jay was already looking past her, thinking of the exit.

"It won't be long before she figures out—"

"Tammy," Jay interrupted. "We went on, what, two dates? A million years ago. What do you want from me? An apology? I'm sorry. I was having a bad week and I treated you like shit. Is that what you want to hear? Can you move on now?"

"I really couldn't care any less about you, Jason. And I don't care about your stupid apology."

"You seem to be expending a lot of energy on someone you don't care about. What was with all that crap you told Courtney, anyway?"

"I just thought she should know what she was in for."

"Then tell her the truth, not all these bullshit lies." He shook his head. "Forget it. Just leave me alone."

Jay finally got around Tammy and stormed off. His cheery mood was totally gone, and it was all because of Courtney. Well, it was all because of Tammy, really, but he was grumpy enough now to share the annoyance around. He decided to go and find his lover instead of going straight home.

Fourteen

APRIL GRIPPED ADAM'S hand tightly as they walked up the path to her house. She had promised Adam that if she spent Christmas at his parents, he would get to meet hers. He wasn't sure what to expect; she had always been so vague about her home life, apart from the friction between her and her stepfather.

"Who's this?" A man had opened the door before April had a chance to get her keys out. Adam figured it must be the stepfather, Henry. He hadn't even made it all the way into the house and the guy was giving him a death stare. What was with this family? Did they always hate people on sight?

"This is my boyfriend, Adam," April replied.

"What's he doing here?"

"I wanted Mum to meet him." April pushed past the man, into the house, dragging Adam with her. "Adam, this is my mum, this is Janey, and that's Maz."

"Hello, Adam," April's mother said. She hadn't gotten up from her chair to welcome them, but she looked more like she didn't have the energy to rather than that she didn't care.

Maz was the teen lying across the floor. She hadn't bothered to get up either. Janey was the kid who had gravitated towards them as soon as the door opened. She was looking at them both with wide eyes.

"Sit," April's mum said courteously. "Both of you."

April pulled Adam down with her into the seat next to her mother. Janey sat on the floor in front of April. Maz continued to stare from across the room, while the stepfather went back to his chair and pretended to read the paper.

"April's told me a lot about you," Mrs Bradbury said. "She said that you convinced her to apply to university."

"No. I just... we talked, went through the options and stuff," Adam said.

"Adam's just finished his degree," April said.

"In what? Decorating? Floral arts?" Henry said from behind the paper.

"Information Studies," Adam clarified.

"And what exactly is 'information studies'?" Henry said the words like they were noxious.

"Information management, librarianship, archiving, that sort of thing."

"Humph." Henry shook his head as if he knew it would have been some kind of drivel like that.

"Adam's got a job at the National Library in Canberra. It's the most prestigious library in the country," April told her mother.

"So that's what all this Canberra nonsense is about," Henry grumbled.

"I'm sure it's a very good opportunity for the two of you. Just..." April's mother hesitated. "You're both young. There's no need to rush into—"

"We're not rushing into anything," April said.

"You're going to be living with the bloke, aren't you?" Henry said.

"How about you mind your own bloody business, Henry?" April said.

"After what he did—"

"Henry," April's mother interrupted. "Maybe we should—"

"You saw what he did to her eye, Nicole."

"What *I* did?" Adam was confused. What was this guy's deal? April had told him that it was Henry that had hit her... hadn't she? Or had he just assumed?

Janey chose that moment to grab onto April and start tugging her free hand.

"Come and see what Dad got me for Christmas, April."

"Sure, Janey."

And April left, like her boyfriend hadn't just been accused of domestic abuse. Adam opened his mouth to deny it himself, but the guy was glaring at him again, with enough intensity to melt Adam into a gooey puddle. April would probably clear it up later anyway.

IT SURPRISED ADAM that April's stepfather was helping to serve lunch. He couldn't imagine his own father ever offering to do that. Then he saw

April's mum passing Henry a bowl with the salad. Her hand was shaking badly, and Adam figured this must have been the reason that Henry was helping.

He wondered briefly what was wrong with her. The flu maybe? She had seemed very tired since they got there.

Adam made the obligatory comments about how nice the meal was. It was pretty average really, but it was the done thing. After thanking him, April's mother appeared to be racking her brain to try and think of a new topic, or more likely one that wouldn't have April and Henry at each other's throats again. Adam sympathised. He usually found himself in the same situation with April and Jay.

"April said she had a lovely time with your family over Christmas," the woman finally settled on. "It was nice of you to invite her."

"Very nice. Taking a child away from her family at Christmas," Henry said. Adam could feel the hostility from across the table.

"Henry..." April's mother frowned. It obviously wasn't the safe topic she'd been hoping for.

"April should be old enough to realise that her place is here—especially now—not gallivanting around with some limp-wristed nancy-boy."

April put her hand on Adam's leg. In comfort or warning, Adam wasn't sure.

"Christmas is a very important time for families," he said.

April's nails dug into his thigh, and he realised it must have been warning. Everyone else at the table ignored him, though. April's sisters were absorbed in their plates. Probably a sound strategy. Adam lowered his gaze as well.

"Don't you think your mother has enough to worry about?" Henry said to April.

There was a bug in Adam's salad.

"I thought you might be finally growing up now that—"

"Henry," April's mother interrupted. "Let's just have a peaceful meal."

It looked like a small green caterpillar thing.

"She keeps telling us that she wants to be treated like an adult. How are we supposed to do that when she persists in this childish defiance?"

It poked its head out above the lettuce and waved around some.

"I never told you shit," April said.

Adam put his fork down. He'd lost his appetite.

"This is exactly what I'm talking about, April."

Feeling a little nauseated actually.

"Please don't fight," April's mother said. She spoke quietly and without any force, but it silenced both her husband and daughter.

Adam looked up and saw that April and her stepfather were glaring at each other over the table. April's mother had a pained expression, like this was a recurring theme that she was sick of hearing about.

"Bathroom?" Adam asked.

"Sorry?" It was April's mother who responded. When her eyes met Adam's, he realised that the pained expression was not because of the argument but from actual pain.

"Where is your bathroom?" he asked again.

Before she had finished explaining, Adam was out of his seat and gone. He could feel the bile creep up the back of his throat, and he swallowed it back. When he found the bathroom, Adam closed the door behind him and waited, but the little food he had managed to eat decided to stay in his stomach after all.

April was ready to leave as soon as he reappeared. They couldn't have spent much more than half an hour with April's family. After that, they headed over to the beach at Glenelg.

Taking a walk along the foreshore, April cuddled into him like it was any other day. It didn't feel that way to Adam.

"Adam, you're a really nice guy, you know," April said.

"Isn't that friends? What girls say to guys they want to be friends with?" Adam stumbled into the conversation. He had been miles away.

"Well, those girls are missing out. You're the whole package: nice, cute, smart... good in bed." April glanced over to watch him blush. "How did I end up with such a sweet guy?"

"Hmm... Um. Luck?"

"Yeah. Thanks." April laughed.

"No. I didn't mean it like that. You're great, April. You deserve better than me."

"No, I don't."

"You do. Look what you've done for me. We're going to Canberra. I never would have done that on my own."

"Yeah. Well." April shrugged. "I appreciate what you've done for me too, Adam. A girl always likes to have a shoulder to cry on."

"So your mum... she's, um... is she... April, is she okay?"

"What do you mean? Don't you think she liked you? Of course she did. Who wouldn't like this face?" April pinched his cheeks.

"Yeah? Well, that's not really... What I mean is—"

"Hey, you want some ice cream?"

"Not really."

"Come on. How about cookies and cream? Or triple chocolate? Who could say no to triple chocolate?"

"April."

"Well, I definitely want some."

"April!"

"She's fine," April snapped. Then she pasted the smile back onto her face. "I'm gonna go get some ice cream. Back in a sec."

April hurried off before Adam could stop her. He didn't know what to say anyway. Her mum was obviously not fine, and April obviously didn't want to talk about it. What was he supposed to do?

Adam continued to be quietly troubled for the rest of the afternoon. He wasn't sure what to do with this new information—if he should do anything—or even how bad it was. Maybe he was overreacting and April's mother really was fine. Not likely, though.

As soon as he had gotten rid of April, Adam hurried back to the flat. He needed to talk to Jay about it. Jay would know what to do. Adam eagerly turned the key to enter but stopped dead in his tracks as soon as he pushed the door open. The keys were still swinging from the keyhole, but Adam was too stunned to reach out and grab them.

Jay was sitting on their kitchen bench, hands flat on either side of his thighs and a man between his legs. As Adam watched, the man turned around and smiled. Adam had never seen him before.

He was tall, had to be at least in his mid-thirties, and... What the hell was he doing standing between Jay's legs? Had they just been kissing? Jay had a soft-focused, just-kissed look in his eyes.

"Hello, Adam. Nice to meet you," the stranger said. "I've heard a lot about you."

Adam stared at the man. "Who are you?" he said.

"I told you about Jack," Jay said.

"No, you didn't," Adam said, his voice devoid of inflection.

"Yeah, I did."

"When?"

"We were talking about the mysterious Bradburys, and I said I had met Courtney's dad and that he was a nice guy."

"Why, thank you, Jason," Jack said.

"You're welcome," Jay said back. "How did it go with the mysterious Bradburys anyway? You weren't gone long."

"Courtney's father? This is Courtney's father?" Adam said.

"Yes, Adam."

"Your girlfriend, Courtney, her father?"

"Well, girlfriend's a relative term..."

"And does she know you've been telling everyone she's your girlfriend?"

"You've never worked with butchers. Nasty bunch. Always asking her out. Trust me, it's better this way. She knows that. Besides it's not like I ever actually said she was my girlfriend, you just assumed."

"You never said she wasn't."

"Yeah I did. You laughed."

"Maybe I should go," Jack said.

"No." Jay put a hand on Jack's arm and tightened his legs around the man's waist. It looked like it was already a familiar gesture.

Adam turned and walked out, shutting the door on them again. He made it all the way back to the car before he realised that his keys were still in the outside of the door to the flat.

Fifteen

NEW YEAR'S EVE. Adam actually had plans for a change. He and April were going to watch the fireworks in the city. At least, that had been the plan. As soon as he got to April's place, she informed him that some girl she knew from school was having a party and April had agreed to go.

Adam said the change was fine. He almost meant it too. He hadn't really liked high school parties when he was in high school, but it would have to be better than spending New Year's at home.

"So these are good friends?" he asked as they drove to the girl's house.

"Me and Allie have been friends since we first started school together. At least we were friends, until this year."

"You had a fight?"

"Yeah, something like that. Cassie, another friend, she thought it was about time we made up. Her words."

"What was the fight about?"

"Stop."

"Huh?"

"This is Allie's house." April pointed to a house on the corner, and Adam looked around for a park. The problem was that the street was already filled with cars. "Why don't you just let me out and you can go back and look for a park."

"Um, okay," Adam said, so April got out and waved at him before heading over to the house where two girls were sitting on the veranda, talking.

By the time Adam had parked and walked over there himself, April was arguing with one of the girls. Adam assumed the girl was Allie. April obviously hadn't sorted out whatever it was they had been arguing about all year. Another girl was sitting on the steps between them, looking from one to the other with a defeated look.

"You might not care what they think, but I do," Allie was saying.

"God, Al, that really is all you've ever cared about, isn't it?" April said. "I bet you weren't even upset about what I did that night. You were petrified about how it would make you look to the pathetic mob of sheep you call friends."

"There's nothing wrong with caring what people think, and that doesn't make what you did okay. You totally—"

"Oh get over it! It was one event, nine months ago. It didn't ruin your life. It didn't kill you. You're still walking. You never even stopped being friends with Ralph. It was just as much his fault as mine."

"He's a guy."

"So?!"

April and Allie's voices had gotten to shrieking level, and people were starting to wander out from the house to see what was going on.

"What did you expect him to do when you practically undressed in his lap?" Allie said.

"Is that what he told you?" April laughed. "You really are a stupid cow."

"I'd certainly believe him over you."

"I was your friend. He was—"

"Was. Not anymore."

"No, you're right. Not ever again. And not because of what I did, but because I finally realise how utterly worthless you are. You are a total waste of breathing space."

"April." Adam put his hand on her arm to try to defuse her anger. He also wanted to let her know he was there. She hadn't told him about any of that.

"Ha. Is this the best you can do now?" Allie said, talking about Adam. "He looks like a before shot in a makeover show. I bet he is a complete donkey in bed."

"April," Adam said, pulling on her arm. He wanted to get her out of there before she did or said something she'd regret. "Come on. Let's just go."

Adam kept tugging at April's arm until she pulled it out of his grasp, angrily, but when she saw his face, she must have thought better of whatever it was she was going to shout back at Allie. She pushed past him and walked away from the party instead. Adam followed.

"You stay away from him, April," Allie yelled after them. "I'll give you *another* black eye if I see you around here again."

The girl kept hurling names at April but April just walked on, head held high, not looking back, as if the rest of the world didn't exist. Adam was full of curiosity about the incident: why she hadn't told him about the fight with what's-her-face and, more importantly, why she had lied to him about who had given her the black eye.

When they got back to the car, April turned her face away from him, either not wanting him to see how this was affecting her or maybe not wanting to see how it had affected him. Adam wasn't sure. It didn't seem like the right time to cross-examine her. He drove them well away from the scene before deciding it was safe to speak.

"Donkey? Is that meant to mean something?" he asked.

"The opposite of stallion," April answered in a monotone.

Well, that clarification certainly made him feel better. They subsided into silence again.

"That girl was calling you some pretty awful names back there," Adam said after a while.

"Yeah," April replied.

"You want to talk about it?"

"Not really."

Adam let the silence fall again as he tried to come up with something helpful to say.

"I guess the whole making up thing didn't go so well," he finally said.

"I was stupid to ever think it would. I should have known better when Cassie suggested it. I just..."

April paused, and Adam could hear her choking back the tears. Adam glanced at her, but she was still turned towards the window.

"I'm just so sick of being alone," she said.

"You don't have to be," he replied, putting his hand over hers. April pulled it away from him.

"Could you please just take me home," she said. "I don't feel like celebrating anymore."

"If you're sure you—"

"Yeah."

WAKING UP WAS a little disorienting. Too much space. Having to extricate himself from his best friend in the morning had become part of Jay's morning routine. Adam had never seemed to grasp the idea of personal space. That morning, though, Jay was surrounded by empty bed. Something he would need to get used to now that Adam was moving out.

He stretched and rolled over. It was a nice bed, lots of room to spread out, and unbelievably comfortable. Typical of Jack. If you were going to have something, it should be the best. If you were going to do something, do it properly. Who knew what he saw in Jay. Well, there was something, Jay thought, grinning to himself.

"What are you so happy about?" Jack said as he came back into the room.

Jay sat up and saw that Jack was carrying a tray. He had actually made Jay breakfast in bed. How... weird.

"I had a really good night," Jay said, smiling wider.

"So did I," Jack replied, sitting on the edge of the bed and giving Jay a quick peck on the lips.

"You have an unbelievably comfortable bed. I mean, amazing. I could definitely get used to this bed."

Jack laughed. "I'm glad," he said. "Here I was, thinking that I could impress you with my excellent kitchen skills. If I'd known you were already impressed, I would have skipped breakfast."

"We could still skip breakfast."

Jay leaned forwards and claimed Jack's lips again, this time in a long, lingering kiss. It would have turned into more but for the tray placed in between them. Jack looked down at it, then back up at Jay.

"Breakfast," Jack said dismissively. "It's not an important meal anyway."

Jay finally glanced at the tray and saw a very unimpressive attempt at cooking. The eggs were over-fried, the toast was black on the edges but somehow managed to be almost white in patches in the middle, and the bacon... damn, didn't anyone make it crispy anymore? Still, no one had ever attempted to give Jay breakfast in bed before.

"It's the thought that counts anyway," Jay said as he removed the well-meaning offering onto a side table. "Maybe there's some other way you can impress me."

"More than the bed?" Jack asked.

"Or involving the bed maybe?"

Jack climbed back in, and Jay continued being completely happy for the rest of the day.

"SO TELL ME again why we're up this early," Jay said.

He was wearing sunglasses but still squinting at the sunlight. That and the crowd of people they were walking through would have normally made him grumpy, but he'd had too much of a good couple of days to really care about anything.

"Stop complaining. You already spent all of New Year's Day in bed recovering. Time to be up and about in the sunshine." Jack appeared to be in an even better mood than Jay.

"I might have spent all day in bed, but I wasn't recovering, Jack."

Jay lowered the sunglasses and gave his lover a look that spoke of all the things New Year's Day had been. Jack returned the heat, and Jay knew it was not going to be a very long shopping trip. Good. He wanted to get back in that impressive bed with its equally impressive owner. Jack was Mr Smooth in all the right ways. His dark hair was always perfectly in place (until Jay got to it anyway). His body was lean and manscaped. And his smooth moves in the bedroom had Jay gasping and whimpering like a novice.

"I thought you wanted a new microwave," Jack said.

"It doesn't have to be today. The other one's been playing up for months."

"And you've been bitching about it ever since I met you."

"Yeah, but if I get a new one, what will I bitch about?"

"You'll think of something."

"Hmm. I think you just like the idea of being my sugar daddy. What's it gonna be next? A car? A Porsche'd be great."

"Aren't sugar daddy's supposed to buy jewellery, not cars and microwaves?"

"Maybe if I was a girl. Everybody knows the way to a man's heart is through his stomach."

"And what would be the purpose of the car?"

"Porsches don't have a purpose. They're just awesome."

They had arrived at the microwaves, but Jack didn't turn his attention from Jay. Jay didn't mind. He liked the way Jack looked at him. The look was the closest Jack would ever come to a caress in public, and Jay was damned if it wasn't hotter than any grope he'd enjoyed with a girl.

The shop assistant found them way before Jay was ready to give him any attention. The guy was blathering about something. Jay pointed at one of the microwaves and said they'd take that one. He didn't even notice which one he'd picked, he just wanted to shut the guy up. Shame it didn't work. The guy kept going on and on: it does this, it does that, it comes with blah blah blah...

"Dude, you've got the sale. Shut the hell up before I change my mind and buy it from Target," Jay snapped.

"I'm not buying a microwave from Target," Jack said.

"Why? You won't be using it."

"It's the principle."

"What has Target ever done to you? Are you a microwave snob?"

Jack leaned closer to Jay and whispered, "Target is a lot further from my house than Harvey Norman's."

"Good point. We'll take that one," Jay said again, not even noticing that he had pointed to a different microwave.

The salesman tried to explain the differences in his first and second choice, but Jay gave him such a glare that he gave up. What did the guy care if Jay settled on the cheaper model anyway? Did he work on commission or something? He should have just rung up the first one then.

Sixteen

ADAM COULD HEAR noises coming from Jay's room. He walked towards the door, but it was like going in slow motion, not sure if he wanted to get there or not. Finally, he had the knob in his hand, but the door wouldn't budge. It couldn't be locked. Jay never locked him out. Almost never.

Adam could still hear the sounds coming from behind the door. It was Jay. Adam was sure it was Jay. And something was happening to him. Someone was hurting him. Adam put all his weight on the door and forced it open, but what greeted him on the other side was not what he had expected.

Jay was on hands and knees on the bed, and Jack was behind him, inside him. Every time Jack moved, Jay cried out. On this side of the door, Adam could also hear the whimpers. He had never heard anything like that before. Jack was hurting Jay. Wasn't he?

Adam strode forwards and called Jack's name. The man turned around and smiled but did not stop what he was doing. He just kept smiling at Adam as he moved, and Jay whimpered. NOT ACCEPTABLE!

Adam pulled the man off the bed and away from Jay. He looked down and saw Jack's member—huge and pulsing. It was like Adam could actually hear it pulsing. So he raised the axe in his hand and chopped it off.

Blood spurted all over him, and he laughed triumphantly, but he could still hear the pulsing. Adam looked down further. Jack's dick was vibrating across the floor like a mobile phone with the vibration setting on. Adam brought the axe down again and again and again. But it wouldn't stop.

"Stop. Stop. Stop," he mumbled and opened his eyes.

A second later he realised that the pulsing noise was actually Jay's mobile phone sitting on the table in the lounge room. He realised this just as the ringing stopped.

Adam sat up. He had fallen asleep on the futon again, and his head was pounding. He shook it, thinking, *What a stupid dream*. This only made the headache worse.

He walked to the bathroom to find some Panadol. On his way back, he heard Jay talking. Jay must have been calling whoever it was back, and he didn't sound too happy with them.

Maybe Jay was having a fight with Jack. But then, thinking of Jack made Adam remember the dream. He didn't really want to do that.

"What do you mean you can't go?" Adam heard Jay say into the phone. "Terry, I got these tickets for you. You're the one who wanted to go. It's not like I can get the money back. ... That's not the point. ... Like who? ... I don't know. ... No. ... Maybe. ... I guess I could call her. ... Yeah, all right. Feel better, okay. See ya." Jay put the phone down and sighed.

"Problem?" Adam asked.

"Nah. Terry wanted to go to this charity film screening, but now she's sick and I'm dumped with the tickets."

"Can't Jack go?"

"He's working. Besides it's a chick flick. I don't think he'd want to."

"You could not go."

"That's what Terry said. 'The money's going to charity anyway'. Blah, blah, blah." Jay made a face.

"You look like your sister when you do that."

"Heaven help us." Jay's attention wavered. "I guess I could call Courtney, maybe she'll go, if she's not already busy. We never did have that date."

"You aren't seriously talking about going on a date with the daughter of the guy you're..."

"Sleeping with? Fucking? Performing acts of a—"

"I could go," Adam interrupted. Jay just looked at him. "I could go to the movies with you. If you want."

"To a chick flick?"

"I was gonna ask if you wanted to do something this weekend anyway. We're leaving next week and..." He shrugged. "I thought you and I could spend some time together before we go."

He waited as Jay thought it over. It had been a while since Adam had offered to spend any time with him, and Jay looked suspicious at the sudden invitation.

"Why not?" Jay finally said.

JAY AND ADAM were among the few men at the screening. The only ones who had not come with girlfriends or wives. They hardly said a word to each other on the way over. Adam wondered how and when he had got to the stage where he only exchanged pleasantries with his best friend of twelve years. They had talked about the weather for God's sake. The situation was making him so uncomfortable that when Jay handed him his complimentary glass of champagne, he downed it in a gulp.

All around them, people were engaged in lively (if not very interesting) conversation while he and Jay stood in silence.

"Mandy. God, I haven't seen you in ages. How was your New Year's?" Adam heard from one side.

"Did you see the first film? I saw it five times," someone on the other side of Adam said.

"I heard she had real trouble getting the weight back off this time." That was from behind.

"Would you like to buy a raffle ticket?"

"Crap," Jay said.

"What?"

"A41." Jay gestured to the raffle ticket in his hand.

"Is that bad?" Adam asked.

"I had A41 in the Woolies raffle. Terry had A31 and she got a Blu-ray player. Which sucks because she already has one anyway. Court had A51 and she got a DVD. I, as usual, got shit."

"How many prizes were there?"

"Three, why?"

"Well, a lot of people work there. That's pretty crappy odds."

"Doesn't matter. If there were six people and five prizes, A41 would still lose."

"That's the spirit." Adam laughed.

"So, how was your New Year's anyway?"

Adam paused for a minute, remembering. In the end, it hadn't been that different than previous years, watching the New Year's special on TV until he fell asleep. He used to be waiting for Jay to come home with his flavour of the month. This time he had been worrying about April after that bizarre scene at her friend's party. And waiting for Jay to come home. Guess some things never changed.

"Good," he said. "Yours?"

"Great," Jay replied.

"You went out with Jack, right?"

"Ummhmm."

"How long have you been seeing him, anyway? It's strange that I never saw him at the flat before the other day."

"Not really. He's almost forty, Adam. He has got a place of his own."

"With Courtney. Isn't that a little weird? Being together around her."

"She's the one who introduced us," Jay said, biting into the strawberry from his champagne glass.

"But it's not like she wanted you guys to... you know, like, 'Dad, here's my boyfriend. Boyfriend, this is Dad. Now why don't you two go make out?'"

Jay frowned. "I wasn't her boyfriend."

"But it must be weird for her."

"Not really... Come on, the cinema's opening." Jay moved towards the double doors. Adam followed.

"Doesn't the age difference bother you?" Adam asked, as they sat at the back of the cinema.

"Nope."

There was a pause.

"He's old enough to be your father."

Jay laughed. "Wow, a whole fifteen seconds. I'm proud of your control. You've obviously been itching to say it for weeks."

"No... Maybe. It just seems weird. You never mentioned him and then there he was. And he's so... well, he's a *he*."

"*He*s usually are."

"What?"

"Everybody take a seat," a voice came from up the front. "We'll be drawing the raffle shortly. First, Miss Webb, from the Cancer Council, would like to say a few words."

Another woman started thanking everyone for coming and explaining what their money was going towards.

"Have there been any other boyfriends you've been hiding from me?" Adam asked Jay.

"What are you talking about?"

"Have you been with any other *he*s, you know, other than Jack?"

"That's a stupid question, coming from you."

"I mean other than me."

"Does it matter?"

"Yes, I want to know."

"Shut up. I want to hear the draw."

"Tell me... Jay... I want—"

"No." Jay said this loud enough that the people around them turned and gave them dirty looks. Adam ignored them.

"No, you haven't?" he persisted.

"No, I haven't," Jay replied. "Now shut up."

"Purple A20. Purple A20," the woman from the front said. She waited for someone to indicate they had the ticket. "Next prize is a basket of nuts and a bottle of wine. Green C7. Green C7." The person with that ticket got excited. Adam didn't get it. They were just nuts. "The next two prizes are for perfume and DVD packs. One goes to Purple B28. Purple B28. The other goes to Purple A41. Purple A41."

Adam turned to Jay.

"Mine's orange," Jay said.

"Enjoy the movie," said the woman, once everyone had collected their prizes.

The lights dimmed, the movie started, and Adam settled back into his chair. They didn't get another chance to talk. This probably wasn't a bad thing, Adam figured, as all he seemed to be doing was irritating Jay. The whole situation had just blown him away. It had never occurred to him that Jay might be attracted to other men. Adam certainly wasn't. For him, it had only ever been Jay.

The movie wasn't too bad, funny. Every now and then Adam would jab Jay's arm to share the humour. It was almost like old times, he thought. Except that it wasn't old times. As the movie played, Adam grew more and more aware of Jay's physical presence next to him. They never sat that close anymore. God, they hadn't been that close since he had come back from the interview in Canberra. Maybe even before that.

Every time he touched Jay's arm, he thought of how long it had been since he had touched his friend. How much he missed the other man. He laid his own arm next to Jay's on the armrest and left it there, skin to skin. Now that he was moving, it might be the last time that their skin ever touched.

Jay didn't move his arm away. What did that mean? Did Jay miss Adam too? Shit, now he was getting all worked up because his arm was touching someone else's. Adam couldn't help laughing at the little melodrama going on in his head. Everyone around him laughed as well. It was a second before Adam realised that they were laughing at the movie. He hadn't been watching it.

Seventeen

JAY ALWAYS SAID that he and Adam had known each other since kindergarten. This was strictly true. It was a small town. They'd seen each other around and they'd probably said hi to each other occasionally. Adam's mother even used to give Jay a ride from school over to the library sometimes if his mum couldn't leave to pick him up. Or Mrs Porter would drop Adam home when he wanted to stay later at the library and his mother didn't have time to wait for him. But they'd never been friends back then.

Mrs Porter used to talk about her son a lot, and Adam remembered watching Jay come bounding into the library, all smiles, with some new story about the day. Adam would already know the details because they went to the same school, but it would sound much more exciting when related by Jay in his breathless, laughing way. In truth, Adam had always been a little in awe of the other boy. Until *that day*.

They would have been about eight or nine because it wasn't long after Jay's father had left. Adam had already noticed a change in Jay. His jokes were louder and more frequent, but Adam thought they seemed to have less real joy in them. Jay would come back to the library after school more often than not, instead of hanging out with his friends. Adam wasn't sure whether this was Jay's choice, his friends' choice, or more to do with how their mothers seemed to be shunning the "abandoned woman". Even Adam's own mother. She always came back to the library to pick him up after Mr Porter left. No being dropped home by Mrs Porter.

That day she must have forgot, though, probably in one of those not-an-argument arguments with his father, because Adam was at the library late, just before closing. He was looking for a book in the back when he rounded a corner and came across Jay.

The boy was sitting hunched at the end of the aisle with his head on his knees and his back to Adam, but Adam could see his shoulders hitching. He must have come as far as he could away from his mother and sister so that they wouldn't see him crying. He was doing it quietly, which was why Adam hadn't heard him before he was almost on top of him.

Adam hadn't known what to do; he had never seen Jay cry. In his confusion, trying to turn away and towards at the same time, Adam managed to kick the metal bookshelf, making a loud clanging noise. Jay looked up, saw Adam, and froze. Adam froze too. He didn't think Jay had ever really looked at him before.

"Jay." He'd meant to say Jason, but it hadn't come out right. Adam swallowed and tried to keep talking, keep Jay looking at him. "What a dumb arse." It was the worst name he could think of at the time. "If I had a family as great as you, and Mrs Porter, and Julie, I'd never leave."

Jay stood up. "Adam, right? Mum's little golden boy." He paused, but Adam hadn't known what to say. "Welcome to the family then, Adam. We've got a spot open."

From that day, it was like Jay had adopted him, like in that moment Jay had decided Adam would be his new best friend and so Adam was. They were always together, and it wasn't long before everyone talked of "Jason and Adam" in one breath.

Adam didn't know what magic words he'd spoken that day, maybe it was just that he had acknowledged the absence where others had gone out of their way to avoid mentioning fathers at all around Jay. Whatever it was, Adam was thankful for it. He couldn't imagine what his life would have been like without Jay. Less exciting, less happy, and so much emptier.

Now he *was* facing a life without Jay. There would be no Jay in Canberra. How would that even work?

Adam collapsed on the futon, letting out a groan.

"It wasn't that bad. I thought the film was funny," Jay said. "I actually had a pretty good time."

Adam had guessed as much. Jay had been humming along to the radio again on the way home. It was a sure sign he was happy.

"You want some?" Jay motioned towards the iced coffee he was pouring in the kitchen.

"Yeah," Adam said.

Jay brought the drinks over, handed one to Adam, and sat down. Adam left his drink untouched. He just sat and watched Jay swallow.

"What?" Jay finally said.

"You're not gay," Adam blurted out. He hadn't even realised that was what he was going to say.

"Oh-Kay," Jay said, putting down his drink.

"You're not, so why... Why?"

"Why what? Why am I fucking Jack? That seems fairly obvious. My original fuck buddy decided to up and move to Canberra."

"But Jack? He's just... He's so old." As soon as the words came out, Adam knew they were the wrong ones.

Jay stood up and fixed his gaze on his friend. Adam anticipated a tirade, but when Jay spoke, his words came out calm and quiet.

"Let's be honest with each other here, Adam," Jay said. "You're going next week so what have we got to lose? We're never going to see each other again anyway. Hell, it's been like you've already gone for months."

"That's not—"

"It doesn't matter who it was. Whoever it was, you would have found something. You would have said something. There is nothing wrong with Jack. He's the only person I know who looks at me and sees more than the small-town loser or the local slut... He's the only one who's ever told me I'm beautiful. And there's nothing wrong with that.

"Maybe I am gay or bisexual or whatever other bullshit label you want to put on me. I don't know. But you never judged me when it was your dick up my arse. What does that say about you?"

"I'm not gay," Adam replied.

"No, you're just a hypocritical son of a bitch," Jay spat out. Then he strode from the room.

Adam and Jay had fought before, that certainly wasn't anything new, but Adam had never seen Jay express his anger like that. All cold and quiet. It was something beyond his usual yelling and snark. This was Jay not just pissed but furious to a level that Adam might not be able to fix. He couldn't leave knowing that he'd broken them that badly.

Jay had only stormed off as far as the bathroom. He was splashing his face with water when Adam came in behind him.

"Nothing good can come of opening my mouth right now, can it?" Adam said.

Jay turned around to face him.

"Depends on what you're going to do with it," Jay said.

He probably meant apologise, but Adam had a better idea. He dropped to his knees on the bathroom floor, pulling at Jay's belt.

"Adam, I didn't mean..."

But then Adam's hand found its way inside Jay's jeans, and Jay appeared to forget what he was going to say. As for Adam, all he knew was that he missed Jay and he was going to be missing him for a long time. His body took over from there.

"I always thought you were beautiful," he murmured, not sure if Jay heard him, not sure if he cared either way.

His world narrowed to that room and those two bodies. He had managed to get Jay's jeans around his ankles and took Jay into his mouth. Something they'd done so many times before but now something he could never have again. Something that was no longer his. If it ever was to begin with.

Maybe this wouldn't change anything. Wouldn't make up for anything. But at least it was a better memory to leave them with than the argument. At least it was something that wasn't going to make the situation worse, which was all his mouth had been doing that night.

His mouth couldn't get him in trouble wrapped around Jay's cock. Adam concentrated on bringing Jay to the magic point. The point where his beautiful talker couldn't get out more than groans or pants. Adam had always enjoyed that. And it was so goddamned easy.

He soon got lost in the sensations. Jay's hardness pressing against his lips. Licking the pre-cum off the tip. Making his way down. Always listening for the groans he knew were coming.

Adam was so into what they were doing that it took Jay's fist yanking his head back to make him realise that they were no longer alone. Jay was staring behind him, and when Adam looked around, he saw April standing shocked in the doorway. He must have left the front door unlocked. Their eyes met long enough for Adam to see the hurt and confusion in hers, and then she was gone.

Adam bolted after her as she retreated to his bedroom. He closed the door behind them, but before he could formulate anything to say (and who knows what that could have been anyway), April said, "My mum's in hospital."

THE NEXT TWELVE hours passed in a blur. It seemed like April didn't even stop crying in her sleep. The hospitalisation had ripped her out of denial about her mother's condition. She hadn't admitted to Adam that her mum had cancer until that night. The doctors didn't think the woman would make it back home.

Adam was having a hard time keeping it all together. He desperately wanted to make April feel better, to make up for what he had done to her. What he had done at the worst possible moment for her. But he didn't know what to do. This was outside anything he had ever experienced. He felt helpless and worthless.

April was finally sleeping somewhat quietly, and Adam had come out to the lounge room to think. He wasn't doing much of that, though, just staring into space as he sat sprawled on the lounge room floor. He barely noticed when Jay entered the room behind him.

"Figure you guys are sticking round for a while longer," Jay said.

"Yeah. April wants to be here when..." Adam sighed.

"I heard a bit of what you guys were saying last night. Her mum's really... dying?"

"Yeah. Jay, about yesterday—"

"Don't. Just forget about it."

"Forget about what?" April said, moving into the room.

She had looked sound asleep when Adam had left her. Adam must have been wrong about that, or he had been staring at the wall for longer than he'd thought.

"I can't remember," Jay replied. "Jeez, you really know how to sneak up on people."

"What's with the bag?" April asked.

Adam hadn't noticed that Jay was holding a duffel bag until April asked.

"I'm going up to see Mum for a couple of weeks."

"Why? Is she dying?" April said it without the snarky tone she usually reserved for Jay. She just sounded tired.

"April, you don't want me here. I don't want to be here. Let's just leave it at that."

"What about Woolies?" Adam asked.

"I had the time coming, and Kevin said he'd cover. I'll see you around. Or not." Jay headed towards the door, then turned back. "Look, April, I know this isn't going to mean much, but I feel bad for you. If there's anything..." He trailed off, then left without finishing the offer.

"I'm gonna go to the hospital," April said.

"Want me to come with you?" Adam asked.

She shook her head, cried, and went back into the bedroom. This time Adam decided to go after Jay instead. If you could even call it a decision. Adam was running on so little sleep, it felt more like an instinct.

Adam caught Jay just before he pulled out of the parking lot. He knocked on the window, and Jay rolled it down.

"You're really leaving?" Adam asked, a panicked edge to his voice.

"Yeah. I think it's a good idea," Jay said.

"You always do this. When there's a problem, you just piss off."

"She's your problem, not mine."

"After what happened—"

"Especially after what happened."

"But, Jay... I don't know what to do."

"Do you honestly think I can help you with this?"

"I don't know what to do," Adam said again. "I don't know what she needs."

"She needs you, Adam, that's all. She sure as hell doesn't need us. We don't even need us."

"What does that mean?"

"You know what it means," Jay said. "You need to be there for your girlfriend now."

Jay rolled the window back up before Adam had a chance to respond. He didn't know what to respond anyway, so he just stood there, watching Jay leave. No, not leave, *leave him*. Jay was leaving him.

It wasn't like Adam hadn't known the goodbye was coming. But it was supposed to be him leaving, not Jay. And he hadn't realised it would hurt this much.

Eighteen

JAY HAD BEEN "home" for only a few days, but already it was like he had never left. Like he could just slip back into the life he had escaped and have it all feel so familiar. Depressing is what it was.

His mother had sent him to the store for some chocolate chips. Why on earth she wanted chocolate chips he had no idea, but he'd been doing everything she asked from a desire to punish himself.

He didn't think he would ever forget the look on April's face when she walked into that bathroom. He knew as soon as he saw her that not all of that hurt was because of them. It didn't lessen any of the guilt that sat heavy in his chest, though. It was definitely not what she needed that night. He hated April, but no one deserved that kind of pain. Jay couldn't imagine not having his own mother in his life. Not having the option of running to Ashdon whenever he was really down.

So there he was, standing in line with a box of chocolate chips in one hand, when he felt someone touch his arm.

"You're a hard man to find," said the woman behind the touch.

"I'm a little surprised you did, Terry."

"What was I supposed to do? You were just *gone*, and you weren't answering your phone. I was worried about you."

"I'm fine."

She frowned at him.

"When did you become super sleuth stalker anyway?" he said. "Have you got a tracker on me or something?"

"Kevin said you'd gone home. I remembered where you said you grew up. I do remember shit you tell me. Google did the rest. And fate, I guess, because I actually had no idea where to go from the little dot that said Ashdon Harbor. Now that I am here, are you going to tell me why you are? I thought you hated this place."

"I'm just... visiting my family."

"Sudden urge? Because you seem to have left in an awful hurry."

"And you don't seem to be sick at all."

"Cough, cough?" Terry tried a half smile. "Was the movie any good?"

Jay just groaned.

He invited Terry to come back to his mother's house without really thinking it through. As soon as the two of them entered the lounge, his sister and mother were hovering over him again. They'd been doing it since he'd gotten to Ash, so he should have known they would.

"I got your chips," he told his mother.

"Looks like you picked up more than that," said Julie.

"This is Teresa. We work together. I ran into her at Belfin's. Terry, this is my mum and my sister, Julia. That's Tim."

"Tom," Julie corrected him.

"Whatever."

"You ran into Jason at the store? What brings you up here?" his mother asked.

"Just take the chips, Mum." He handed his mother the packet and led Terry to his room.

"Don't we get to talk to your guest?" Julie called after him.

Once he had shut the door behind them, Jay collapsed on the bed.

"Guess what?" Terry said brightly. "Tammy quit. She mustn't have been able to handle being around such a stud muffin like you. What with you—"

"I have so completely fucked up," Jay interrupted her.

Terry sat down next to him and put her hand on his shoulder.

"Porter, if it's that bad you should talk to someone. Maybe you don't want to talk to me, but someone... before you..." She shrugged.

"What? Blow up government house? Eat Mexican food? Become a butcher?"

"I was actually thinking top yourself."

"Huh. Never thought of that one. Thanks."

"Jason." Teresa let out a breath, sounding thoroughly exasperated with him.

"You were with butcher-boy that night, weren't you?" Jay asked.

Teresa hesitated.

"Weren't you?"

She looked away. "Yeah."

"After all that, you took him back."

"I love him."

"So you take him back? Just like that?"

"No, not just like that. We've been talking, working things out..." She stopped. "Is that why you disappeared up here? Me and David?"

"April's mother is dying."

"Okay," Terry said, sounding unsure of how that answered her question.

"Makes you think, huh?"

"About what? Jason, will you just tell me what's wrong?"

"If butcher-boy had cheated with another guy, would you still have forgiven him?"

Terry looked confused. "What does that—"

"It shouldn't make any difference, right? If you love him, what difference does it make who it was with?"

"Did Courtney..." Terry started, but Jay shook his head. "Then just tell me. I suck at guessing and—"

"April found me and Adam together. On the day her mother went into hospital."

"Together? You mean..."

Jay nodded, and there was silence. He was too scared to look at Terry to see her reaction.

"Was it the first time you'd..."

Jay shook his head.

"When we were together?"

Jay nodded but still couldn't meet her eye.

"The whole time?"

Jay nodded again.

There was more silence, then *SLAP!* The sting of the blow lasted far longer than it took for Teresa to leave the house. Jay welcomed the pain. He deserved it. But then she hadn't deserved the pain he'd just given her. He hoped he hadn't just fucked up another friendship.

THERE WAS A chocolate cake lying on a rack in the kitchen when Jay walked in for lunch. His family must really be worried about him. Jay's mother never baked.

"That was a pretty impressive storming out," Julie said.

"Mmhmm."

"Have you known each other long?" Mrs Porter asked.

"About three years," Jay replied.

"What brought her to Ashdon Harbor?"

"Me," Jay said.

"Is she your girlie?" Tom leered.

"Not anymore."

At this, his mother and sister looked at each other like they had solved the mystery of the pyramids. Jay didn't bother correcting them.

JAY LAY ON his bed, staring at the ceiling. It was very quiet. The CD he had been listening to had finished a while back, but Jay didn't move to change it. What was the point?

It was also quite hot in his room, and there was a small spider crawling across the ceiling. Normally these things would bother him enough that he would take some kind of action against them. Put on the fan. Find something to poke the spider.

Jay just lay there, watching the spider crawl across the ceiling. He wanted to call Adam, see how he was coping, but each time he got as far as bringing up Adam's name in his phone, he couldn't go through with it. Whatever had been between the two of them over the last few years, it wasn't healthy. Terry's reaction had confirmed that for him. He had been right to leave. Now he just needed the willpower to stay away until Adam was gone. Adam would be better off that way. Jay wouldn't make things worse for him.

From a distance, he heard his mother start rattling around in the kitchen, then a crash and swearing. This finally made him get off his arse. Julie was out—studying, or joyriding, or something. His mother couldn't be trusted in the kitchen alone. It wasn't that she couldn't cook; she just wasn't able to keep her attention on anything for very long so things remained unfinished or got burned.

When he got to the kitchen, Jay found his mother picking up pieces of chopped vegetables off the floor. She must have stumbled over one of the boxes and knocked the frying pan off the stove again. The kitchen was small, but Jay's mother seemed to have a bigger image of it in her head because she kept filling it with junk. The table in the middle took up most of the room, then there was a set of draws on wheels, a cabinet with the telephone and message pad on it, and a stack of boxes filled with who knows what—mostly food and books.

Why books in the kitchen? There were books in every room of the house. The kitchen was usually where new books came in and, if they were very bad, stayed to die. Jay used to wonder if he and Adam had been switched at birth; Adam was so like Jay's own mother, with the love of books, the constant clutter, and the absentmindedness about anything practical. But Jay didn't want to think about Adam, so he moved over to the table and silently started to chop more vegetables. His mother started babbling on about something he didn't listen to.

"Mrs Barrett wanted me to get one of those Anita Blake books. Can you imagine that little old lady reading about sex with vampires and werewolves? I thought she was going to ask for Jane Eyre or Wuthering Heights, or that other Bronte's book. I guess everybody needs to get their kicks somehow. It had me flummoxed, though. People always surprise you. Like when Old Beanie asked for the Dexter books. Although I suppose he always was a little creepy. It wouldn't really surprise me if he *was* a whacko serial killer. Did you ever see the way he looks at Lydia Planter? Creepy eyes. Not that she'd ever notice. Talk about head in the clouds. Never could get her interested—"

"Mum..." Jay interrupted her but then said nothing.

"What is it, honey?"

"Are you proud of me?" Jay asked. He didn't look up from what he was doing.

"Of course I am. Don't be stupid."

"Why?" Jay persisted.

Jay's mother came around the table to get a better look at his face. His expression was serious.

"Why do you need to ask? Jason, you're my son, I'm very proud of you. Just look at you. Why wouldn't I be proud?"

"I'm not," Jay mumbled.

"Oh, Jason." She kissed Jay on the top of his head and cradled him into her chest, like she had when he was very small. It surprised him. Not because it was unexpected but because it actually made him feel a tiny bit better.

"Jason, you're strong and independent. You've always gone after what you want, and usually gotten it. You're loving and caring, and make me laugh... And I know you'll never make the same mistakes I did. What more could a mother want?" She turned his head so she was looking into his face. "And when you want to talk about whatever happened in Adelaide, I'll be here. Okay? You can talk to me, Jason. Okay?"

"Yeah. Sure. Okay," Jay said at last, pulling out of her grasp. Loving? Caring? Yeah, she really knew him. He could never tell her what happened.

Nineteen

ADAM HAD COME to the conclusion that it was best to leave April alone. Every time he opened his mouth, the only things that came out were useless platitudes like "I know how hard this must be for you" or "I'm here for you". She must realise that he was totally full of shit. Of course he didn't know anything about what she was going through. How could he? His mother was still alive.

April probably wasn't taking in what Adam was saying anyway. Since she'd gotten the news about her mother's death that morning, whatever he said, she just stared, unmoving, with her back against the wall and her knees in tight to her chin, as if holding in her grief. Most of the time, she wasn't even staring at him. Or anything really.

When he heard the knock on the door, the first thing Adam thought was that it might be Jay. That was how badly his head was screwed on at that point. Jay had a key. Why would he knock on the door? Turned out to be April's aunt—Kay, he thought her name was—and her son, Steve, the not-cousin.

"I just wanted to see if she was okay," Kay said.

"Of course," Adam waved them inside. "I'll tell her you're here."

He stuck his head into the bedroom. April hadn't moved.

"Your aunt's here," he said quietly. "Are you up to seeing her?"

He waited, but when April didn't speak, move, or even look at him, he figured she probably wasn't up to it. He was going to go and tell her visitors that when she called his name.

"It's okay," she said.

It was only a whisper, but it was more than he had got out of her all day. She still didn't make any move to get up, though, so Adam went and told her aunt to go through to the bedroom. Kay headed in, and Adam turned to the not-cousin.

Steve had his back to Adam, apparently examining Jay's DVD collection. Adam eyed the back for a while, but Steve didn't turn around or offer any kind of conversation. What *was* there to say in this situation? Adam had no idea whether Steve had been close to April's mother. They were not related.

The only thing Adam really wanted to say was "what the hell am I supposed to do with her", but he didn't think he knew Steve well enough to actually say it. Besides, Steve would probably just give him the same look of contempt that he had at the football club. A look that said a real man would know what to do for his woman.

Eventually Adam gave up and shuffled back to the bedroom. April's aunt had sat down on the bed next to April. She tried to put her arms around April, but April remained stiff and held her position against the wall. Kay dropped her arms.

"You know I'm here for you?" Kay said. "I said the same thing to Mary, of course. You and your sister are both welcome at our place whenever you need."

"Will you be there?" April asked. "Thursday?"

"At the funeral? Sure. If you want me to come, I will." The woman smoothed back April's hair. "It'll be okay. Not for a while but it will."

"Do you think Dad will come?"

Kay's hand stilled, and she opened and closed her mouth a few times before getting out one word: "April..."

April just looked at her, waiting for an answer.

"April, my brother... he's not... things didn't end well with him and your mother, and... no, I don't think he'll come."

"Have you asked him?"

"Not—"

"Have you even told him that she died?"

"I wouldn't know where to find him, sweetheart."

April blinked twice, then put her head down on her knees and ignored the stupid woman until she went away. Adam had been hoping she would know what to do, but she had been even more useless than he was.

APRIL'S HAND WAS feather-light on Adam's arm as they entered the small room. They sat at the back of the chapel just as the service was about to begin. At first, April's eyes projected hatred at her stepfather where he sat in the front with her sisters. Then, as the man giving the eulogy spoke, her head fell forwards and Adam couldn't see her face. He couldn't imagine what was going through her mind right then, or if his presence was any help to her at all.

There were many times in his life that Adam had wished to be far away from his family, but sitting in that chapel brought home to him just how lucky he was. His parents might have their faults, but they loved him, and he knew they would always be there. Of course, April had probably thought that about her own mother.

She had avoided talking about her mother for such a long time that Adam had assumed they weren't close, but after the initial shock of the news, it had all poured out: about helping her mother with baking all the time when she was little; about her mother comforting April after the nightmares she'd had as a kid, staying with her the whole rest of the night when she'd wake up scared; about April being nervous when she started school and her mum waiting for her at the gate every afternoon of the first week with chocolate so she'd have something to look forward to. How her mother had always been there for her.

April's mother sounded really great from all April had said about her. Adam wished he'd had more time to get to know her.

When April had found out about her mother's illness, it had gutted her. She had gone out and got drunk and slept with her best friend's boyfriend—the girl from the party. But April hadn't wanted to talk to anyone about her mother so the girl had assumed April was just a... well, she'd had some lovely names for April on New Year's Eve.

Adam had been an excellent distraction apparently. Somewhere to go to forget everything that was going on at home. Hearing that had made him feel a bit better about his uselessness.

When the service ended, April remained in the pew with her head bowed. The people around them all started filing out into the other room, but April didn't notice. Adam squeezed her hand, gently.

"April," he said. "Did you want to go and see your family in the other room?"

April shook her head but stood and started wandering along behind everyone else. As soon as April's sisters noticed her, they made their way over, Janey suctioning on to April without a word.

"April... We all... I don't... Oh, April." Maz had been trying to hold back her sobs, but eventually she let go and joined her younger sister in hugging April. "You should have sat with us."

Janey disengaged herself from April's side and grabbed April's hand instead. She pulled April across the room. Adam hung back, thinking it would be better for April to be with her sisters. He didn't realise where Janey was leading April until she was a few steps away from her father, April's stepfather.

The stepfather was talking with April's aunt and another man. Adam thought April had muttered something earlier about him being her stepfather's brother. Adam walked over behind them, in case April needed him to extricate her from the situation. She hadn't seemed to notice who was standing in front of her yet, but she'd been adamant about avoiding her stepfather.

"The poor girls," Kay was saying. "It's going to be hard for them without a mother."

"A girl needs a mother, sure," the stepfather's brother said. "But a man needs a woman too. A cold bed is a lonely place."

Adam could see April tense up at his words.

"But then it won't be forever, hey, Henry," the man continued. "Who knows, you might meet someone—"

"I suppose..." Henry said.

Adam thought he said it more to stop his brother from talking than anything else, but April was furious.

"You BASTARD!" she screamed. "You haven't even made it to the wake and you're already interviewing replacements?"

"April, I didn't—"

"She was better than twenty of you put together. You didn't deserve her. You don't deserve anyone. I'm glad I'll never have to see you ever again. Any of you."

And she ran. Adam had to move fast to catch her before she could take off down the highway. He figured she probably wasn't in the right frame of mind to be on her own. But then, she didn't seem all that happy to be with him right then either. He got the impression that she only left with him because getting into his car would allow her to be away from there a lot quicker than running along the highway. So much for him being a great distraction. Now he was just transport.

ONCE AGAIN, APRIL was sitting on Adam's bed with her knees drawn up to her chin and her arms around her legs, completely ignoring

Adam's presence in the room. Her bags were packed at the foot of the bed so she had roused herself enough for that.

It was their last night in Adelaide. That was the plan. The next morning they were supposed to drive to Canberra.

"You want me to put those in the car?" Adam asked her.

"Leave them for the morning," April replied, not bothering to look at him.

"It'll be good to have a new start, huh?"

"Yeah."

"But if you want to wait, stay for a while..."

"No. There's nothing to stay for."

"Well, what do you want to do for our last night?" Adam tried to sound cheerful, and April finally turned to him.

He thought he had said the wrong thing for second, but then she leaned over and kissed him. It wasn't what he was expecting. His response was pure reflex. He put his arms around her, and she clung to him. It was nice, he thought, being able to hold her without it all being about grief and comfort. Until he tasted her tears as they trickled down into the joining of their lips. He tried to pull away then, not take advantage of her, but she wouldn't let him go.

He lowered her onto the bed, and she put her legs around his waist, drawing him in closer. Maybe this was what she really wanted. What she needed. A distraction, that's what she'd called him. He could give that to her. He could finally give her something.

THE FIRST THING Adam noticed when he woke up was April's absence. She wasn't in bed. As he sat up, he saw that her bags were gone too. She must have put them in the car herself. He could have done that.

He got out of bed to look for her, but the flat was empty. She wasn't making breakfast. She wasn't having a shower. She wasn't out at the car either. They were supposed to be leaving in an hour. Where was she?

After a few paces around the flat, he finally noticed the piece of paper next to the bed. It said simply: "I can't. I'm sorry".

He sank to the bed, April's note clutched in his hand. She'd left him too. What was he supposed to do? Go to Canberra on his own? Try and find her? He had no idea where she would have gone. And his body was seized with apathy. He had no desire to go anywhere.

ADAM SPENT THE day wandering around the flat, not knowing whether to go or wait in case she changed her mind and came back. Mostly he just procrastinated making a decision either way.

Without April and her problems filling the flat, and with all Adam's stuff packed, the place felt empty and depressing. It would have been different if Jay was still there. The atmosphere of the place was different without him. Not home, just space.

Adam had only talked to his friend once since Jay had left him to deal with April's grief. Jay had called to say that he would stay with Jack until the two of them had moved on to Canberra. Stay out of April's way was what he meant. He didn't have anything else to say, not even a lame joke that was unintelligible to anyone but him. Totally unlike Jay. Adam had felt like he was talking to a distant acquaintance. Someone he barely knew.

Adam badly wanted to talk to his friend. But what would he say? April left me? Would Jay care? Would Jay take it the wrong way? Adam didn't want someone to screw. He wasn't looking to resume their situation. He just wanted to talk to his friend. That's what they had been before any of this. Before they had even come here. Best friends. And he'd gone and fucked everything up.

Twenty

"COUGH UP, LOSER," Courtney said as Jay landed on one of her squares again.

It had become a habit for them to play board games while they waited for Jack to get home, especially on a Friday night. Courtney liked to be by the window so that she could tell when he arrived. Or more precisely, when his car was back so she could borrow it. If she was as good with real money as she was amassing Monopoly money, she could have just bought her own, but she got huffy when Jay had tried to point that out earlier.

What was Jay's reason for playing? He wasn't really sure. Partly because Courtney was hilariously ridiculous whether she was winning or losing—something about being an only child seemed to have given her poor social skills—partly because Jay just didn't have anything better to do.

"You've just about cleaned me out," Jay said as he counted what was left of his Monopoly money.

"I could always give you a loan, high interest," Courtney replied.

"You like playing this game way too much."

"I've never won before. Dad is not the kind to let you win because you're a kid. It's cool to have a brother to play with."

"I'm not your brother."

"Like the brother I never had."

"What does that say about your dad?"

"Hey, I could always call you my new daddy. Would you like that better, New Daddy?"

"Shut it, Court."

"You know my real dad would never get me a pony as a kid either. How about it, New Daddy? Can I have a pony? Please, please, can I, please?" Courtney clasped her hands in the beg position and pushed her lower lip out in a pout.

"You keep calling me New Daddy and I'll shove your pony..." Jay never got to finish because Courtney heard a car turn in the driveway and bounded out of her seat to the door.

"Oh. Real Daddy's home."

Courtney picked up her bag on the way out the door while Jay started putting the Monopoly pieces back in the box. By the time he had placed the box back on the shelf in the lounge room and ambled over to the door himself, Courtney had already taken off in Jack's car. Jack was standing on the front veranda looking after her.

No matter what Courtney said about "Real Daddy" not giving her things, Jay could see that she had her father wrapped around her little finger. He figured Jack probably would have given her a pony if she had asked for one, and he couldn't blame the man. Courtney could be very charming when she wanted to be.

Truth be told, she reminded Jay a bit of his own sister now that he'd gotten to know her better. Their relationship *had* fallen into a kind of easy sibling-like flow, not that he was completely comfortable with her casually labelling him as "brother". Jay couldn't tell whether her ready acceptance of his place in her father's life meant she was extremely well adjusted or the exact opposite.

Of course, at that moment, she was gone, and Jay had plans for the empty house. He went over to Jack and touched him on the arm, briefly, to get his attention. Jack turned and smiled.

"Hi, honey. I'm home," Jack said.

"Don't you start," Jay said, placing his hands on Jack's neck and pulling him down for a kiss.

It always felt good to have Jack's arms around him. Being with Jack was the only thing that kept Jay's mind away from how crappy the rest of his life was. He could have stood there all night kissing Jack, but that would mean foregoing his plans, which just wouldn't do.

"Come on, I made dinner," he said, still with his hands on Jack's neck.

"You're making dinner for us now? No wonder Courtney's calling you New Daddy. You're putting me to shame." Jack smiled as he said it, but Jay groaned and pulled him through the door.

"I didn't make dinner for Court. I made dinner for us. Us, alone in the house, all night."

"And you want to have dinner?" Jack asked, still smiling.

"First," Jay replied. "I want to have dinner first."

Jack's smile got wider, and Jay knew that the effort he had gone to would bring him high reward later. Jay had learned that having a more experienced lover could be a very, very good thing.

JAY'S SHIFT HAD just ended at Woolworths when he spotted Terry at the other end of an aisle pushing a trolley. According to Kevin, Terry had quit her job. Jay hoped it wasn't because of him. By the time he'd got back to work, she'd already given her two weeks' notice.

He trailed along behind her, watching her put things in her trolley and thinking of the message from her that he still had on his voicemail. He felt a stab of pain every time he listened to it, but he always chose to save it. That's probably *why* he chose to save it. She'd left it the night after he'd told her about him and Adam, that he'd cheated on her when they were together. He wasn't surprised that she hated him, but it still hurt. She was one of the few people that he would never have wished to be on the outs with.

Maybe she was right; maybe he wasn't capable of a broken heart. That was one of the many insults she had let fly in the message. Jay had immediately wanted to call her back. Apologise. But everything she had said was true. How could he justify any of it to her? So he hadn't called. In fact, he hadn't talked to her in weeks. Not since that day in Ashdon.

Suddenly, she left the trolley in the middle of the aisle and hurried out of the shop. Jay wondered what was wrong. She hadn't looked at her mobile, so she hadn't got an urgent message. She hadn't looked at her watch either, so she wasn't late for something. Jay hurried after her, to make sure she was okay.

She was standing outside the shop with her hands on her hips, looking really pissed and right at him. She must have realised he was following her. His power walk slowed to a stroll to avoid what was obviously going to be a confrontation, but Terry didn't even wait for him to reach her before she started to tear into him.

"Is it really so thrilling, watching me do my grocery shopping?"

"I saw you go past in Woolworths and—" Jay started.

"What? What was so important that you had to follow me?"

"You're not coming back," Jay said. "To work."

"No."

"Because of me?"

"What do you want from me, Porter?"

"I don't know."

"Typical."

"I know what I don't want."

"And how's that working out for you?" Terry started to turn away, not waiting for an answer.

"Wait." Jay reached out to stop her but thought better of it. If she was pissed at him walking behind her, she'd react worse to him touching her. "I just... I don't want to not ever see you again. You're my friend. I don't feel this close to anyone else—"

"Shut up. Just shut up." Terry went to walk away again but then turned back, agitated. "You're seriously going to stand there and talk about how close we are? I don't even know you."

"I'm not sure I do either." Jay sat down on a bench in the middle of the mall and bowed his head. It surprised him how much it hurt to have Terry dismiss their friendship so utterly. If it had been anyone else who'd treated her like he had, though, he would have been right there with her damning the guy. She deserved better.

"What do you expect me to say to that? What do you want? Forgiveness? I'm all out of forgiveness," she said.

"Used it all up on butcher-boy?"

"It's not the same."

"Yes, it is."

Terry sighed and sat down next to Jay. "I broke up with butcher-boy."

Jay knew better than to say anything to that. If he'd kept his stupid mouth shut in the first place, Terry wouldn't hate him.

"Just give me a chance to make it up to you," he said. "To explain..."

Jay glanced over at Terry and found that she was studying him. Was she actually considering listening to his side?

"Is there a good reason you cheated on me?" she asked.

"No."

"All right then." Terry got up. "You can drive me home. The damn car is playing up again."

They drove all the way to Terry's house in silence. Jay pulled up in front and turned the engine off, but neither of them moved.

"Aren't you going to invite me in?" Jay finally asked.

"No."

"I never wanted to hurt you, Terry," Jay said. Terry made a sound of disbelief. "I did really care about you. I do. It's just…"

"Just what?" Terry said. "Is that all you wanted to say? You didn't mean to hurt me? That's lame, even for you."

"I don't know where to start," Jay said truthfully.

"Do you love him?"

"Does it matter?"

"It should," she said. "Does anyone else know?"

"April, obviously. And my sister guessed."

"How long was it going on?"

Jay shrugged.

"When did it start then?"

"Just before we moved to Adelaide." Jay was becoming increasingly uncomfortable with the conversation.

"And how long before that did you want it to?"

"I thought we were going to talk about us?"

"There is no us, remember? You're the one who broke it off."

"No, I didn't."

"Practically. You told me there was no future. You said… Is that why?"

"Why…?"

"You never thought we had a future because you were in love with Adam."

"No."

"Then why?"

"I just… I don't know. Because we didn't."

"Not good enough."

"I guess, we just… we got too serious. I didn't want that."

Terry laughed.

"I wasn't trying to be funny," Jay said, frowning.

"I know. It's just… Jason, this is literally your last chance. I'm going to get out of the car, and then I don't ever want to talk to you again. So if you honestly believe you need to tell me something, tell me now because I can guarantee that tomorrow I won't be listening."

"I didn't want to be that person, Terry."

"What person?"

"Obsessed with 'the one'." He used finger quotations. "There is no such thing as 'the one'."

"Do you mean you never want to be in love?"

Jay hesitated. "It's not worth it."

Terry stared at him, amazed. "You pushed me away because you were afraid you'd fall in love with me?"

Jay shrugged. "Maybe I already was. I don't know. How are you supposed to feel when you're... you know?"

"Jason..." She looked at him with pity. "You can't even say the word. If you won't let yourself love, you're going to end up alone."

"I do okay on my own," he said.

"Then why are you here?"

"I couldn't stand the thought of you hating me."

"I don't hate you. That's the problem. I really loved you. You know, I think maybe a part of me still does. That's why... After what you told me about you and... It hurt. It physically hurt. It was like I couldn't breathe. And I wanted you to hurt too. But when David told me he'd kissed someone else, I felt nothing. Things just went on like nothing happened. That's not normal, right?"

"I don't think I'm the right person to ask about normal."

"I've been doing a lot of thinking over the past few weeks—about what I want. I guess I'm more like you than I pretend because I came up with what I don't want."

"So what don't you want?"

"I don't want to be baking at Woolies forever. I don't want to be married to a butcher."

"Married? I didn't think it had gone that far."

"When I broke up with him, he told me he'd bought a ring. I don't know if it's true. It seemed like he just wanted to say 'see what you're missing', you know. He was a bit of a tool."

"Yeah," Jay agreed emphatically.

"It actually had the opposite effect. I'm twenty years old and I haven't done anything." Terry paused. "I think you should go now. And don't follow me around again, okay?"

"But, Terry—"

"You said you didn't want me to hate you. I don't."

"I also said I don't want to not ever see you again."

"Yeah. I remember that. Really bad grammar."

"Terry."

"Jason."

"Maybe..." Jay put his hand on Terry's knee, but she pushed it away.

"No," Terry said.

"But you said you still have feelings for me. You still love me."

"I do." She shrugged. "Maybe I always will. But it's never going to work, not the way I want it to."

"Maybe—"

"No. I can't. I can't go through all that again. Especially now..." She trailed off, but they both knew what she couldn't say as well as if she had. She wouldn't be with him now, not when she knew he'd been with Adam. "I need to move on. I need to figure out what I want. And you need to figure out what you want."

"What if what I want is you?"

"Can you honestly look me in the eye and tell me that it is?" Terry asked. Jay looked at her but said nothing. "I didn't think so." She put her hand on the door, ready to escape.

"I have a boyfriend." Jay mumbled it, but Terry heard and stopped moving.

"If I was talking to anyone else I'd say 'why the hell were you making moves on me if you have a boyfriend', but that statement actually makes some sense out of the stupid pass you just made." Terry shook her head. "I assume it's getting serious."

"No. I don't know. Why would that—"

"You're doing the same thing to him as you did to me. Looking for any excuse to back away from commitment. Lately I was thinking maybe it was because I was a girl. But then maybe it is just you. Has he told you he loves you?"

"No."

"When he does, it's over. That is how it happened with us, right?"

"It wasn't like that."

"Whatever. I can't keep doing this, Jason. I can't keep falling into your bullshit. I'm sorry, I have to let go. No... Actually no, I'm not sorry. After what you did to me, I can't believe I'm apologising to you."

"Do you think that we could ever be friends again?"

"I don't know," Terry said honestly.

"I miss hanging out with you," Jay said. "I know you're still really pissed at me, Terry. And you have every right to be—"

"Do I? I didn't think you'd notice. You've got this giant wall around you, and I don't think you realise that you can still hurt other people from behind there."

"I'm starting to."

"I hope so."

"If you ever do forgive me… just call okay. I'll always be there for you."

"If you say you really cared for me one more time, I will punch you in the face."

"Fair enough."

The two of them sat in Jay's car staring at each other for a long time.

"I don't know what else to say." Jay spoke first.

"That's because there isn't anything left to say," Terry said.

Terry paused, and for a second, Jay had the glimmer of hope that she might say she forgave him after all. The second passed and what she actually said was: "It's been an experience, Porter." Then she leaned over and kissed him on the cheek.

JAY HAD BEEN tossing and turning most of the night. His little talk with Terry had not been a major success. Sure, she had said that she didn't hate him, but she also said that she didn't want to be friends with him anymore. That, in fact, she never wanted to see him again. Not the best possible result.

He had already drifted apart from most of his friends from Ashdon Harbor, Adam had nicked off, and now Terry was gone. If things kept on this way, Kevin would swear to never speak to him again. Actually, that might not be a bad thing.

Jay sighed, possibly a little loudly and dramatically. Jack rolled over to face him.

"It wasn't your fault, babe," Jack said, his breath whispering across Jay's skin. "It was Adam's choice too."

"I wasn't thinking about Adam," Jay said, scowling.

Jack had been trying to bring the subject of him and Adam back up ever since Jay had told him what happened. Jay did not want to go over it again. But then Jack started to turn away, and Jay didn't want that either. He didn't want to be left with his own thoughts about how lonely he was.

"Was Courtney's mum your first love?" Jay asked.

"Yes. She was. I don't know if we would have stayed together if she'd lived, but I did love her. I'd like to think that we would have remained friends at least."

"I felt that way about Terry too, I think. In my own way. I just... It was like I knew there was a part of me that..."

"Wanted more? Or perhaps—"

"Less. Like there was a part of me that was sick at the thought of being stuck with her forever. But then a part of me was starting to kind of like the idea." Jay frowned. "It was just getting too complicated. Do you think that I could ever be friends with her? Like you said about you and Margaret?"

"I don't know, Jason. I think the problem there is not so much that you were with another man, but that it was while you were with her, that you were deceiving her. She may take time to get over that."

"But she will, right? I don't... I've already lost one friend. I don't..." Jay sighed again in the dark, and Jack pulled him closer.

"It feels like I'm losing everyone," Jay said.

"You haven't lost me," Jack replied. "I love you, and I'm not going to leave you."

Jay hadn't expected that.

Twenty-One

IT WAS THE third weekend that Jay had come up to Ash to get "just a few more" of Julie's prized possessions. When she'd moved into the flat, he had told her as long as she didn't make the place look too girly, he didn't care what she brought. He was starting to regret that.

"God, Jules, how much crap do you own?" he said, half joking, half afraid that she would be dragging him back up there all year.

"None. All my stuff is very important," Julie replied.

Jay lifted up a pink pig ornament with wings.

"That one reminds me of you," Julie said.

"Do I want to know why? A fallen angel..." Jay trailed off.

"Fallen?" Julie sighed. "Okay, why is my pig a fallen angel?"

"What else would you call an angel who likes to wallow in mud?" Jay asked. "Enlightened?"

"What would you call it? Endarkened?"

"Endarkened. I like it."

"Are you going to talk to Adam while you're here?" she asked casually.

"Why would I? I wouldn't think Mum's budget was up for long distance calls."

"I was actually thinking of a drive." Julie let out a gasp of exaggerated surprise as her brother turned to her. "Didn't you know he was back in Ash?"

"Is he? Well, that seems bloody stupid."

"Are you gonna go see him or what?"

"I repeat, why would I?"

"Don't you want to know why he's here, alone?"

"Obviously not as much as you do."

"If you say so."

Jay knew that Julie was baiting him with the news and waiting to see what he did. So he tried to put it out of his mind, give her nothing. But why would Adam come back to Ashdon and not tell him? In a year full of weird behaviour, that might just be Adam's weirdest. Was he avoiding Jay?

On their way back to the city, when he got to the turn towards Adam's house, Jay took it without hesitation, pretending not to notice Julie's self-satisfied smirk.

"HEY, YOU LOOK familiar," Jay said when Adam opened the door. "Didn't we used to be friends?"

Jay forced his face into a smile, but Adam didn't smile back.

"I didn't know you were coming up this weekend," Adam said, looking at him through the screen door.

"Until about an hour ago, I didn't know you were here either... Gonna let me in?"

"Yeah. Sure. I was just sorting out my books. Rearranging the shelves," Adam said as he moved to let Jay in.

"How many times have you done that since you got back?"

Adam shrugged. "You want a drink or something? We've got Coke, diet Coke, vanilla Coke..."

"Coke, Coke, or Coke? Hmm... How about a glass of water?"

"Sure."

They both moved into the kitchen.

"So, you and Jack...You're still..." Adam started.

"Mmmhmm. ... You and April, though..."

"Yeah." There was silence for a while.

"What happened with Canberra, anyway?" Jay asked. "Aren't people supposed to actually go somewhere before they get homesick?"

"I've been away from Ashdon for three years already, Jay. I wanted to come home."

And he didn't have April to prevent him from doing it anymore. But that went unspoken.

"So, you'll be sticking around Ashdon?" Jay asked.

"That was always the plan."

"I bet the library guys were pissed."

"They were actually really nice about it."

"Nice librarians. What's the world coming to?" Jay sipped his glass of water and looked out the window, trying to think of something to say.

"You remember sneaking out your window so we could go to the Good Charlotte concert in Adelaide?"

"I remember you getting pissed off and blaming me for running into the back of that car on the way home."

"Well, if you hadn't started dribbling shit about Gabby—"

"She'd just broken up with me two days before."

"Yeah, and I was supposed to be taking your mind off of her."

"I remember," Adam said, his eyes glazing over as he distanced himself even more from this conversation that he hadn't seemed to want to have in the first place. Maybe he really had avoided telling Jay he was back because he wanted to avoid Jay completely.

"It's your birthday next weekend, right?" Jay said.

Adam nodded.

"Got plans?" Jay asked.

"My parents are giving a dinner."

"A dinner? Sounds like a bitchin' twenty-first."

"You wanna come?"

The question threw Jay a little off balance. "I can't... I have plans and... I thought you were in Canberra so..."

"That's fine."

"I'm sure you'll have a great time anyway. Everyone in the town'll come. The Event of the Year."

"Even an event isn't eventful in this town."

"It's not that bad... well, it is, but aren't you the one usually defending this shithole?"

"Jason. We haven't seen you in a long time." Of course Mrs Pearson would choose the exact moment that he swore to come home, Jay thought.

"I was just leaving. Got to get the last of Jules's stuff into Adelaide. Thanks for the drink, Adam." Jay said all this in a rush, putting his obviously full glass of water in the sink and heading back out to the car. He had left Julie waiting in there.

"So, how did things go with Adam?" Julie asked as Jay got back in.

"We've decided to splurge all our money on one-way tickets to Vegas, where we'll have an Elvis-inspired wedding and start work as showgirls," Jay replied.

"Men can get married in Las Vegas now," Julie said.

Jay snorted and started their trip back to Adelaide.

"Why can't you just admit that you're in love with him?" Julie continued.

"Because I'm not," Jay replied.

"Because you're not gay?"

"Because love is stupid."

"Love is stupid? That's some pearl of wisdom." Julie shook her head, then looked more closely at Jay. "Are you serious?"

"Haven't you ever watched what happens with this love delusion? The guy's minding his own business, doing whatever he wants and then BAM he's 'in love' and expected to drop everything and constantly think of someone else's needs more than his own. How does that make life better? We're just meant to be pathetically grateful that we aren't left on the bench of losers without life partners? Screw that. That bench is infinitely preferable to running around trying to figure out the rules in a game that we never wanted to play in the first place. Love is such a load of bullshit. Can you honestly say that you've seen any love that wasn't stupid?"

"Kermit and Miss Piggy," Julie said, without thinking for a second.

"What?"

"Come on. If two different species can make love work there's gotta be hope for us, right?"

"I don't think they did make it work."

"Didn't they? Well, they're just puppets, that doesn't count."

"Uh-huh."

"Love isn't a relationship, you know. Love isn't actions or words—it's feelings, and you can't make them go away by denying them."

"A few months ago, you thought I was denying my feelings for Terry."

"No. I said that you must have been denying your feelings for Adam by going out with Terry in the first place, but that it didn't make them go away and when things went bad, it made you feel worse."

"Uh-huh."

"If you tell Adam about your feelings for him, yeah it might hurt, and yeah he might totally freak out and hate you, and that'll hurt like hell—"

"This is a great pep talk."

"But so what?"

"So what? That's your big ending?" Jay shot an incredulous look at Julie then turned his gaze back to the road.

"Yeah. So what? What are you afraid of? That you'll end up alone? That you won't end up alone? Hello, if you keep telling people love is stupid, you're gonna end up alone anyway. And actually wanting to be alone, now *that's* stupid."

"Better to want to be alone than to spend all your time daydreaming about someone that doesn't want you."

"News flash. I don't want to be like Mum either. That parade of sorry-arse losers, and pining away for someone like Dad, who wasn't exactly a catch to begin with. But guess what, you've already got the parade of losers."

"I'm not Mum."

"No. You're worse. At least she's tasted love, even if it was with a dud like Dad. You're too scared to even try."

"So I should love like mad and be ecstatic when they leave with some ugly waitress because I've tasted love? Please. Did you not listen to *any* of my rant? Love is not worth it."

"Says someone who's never even given it a try."

"You don't have to fall for a con to recognise it as a con."

"You really suck."

"Jules, I've told you before that saying 'you suck' does not win an argument."

"But you do."

"Maybe, but that doesn't mean that love isn't stupid."

"You are such a downer. It's no wonder you don't have a boyfriend. Isn't gay meant to mean happy or something? Where's your gay abandon?"

"Must have abandoned it."

"Ah! So you admit you had it in the first place."

"Change of subject. Please."

Julie thought.

"Well," she said. "I was in this little café in North Adelaide the other day when this guy practically tripped over the back of my chair. I'm thinking, what a freak, you know. How can someone possibly be so stupid, right? So, I turn around to tell him what a wank he is—"

"Poor guy. I can imagine. Did he wet his pants at your terrifying outburst?"

"What outburst? I didn't say a word. He was gorgeous. Like 'oh my God, I want to have his babies' gorgeous. You would have loved him.

Anyway he was all like 'I'm so sorry' and like touching my shoulder and I'm thinking—"

"Music should be back," Jay interrupted, leaning over and switching on the radio, loud. They had just passed the point where fuzz turned back into music. Julie leaned over straight after he did and turned the volume down, giving him a glare at the same time.

"Hey. I was talking," she said.

"Um. Yeah. That was meant to stop you," her brother replied.

"Jase. I listen to all your shit—"

"No. You go on and on, trying to get me to talk about my shit. Just so you know, if I have to hear about one more 'gorgeous' guy and what you want to do to him, I will kill myself. And you'll be the one cleaning up the mess, so how about we just listen to the music?"

"The guys in Adelaide are way cuter than the ones in Ashdon."

"Larger pool to choose from."

"So you agree?"

Jay laughed. "And we're back to my shit," he said.

"Well, you do have a lot of shit to deal with. You know, coming out of the closet and all."

"To come out, I'd have to admit I was in there."

"Fine. Your shit is all about coming into the closet."

"That doesn't even make sense."

"Of course it does. You have trouble admitting your gayness, which may be a snag in the whole coming out process. You really need to admit it to yourself before you can announce it to the world. So it would be more of a coming in than a coming out."

"Coming in?" Jay made a face.

"I like it. And if you can use endarken, then I get to use coming in."

Jay turned the knob of the radio back up to drown her out.

Twenty-Two

WHEN ADAM WOKE up that morning, he wanted nothing more than to roll over and go back to sleep. When you're a kid, birthdays, Christmases, they're so exciting, you can't wait for them to start. Then you get older and all they signify is one more crappy year having passed. The fact that Adam had reached this point at twenty-one was kind of depressing in itself. Of course, parents don't always recognise that their children are all grown up, so when Adam's mother walked into his room that morning, she was as cheery as she had been every birthday of his childhood.

"Happy birthday, Adam," she said as Adam felt something heavy rest on his legs.

He couldn't actually see it because he'd laid his pillow over his head to block out the light his mother was flooding into the room. He mumbled something, which his mother interpreted as "thank you" (it was more like "leave me alone").

"Why don't you have a shower, and I'll get you some breakfast."

She left the room, but it was now bright enough that Adam couldn't get back to sleep so he got up and stumbled to the bathroom. He didn't bother opening the present first. It wouldn't be a surprise. His parents always just asked him what he wanted and bought that.

Adam went through the motions of showering, but he was still half-asleep and fumbled the soap. As it hit the bottom of the shower stall, he smiled, thinking of Jay. Whenever Adam had slipped into the shower with Jay, Jay had invariably made a joke about dropping the soap. For some reason, Jay found that endlessly funny. But then, the joke always led to shower sex so Adam never minded too much.

Adam could picture Jay as if he were right there, the way he would give Adam a dirty little smile, reach out a hand, and let the soap fall, curving his mouth into an O—as in "Oh, what have I done?" Then Adam would step behind Jay and run his hand down the other man's body, feeling the slicked hardness of chest, abs, and cock.

Adam closed his eyes and let the images flow over him with the water. He ran his hand down his own body, imagining it was Jay. It had been such a long time, and the images his mind conjured were so vivid that his body responded in a big way. He wrapped his fist around the—

Beep. Beep.

Adam's eyes flew open. It was the damn shower timer his parents were so obsessed with. It gave you four minutes before informing you that you'd showered long enough. Adam could reset it, but he knew from past experience that if he ignored it, one or other of his parents wouldn't be far behind, knocking on the door. He'd forgotten how much living at his parents' had sucked, but he was fast relearning.

Adam sent his body a blast of cold water and got out.

AFTER DRYING AND dressing, Adam headed towards the kitchen for breakfast. He could hear his parents before he even got to the room. It was unusual to hear their voices raised like that.

"I'm waiting for the cake to cook," he heard his mother say.

"You could be getting dressed while you wait instead of playing cards." That was his father's voice.

"And you could have started on your chores instead of sleeping in. I don't know how you're going to cope when I'm gone. When I'm not here to do every little thing for you."

"The sooner you go, the better. I'll be just fi—"

"What do you mean, when you're not here?" Adam interrupted his parents' fighting as he entered the kitchen. Yes, they were actually fighting.

"Nothing, I was just talking. It's just something people say," said his dad.

"Why don't you just tell him the truth?" said his mum.

"You're not sick, are you?" Adam asked, thinking of April and her mother.

"No, of course not. I was just talking."

"Beth—" Adam's father started.

"I don't think this is the time," his mother interrupted.

"Time for what? Just tell me," Adam said.

"Your mother and I are separating," said his dad.

"What?" What a sick joke, Adam thought. Neither was smiling.

"It's been coming for a while, Adam. We thought, when you went to Canberra, but..." said his dad.

"Why haven't you said anything before, if it's 'been coming' for so long?" Adam was reeling. It was true, they hadn't been talking to each other much since he got back, but hell, they never had.

"With everything that happened with April, we just couldn't find the right time," his mum said quietly.

"So, my birthday, that's the right time?" Adam said.

"I didn't think so, no." His mother gave his father a terrible look.

"We couldn't keep going like this," the man said.

"And it couldn't wait another day?" his mum asked.

Adam couldn't stand hearing his parents fight again so he slunk back to his room. His parents were separating? And they were miserable now because of him. Because they couldn't give him the trauma of telling him the truth. Great, he had made two more people he cared about miserable. He was getting real good at that. Wait! His mother was leaving! That meant he would be living in the place alone with his father. Shit, his mother was right—this was going to be a disaster.

AFTER HIS PARENTS' big announcement, Adam didn't have the energy to really do anything. He sat looking out of his window for more than half an hour. Staring at nothing. At least in Adelaide he would have seen a car going past every now and again. In Ashdon...

He wondered where April was, whether she had gone to live with her stepfather. He couldn't imagine it, but where else would she go?

He wondered what Jay would be doing that night. With Jack probably. It was the first time in a long time that Adam would not see Jay on his birthday. It wasn't going to be the same without him.

And then there were his parents. They would be putting on happy faces for the night. For the guests. The event of the year, Jay had called it. His stupid birthday dinner. Adam couldn't summon any enthusiasm for it. He wished he could just skip the whole thing. He had never felt less like spending an evening surrounded by people he barely tolerated. Right then, he had a strong desire to be anywhere but Ashdon Harbor.

How had he ended up here, home but alone and miserable? For weeks he had been going over the events of the past year in his head, trying to figure out if he could have done something differently, if things could have worked out differently. He'd spent pretty much the entire three weeks in Canberra brooding on it. The more he thought, the less certain he was about how it should have turned out, how he wished it had turned out. It didn't really matter anyway because there was nothing he could do to change it.

In the middle of this latest brooding session, Adam found himself in his car with his hands on the wheel. There was no intention—he just drove. No surprise where he ended up. The flat. It seemed inevitable somehow.

Of course, it wasn't his flat anymore so he didn't have keys to get in. He knocked, but no one was there. Adam turned his back to the door and slid to the ground. Put his head in his hands. Everything just seemed so...

"You're one of those kids from 2B, right?" a voice said. Adam looked up and saw their neighbour Dan/Craig. "What're you doing out here?"

"I... I'm not sure," Adam stammered.

"You better go in. It's been threatening to rain all day."

"I can't. I moved out. Don't have my key anymore."

"Then maybe you'd better just go home."

"Yeah," Adam said.

Dan/Craig looked up at the sky and moved off. Adam went back to sitting with his head in his hands. He was in almost the same position as April had been when he had come home and found her on his doorstep so many months before. He imagined Jay coming home and finding him there, what Jay's reaction would be.

If there was anyone who knew what to say to bring Adam out of this funk, it would be Jay. But would Jay be happy to see him? Or was Adam a face from the past already? Another discarded acquaintance. Jay had a lot of those.

Things already felt awkward between them when Jay had come by the other day. Jay had mentioned the night of the Good Charlotte concert as if it was like any of the other nights they'd hung out back in high school. Nothing special. To Jay, maybe it hadn't been a big deal, their first kiss.

Jay had always said that he was only trying to get Adam to shut up about Gabby and their break-up that night. Adam couldn't get the kiss out of his head afterwards, though, so he kept talking about Gabby to hide his embarrassment and confusion. If the intent of the kiss had been to shut him up, then it had backfired badly.

And now they were meant to pretend none of that ever happened, Adam supposed. Hell, when he'd last seen Jay, it had hardly felt like they'd ever been friends, let alone anything else.

IN THE END, it was Julie who showed up first.

"Adam?" she said. "I thought you had a party back in Ashdon tonight."

"I do."

"You look awful."

"Thanks. Can I come in?"

"Sure. You are the birthday boy, right?"

Adam moved out of the way so she could let them both in.

"I don't have your present, though. Sorry," Julie continued. "I left it at Mum's. She was supposed to go to your dinner thing tonight."

"That's okay," he said, following her into the flat. It was a flat covered in pig and teddy bear ornaments now apparently.

"Why *are* you so glum anyway? You're finally home. You should be ecstatic." She sat on the futon, but Adam remained standing, looking down at her blankly. "Ashdon. You're back now. That is what you wanted, isn't it?"

"Yeah."

"Come on, Adam, it sucks to see you like this. It's your birthday. What can I do to cheer you up? Tell me..." Then in a singsong voice: "I'll be your best friend."

"The position's open."

"Is that what's upsetting you? That Jase isn't coming to your thing? He didn't even know you were back. Now he knows—"

"He's busy."

"Doing what? Sitting on his arse feeling sorry for himself? You both seem to be good at that."

"He said he had plans. With Jack, I guess."

"Who's Jack?"

"His boyfriend."

"I didn't know he had a boyfriend."

Oops.

"Must be where he disappears off to all the time. He never tells me anything," Julie said. "The guy can't be that great a boyfriend, though."

"Why?"

Julie frowned at him. "Didn't you hear me say that he has been moping about as much as you are? It's not like him."

"Has he said anything about me?"

"Guys always have to make everything about themselves." She rolled her eyes and shrugged. "He was surprised you were back."

There was a pause.

"I think he probably misses you as much as you miss him," Julie said.

Adam shook his head. Julie got up and put a hand on either side of Adam's face, forcing him to look into her eyes.

"Adam, I've known you my whole life," she said. "I love you like a brother. And that's why I'm going to be brutally honest with you right now. You're a complete and utter moron."

"What?"

"I know you always said you were gonna go back to Ashdon, but seriously, you look about as happy as someone whose puppy just got run over by their favourite uncle. Do you really want to be there?"

"Of course. It was always the plan. Where else am I gonna go?"

"Again, Adam, know this is from a place of love." Julie slapped him. Adam brought one hand up to his stinging cheek in reflex, although what he was now protecting himself from, he didn't know.

"Come home, you idiot!" Julie yelled. "Why can't you two put your male stupidity aside for one second and just admit you love each other?"

"What? Me and Jay?" Adam said, one hand still on the spot where she'd hit him. He couldn't believe she'd actually done that.

"Yes, you and Jay. He's in love with you, and you're in love with him. Why do I need to keep spelling it out? Forget everything else and just go get him... before I'm driven to something drastic."

"Julie, I'm not..."

"If you say 'I'm not gay', I swear I'll slap you again." Julie tried to stare him down with her hand raised, ready.

"Jay and me, we're not in love. Jay doesn't even believe in love."

"My brother is even more of an idiot than you. You don't have to believe something is real for it to be real. And he really is in love with you. Don't you feel the same way about him?"

"I... I was in love with April, not Jay."

"Miss Ugly Shoes? She didn't care about you, Adam. All she cared about was what *she* wanted. What about what you wanted? Ashdon Harbor wasn't good enough for her, so you couldn't live there? That's not love."

"It wasn't like that. She just made me see that Canberra was what I wanted."

"Then why aren't you there now?"

Adam had nothing to say to that. Julie had a point.

"Jason always supported you. When you said you wanted to go home to Ashdon, he said 'okay'. When you said you wanted to go to Canberra, he said 'if that's what you want'. That's what love is. Shit, if he only cared about what he wanted, he would have asked you to stay right where you were."

Julie's eyes bored into him, as if trying to press the truth into him. Adam found that he couldn't look away. If what she said was true... No, Jay didn't do love.

"Speak of the devil," Julie said as Jay unlocked the door and came in.

He only seemed mildly surprised to find Adam there. He just nodded his head and dumped his jacket on the futon as he made his way through the lounge.

"Well, I've got places to be," Julie said to Adam. "One afternoon of annoying little sister's absence coming up. You're welcome. Now you can't say that I didn't give you anything for your birthday. And do actually *talk* to him, Adam."

Julie headed out, leaving Adam alone with Jay. Adam's head was spinning with the idea that Julie had planted, and he couldn't think straight.

"Jay..." Adam started.

Jay looked over, but Adam couldn't find any words. He gave Jay a mournful look, hoping it would communicate his misery and confusion. Apparently it didn't.

"I was going to call you earlier. Say happy birthday and everything," Jay said.

"Thanks," Adam replied.

"Had to get away from the party preparations, huh?"

"Something like that."

"It probably won't be as bad as you think."

"It would be better if you were there."

"Yeah. Sorry."

When Adam didn't say anything, Jay kept talking.

"I'm meeting Jack later," he said. "He made these plans... I don't know. I couldn't get out of it... So... Must feel good to be back home, though."

"Pretty much sucks, actually," Adam said.

"Huh. Well, it is Ashdon."

"Yeah. It's not really the same after..."

"After Canberra."

"No. After... us. It doesn't feel right, being up there without you."

Adam searched Jay's face for any sign that Julie could be right. All he found was the same awkward speechlessness that had been there when Jay had come to see him the other day.

"Us?" Jay said.

"Don't do that, Jay. You know what I mean. What we used to be in Ashdon... we're not anymore."

"Friends?"

"We haven't been friends for a long time."

"That's a shitty thing to say."

"We've been more than friends."

Jay frowned and looked away, and Adam laughed.

"We spent almost three years doing that and we never talked about it. Do you think that's weird?" Adam said.

"Shit, Adam. What is there to say?"

"I don't know. I love you?"

Jay snorted. "Julie's been in your ear," he said.

"Maybe she has a point," Adam replied.

"Right. She gives you a pep talk, and you've all of a sudden discovered these hidden feelings? Convenient."

"No. It's not convenient. Do you know how bloody inconvenient it is to..."

"See? Even you can't say it with a straight face. Julie is a romantic. Us? We were just two bored, horny mates who had nothing better to do with their time. There's nothing romantic about that."

"Yeah. Nothing romantic about you," Adam said. "Just forget I said anything. It's pointless."

He turned and walked away, back to the car and Ashdon. He heard Jay call his name, but Adam didn't slow, didn't turn and look. He was sick of obsessing over Jay. Julie was wrong; talking to Jay wouldn't change a thing. All Jay brought was pain.

Twenty-Three

THE TWO BOYS stood close. They were smiling, laughing, and every now and then one of them would grab an arm, punch a shoulder, even kick a shin, to get some contact. It was as if they both had an irresistible urge to be touching. They might as well jump each other in the street; it was that obvious it was what they wanted to do. They were teenagers after all.

The taller of the boys leaned down and whispered into the other's ear. The smaller boy's eyes widened in surprise, and then he burst out laughing. It was unselfconscious and beautiful. The taller one grinned in response, obviously pleased with himself. The other boy punched him in the shoulder.

All of a sudden, the taller boy abandoned the other, without a word. Two teenage girls came out of the arcade, laughing, with their arms entwined and carrying a few shopping bags each. The taller boy went up and tried to put his arm around the blonde. She just handed him her bags and turned to her friend who was holding hands with the smaller boy.

Jay watched the boys leave with their girlfriends, still thinking "maybe"... A girlfriend didn't necessarily signify anything. It wasn't like he hadn't—

Then he shook himself. What was he doing, staring at a couple of teenagers like a fucking paedophile? Who cares what they did or didn't do with each other in private?

Jay looked at his watch. Damn. He must have been spying on them for at least ten minutes. He was going to be late meeting Jack if he didn't start moving his arse. He shook his head again and started moving fast in the opposite direction, not admitting to himself that he had been doing more than watching a couple of kids in the mall. He had been remembering. Remembering a time when he was a teenager, needing to touch so badly that it was like a constant twitch, but having to cover it with jokes and horseplay.

Terry had asked him how long he'd wanted something to happen between him and Adam. The truth was, he didn't know. When he'd finally realised what the twitch was, it already felt as natural as breathing.

When Gabby left Adam so miserable and broken, Jay would catch himself thinking, *I would never do that to him. If he loved me that much, I wouldn't break his heart.* But then he'd realise how crazy that was. He hadn't wanted Adam to love him. Of course he hadn't. He wasn't gay. He'd just wanted to touch Adam. Jay had wanted to kiss Adam and touch him and make him moan the way he had been that time Jay had walked in on Gabby and Adam together.

Okay, maybe that did sound slightly gay, in hindsight, but Jay had been real good at ignoring the unimportant back then. Until *that night*.

Jay had heard about Gabby and her heartlessness so much over the previous couple of weeks, he had begun to feel a bit crazy and heartless himself. So he did it.

He told Adam afterwards that he'd kissed Adam just to make him shut up. Maybe that was part of it. But he'd wanted to do it for a very long time. And Adam hadn't hit him or yelled at him or... well, much of anything. He'd just stood there, looking bewildered.

Jay had also told Adam that he was to blame for the accident because he'd kept talking about Gabby and irritating the hell out of Jay when, in reality, Jay hadn't heard a word that Adam was saying in the car that night. He'd assumed Adam had been talking about Gabby, and Adam hadn't denied it. Jay had been remembering the kiss. How Adam's lips had felt against his own. How Adam's body had felt against his. And how badly he wanted to do it again. He'd been so preoccupied with these fantasies that he hadn't noticed the car in front of him was still motionless when the lights changed. But then, Adam hadn't noticed either.

JAY WAS STARING at the windshield, and had been for some time. Staring from the outside of the car. He had gotten out and leant on the hood, waiting for Jack to come over from his own car. When Jack had come over, though, Jay continued to stare at the window, not noticing Jack at his side.

"You are going to have to decide, you know," Jack said.

"Huh?" Jay had been busy not thinking about Adam and his stupid birthday party. He had been not thinking about it all night.

"Are you going to invite me in or tell me to go home?" Jack asked.

"Of course you can come in," Jay said, finally moving away from his car.

"It's the last time, isn't it?"

Jay found himself nodding. He hadn't thought about it until Jack asked. It was probably for the best, though. He opened his mouth to say so, but Jack stopped him.

"You don't need to explain," Jack said.

"Why?"

"It's obvious you're still in love with Adam. If you want to try to make things work with him now he's back..." Jack shrugged.

"No. That's not even..." Jay shook his head. "It's got nothing to do with Adam. And there's nothing to work out there anyway. We were never like that. But *you and me*... It's been great, Jack, but then, I don't know, I'm just really fucked up right now. You'd end up getting hurt. That's what happens around me. I screw things up."

"You don't have to."

"That's the problem, I don't know how not to. Even with Adam..." Jay paused. "Things have just gotten... complicated." It wasn't the right word, and Jay made a face. "Christ. I don't know what I'm saying. I can't do this now. Let's just go inside."

"Okay."

"Okay?" Jay studied Jack's expression, trying to gauge his feelings, but Jack was already in lockdown, probably regretting he had ever opened his heart to Jay.

Part of Jay wanted to say that he'd changed his mind, that he didn't want to break up with Jack at all. He hadn't planned to do it. And things had been going great. Maybe Terry was right and he was throwing away something good when he should be holding more tightly. The problem was, the other part of him wanted to run while he could.

At that moment, the heavens chose to unleash the downpour it had threatened all day, and Jay did run. It wasn't until he got to the door of his flat that he realised Jack wasn't with him. He stood in the rain for a little while, watching as Jack drove away. It wasn't that Jay couldn't see the logic of going inside. It was just that the place was so empty. Julie was there almost less than he was.

Jay wondered if Adam's dinner party had started. It was still early. He had an absurd notion that at night, with the rain, maybe it wouldn't take as long to get up to Ashdon as it normally did. Yeah, absurd.

BY THE TIME he got to Ashdon, it was extremely dark and still raining. He contemplated turning around and going home, but Adam's parents must have heard the car. His mother stuck her head out of the door and saw Jay standing in the rain.

"Jason?" she called. "Come in. You must be getting soaked."

Turning around without a word would have seemed more than eccentric at that point so Jay just smiled and came in to drip on their front hall carpet.

"Hello, Mrs Pearson," Jay said. "Did I miss the party?"

"You did. Everyone has gone home."

"Right."

Adam's father appeared then with a towel.

"Here you go, Jason. Dry yourself off a bit and you can go and wish the boy a happy birthday. I'm sure he'd be glad to see you."

"It's a bit late." Mrs Pearson frowned, shooting the man a look that Jay couldn't decipher.

"It won't take long to say happy birthday," Mr Pearson said.

"He'd be better off going home and getting out of those wet clothes," Mrs Pearson argued back.

She had a point. Jay was patting himself down with the towel, but as he was soaked to the skin, it wasn't helping much. The Pearsons hadn't noticed. They were too busy arguing. Jay snuck past them towards Adam's room. He didn't think he'd ever seen the Pearsons argue before. It had been a real weird year.

Adam was sitting at his desk, staring out at the rain when Jay came in.

"Yep," Jay said. "Definitely raining."

Adam spun round at his words and looked taken aback, as if seeing a ghost.

"What are you..." Adam started.

"Thought I'd come to wish you happy birthday after all."

Adam just stared at him.

"Happy birthday," Jay said.

Still staring.

Jay closed the bedroom door and leaned on it.

"Come on, you didn't think I'd let the day pass without your traditional birthday blowjob, did you?" Jay smiled.

He had always used humour as a defence, but sometimes (like that very moment) it turned out to be the worst thing he could do. Adam's stare turned into a glare.

"You drove three hours and got soaking wet just to say that? Okay. Sure." Adam stood up and undid his fly. "What's one last orgasm between mates, right?"

Jay shook his head. "It's not what I came to say. I just... I've missed you. The flat feels empty without you." Jay took a couple of steps towards Adam and stopped. "You're my best friend."

"Are we going to fuck or what?" Adam said, closing the distance between them.

"Adam."

Jay didn't say any more. Adam looked into his eyes, like he was waiting for something, but that was all Jay had. After a few seconds, Adam gave up, turned his back on Jay, and started pulling his fly up.

"Just go, Jay."

"Can't we go back to the way things were? That's what you wanted wasn't it, when you came to the flat today?"

Adam turned around again, and Jay almost wished that he hadn't. Jay had never seen Adam look that upset, like he was angry and hurt and miserable and confused all at the same time. Had Jay done that?

"You want everything to go back to the way things were?" Adam asked.

"More than anything," Jay replied.

"Do you even realise how miserable I was? All those women you brought home. Constantly. And I knew exactly what you were doing. Exactly how you'd do it. And every time I'd want to crawl into your bed afterwards. Erase any trace of her. Whoever she was. Make you forget. But you'd just bring another one home. Did you ever think about how that made me feel?"

"Um... I don't know."

Adam shook his head. Jay had obviously given the wrong answer.

"When April came along," Adam said. "I thought it was finally my time to have someone. I thought I was in love with her, but I couldn't let you go. I couldn't... Did you even realise that I'd fallen in love with you?"

This time Jay kept his mouth shut.

"Yes. I can say it, Jay. But I can't go back to the way things were. This sucks." Adam swept his hands around, meaning the room or the house or even the town. Jay wasn't going to ask. "But I won't go back to that. I won't go back to pretending that I don't feel something for you. That I don't... I've been sitting over there, thinking about this for hours. I don't know if it makes me gay or whatever. I do know that I love you. I'm sure of that. But I don't want to." Adam's eyes locked onto Jay's, looking for a reaction. "Say something, Jay."

"What do you want me to say?"

"Say you love me too."

"Adam..."

"You're the one who can't say it. I knew that's how it would be. You've never let yourself go there with anyone. Why would I be any different? I don't want to love you without getting anything back. I don't want to be like all those girls breaking their hearts in your bed."

"Just because I don't say it doesn't mean I don't... you know... feel that way about you. Why is it so important to say—"

"It just is."

"Ugh. Come on, Adam."

"Say it, just once. Please. If you want things to go back to the way they were, at least give me that. At least give me something that makes me different. If you really feel that way..."

"God. Fine. I love you too, you moron."

Adam stood, stunned, for a moment.

"Are you serious?" Adam said.

"Yes," Jay said. "You are a total moron."

Adam grinned so hard that Jay thought for sure he'd pull a muscle. Then Adam's body was thrust against his, Adam's lips met his own, Adam's tongue was in his mouth, and Adam's hands were on his skin.

So this was love. It didn't feel so bad.

"Adam," Mrs Pearson said, opening the door.

Jay and Adam jumped apart. Jay ended up standing on the opposite side of the open door, hidden from the view of Adam's mother.

"Jason was here," the woman said.

"Yeah?" Adam said, still breathing heavy.

"He must have gone to his mother's to get some clothes. He was soaked. You should probably go over there tomorrow and see what he wanted."

"Oh. Okay. Sure."

"It's a bit late to call there. Although, he would've gone and woken them up anyway. That boy." She paused, almost certainly shaking her head at Jay's thoughtlessness. "Just get some sleep. Or... whatever it was you were doing."

Adam's mother left abruptly, and Jay started laughing quietly to himself.

"Why didn't she know you were here?" Adam hissed.

Jay shrugged. "They were arguing. I guess they missed the part where I walked right past them."

"It's not that funny."

Jay continued laughing and nodded down. Adam's fly was open again and the front of his clothes were wet from where he had plastered himself against Jay.

"Dude, you look like you were jerking yourself out the window into the rain," Jay said. "That's a little odd, even for you."

"Let's just get out of here," Adam said.

"Where do you want to go?"

"Home."

"You are home."

Adam glared at him, and Jay grinned. This was more like it. This felt right. Like them.

"Are you gonna sneak out the window again?" Jay asked. "It's still raining."

"How much wetter can I get?" Adam replied.

"A lot actually. Trust me."

"I do."

Jay held out his hand, and Adam took it. They both climbed out of Adam's window into the rain and ran to the car.

They didn't make it far before pulling over for another embrace. It just felt too good to be together again. And all it took was one four-letter word. The word seemed so small now, not worth the heartache of the last twelve months. Jay tried it out again.

"I love you," he breathed into Adam's mouth.

"I love you too," Adam replied. "Idiot."

Twenty-Four

"MUM, DAD, THERE'S something I need to tell you," Adam said. He ushered them into the lounge chair and sat across from them, all with an air of sombre concern.

"What's the matter, son?" his dad asked, picking up on Adam's unease. "Has something happened?"

"Well... in a manner of speaking."

"What is it, dear?" his mother asked.

"The thing is, Jay and I, we've been... well, a couple, I guess. Or at least we are now."

His parents said nothing.

"We're seeing each other," Adam continued. "You know... as lovers."

His parents were still placidly watching him in silence, as if waiting for the momentous news.

"So... aren't you surprised?" Adam asked.

"Of course not, we always knew you were different," his mother said.

"Different? In what way?"

"It's hardly a secret, Adam," his father said. "Just look at you. You're a freak."

Surely Adam had heard him wrong.

"You don't mean that," Adam said.

"What your father means is that you're not normal," his mother added.

"How can you say that? I'm your son, your—"

"No. You're no son of ours," his father said.

Adam stared in disbelief at his parents. He had thought that they wouldn't take it well, but this was unbelievable. They were speaking calmly and rationally, like they were discussing the weather, not disowning their only child.

"Adam, this can't be a shock to you," his mother said. "You're not one of us. Never have been."

"Just look at you. Freak," his father said.

"Not freak, Stuart. Alien," his mother said.

It was then that Adam realised he was floating a couple feet above the lounge chair. Just hovering. Stress always made him do that.

"When we found your ship as a baby, we knew that you would grow up different to all the other boys," his mother continued. "You weren't human, after all."

ADAM WOKE UP when Jay attempted to untangle himself enough to actually get out of bed. He must have been latching onto Jay in his sleep again.

"Didn't mean to wake you," Jay said. "Go back to sleep. I just had to get up to go to the bathroom."

"I had the weirdest dream," Adam said.

"Yeah? About what?"

"I told my parents about us, and they told me that I was an alien. Not human. And I was floating. Which apparently I did."

"Weird." Jay opened the door to leave.

"What do you think it means?" Adam asked.

"That the possibility of ever telling your parents about us exists only in the realm of science fiction," Jay replied.

Adam sat up in bed and looked at Jay. "Seriously, Jay. What if I tell them and they disown me?"

Jay sighed. "Adam? You're not planning on telling them, right? So why worry about it?"

Jay left the room then, leaving Adam to stew about it on his own. He should have known Adam better than to say that. Adam worried about everything.

They'd been a couple for a number of months by that point, and it was not the first nightmare that Adam had experienced. It was funny. When they were just fooling around, Adam had never worried about people finding out. Now that it was an actual thing, Adam thought about it all the time. Maybe it was just because Julie knew—made it more real somehow.

Adam lay back down and tried to put it out of his head again. He'd be able to go back to sleep once Jay returned from the bathroom. He could wrap himself around Jay and breathe in his calmness. It always made Adam feel better.

Twenty-Five

JAY STRUGGLED TO keep his eyes from drifting closed. He had never been so bored in his life. And that was including the time his mother had decided they should all go on an outing to see the tree that she had climbed as a child. After all the hype, the tree was, quite expectedly, a tree. This new torture, however, was mind-numbingly worse. He must have really loved his sister.

The sister in question popped back into view, holding another armful of long, tightfitting dresses that would undoubtedly look just as hideous as all the previous versions of exactly the same damn dress.

"What about this one?" Julie asked, holding one out for him to inspect.

"Sucks," Jay replied, barely even glancing at her by that point.

"This one?" She held out another.

"Sucks."

"This one?"

"Sucks."

"What about this?"

"Actually, it's surprisingly tasteful and elegant."

"Really?"

"No. It sucks."

Julie gave him the look of a long suffering sister and moved to put them all back.

"Jules, can I go now?" Jay whined, not for the first time.

"No. You said that you would shop with me."

"I said that I would take you to the city after school when you asked. There was nothing in that request about being dragged all through the mall looking at dresses."

"Didn't you wonder why I wanted to go to the city? Honestly, brother, it's not my fault if you lack the foresight to have seen this coming."

"And it's not my fault that you don't have any friends."

"I have friends."

"Then why couldn't you have gone shopping with them?"

"Because their fashion style ranges from skanky to terminally boring."

"And what, supposedly, is mine?"

"Gay chic." Julie said this like it was entirely obvious.

Jay tried to convey his utter disdain for this sentiment, as if his being in a relationship with another man automatically made him stylish. He had never been interested in fashion. He was beginning to think that Julie was torturing him on purpose for her own amusement, not that she actually wanted his advice.

Having put the armload of clothing back, Julie headed out the store, only to pause at another a few doors down.

"Julie, no," Jay said, trying to put a stop to this nonsense before she made him go through every store in Rundle Mall. Come to think of it, Jay was pretty sure that they had been into this one before.

"Come on. I won't be much longer," Julie said.

"Jules, we've already been here for hours," Jay replied.

"Have we?"

"The Formal is ages away. Why do you even need a dress?"

"I'm not going to buy one today," Julie scoffed. "We're just looking."

She turned her back on him and went inside the store. Jay hesitated a few beats, then turned the other way and left her to it. He walked slowly, waiting for Julie to realise that he hadn't followed her in. She caught on eventually.

"Oy," she said as she reached him. "Where are you going, doofus? You just left me there."

"I figured you'd had enough fun torturing me for one afternoon. I'm going home."

"What are you talking about?"

"Jules, there is absolutely no reason for me to be here, other than for you to enjoy watching me suffer."

"No. I wanted you to come. I wanted to hang out with my brother and... well, okay, I admit that I was wondering how long I could drag you around before you cracked. To be honest, you lasted longer than I thought you would."

"You are an evil little wench."

She laughed. "It wasn't pre-planned or anything. It just occurred to me when we got here and I went into that first shop."

"We went into the same shop more than once, didn't we?"

"Maybe." She laughed again.

Before Jay could unleash his wrath, someone yelled his and Julie's names.

"That would be us..." Jay said. "Who the fuck are you?"

The guy looked hurt. Jay *had* recognised him. He was from Ashdon Harbor. A couple years older. He'd always been coming into the library asking for sponsorship for something or other throughout high school. He'd be all like "I'm collecting donations for CanTeen" or "I'm running in the fun run" or "I'm selling tickets in this raffle" or whatever bullshit thing he'd wanted money for that month. He'd never be in there for an actual book. Only money. Jay's mother had handed some over happily for whatever cause it was, but Jay had been sceptical. The money was probably going into the guy's wallet every time. Nobody had that many causes they were passionate about.

"I think the more pertinent question, Sammy Turner, would be why are you jumping on us in the middle of the city?" Julie said.

"You do remember me?" He beamed.

"It would appear so. But you didn't answer my question."

"It was just nice to see some familiar faces. Adelaide can be kind of lonely, don't you think? You going to school here now?" Sam asked.

"That would explain the uniform," Julie replied, referring to the private school get-up that she spent so much time in these days.

"Either that or a kinky boyfriend," Jay added.

"Right." Sam looked a little lost for words at that, but apparently the correct response was to change the subject very quickly. "So, I'm working here now. Got a job—promotion work for this cancer charity. It's okay, I guess, but the boss is a real nightmare. I don't know. Makes me miss Ashdon a bit."

Jay cut in to say in a singsong voice: "He is not happy, Sam-I-Am. He does not like his boss, oh damn."

"Would he like him on a boat?" Julie asked.

"No, not on a boat, or wearing a coat, or riding on a pageant float. He does not like him here or there. He does not like him anywhere."

Sam stared at them, dumbfounded. "Were you guys always this weird?"

"Oh, yes," Julie said.

"Quite," Jay added.

"You just didn't know us that well," Julie said.

Sam looked from one of them to the other, then must have come to the conclusion that his nostalgia for their hometown was not strong enough for him to put up with them.

"See you around then," he said, moving off, a lot less happy to have found them than he had been a few moments ago.

"Bye, Sam," Julie called out loudly, waving.

"That was nice," she said, turning to her brother.

"He'll never talk to us again," Jay replied.

"Yeah." Julie sighed contentedly. "You know, I don't think we've ever called him Sam-I-Am to his face before."

"I live dangerously."

Julie snorted. "I think it's more likely that he never directly spoke to us before."

"That was the best policy all around, really. He understands now."

"Hey, on the way home—"

"No. Just assume that from now on, the default answer is always no."

Julie just laughed.

ANOTHER DAY AT work, another day of quarantine. Adam spent all his time in a back room doing cataloguing, circulation, and item maintenance. They let him out, occasionally, to shelve, which was almost an adventure after spending so much time in front of a computer.

He knew that he had only been there for a short time, and as the new guy, he couldn't expect to be trusted with anything too important, but when were they actually going to let him near the patrons? It wasn't like he was a total neophyte. He had worked in a library before; he knew how to handle patrons. He wasn't going to discredit them.

He shouldn't complain; Adam knew that. Most people would probably consider his move back to Adelaide a success. He had a job. And it wasn't an awful job, really. He had a roof over his head and a means of transport. He had a... significant other. That term sounded odd to him, middle-aged. But Adam couldn't bring himself to say boyfriend, even in his head.

Adam settled himself into place among the other people waiting for the green go-signal to cross over and walk to where his car was. He was going home, and Jay wasn't working, which meant that they could spend some time together.

The pedestrian light turned green. Adam was about to step off into the street when he saw something that couldn't be—shouldn't be—a girl with long blonde hair flowing down her back and blue jeans hugging her behind. April? The height and build was about right, but he hadn't seen her since the night before they were meant to go to Canberra.

Adam pushed himself back through the knot of pedestrians and followed the blonde. He didn't rush. If he caught up with her, he would discover whether she actually was April, and he wasn't yet sure whether he was hoping she was or wasn't.

The blonde turned into one of the side malls and walked into a store. Adam followed her in and found himself surrounded by Apple products. He stopped in front of the MacBooks, as if he were considering their features, while eyeing the blonde, who was reading the back of a box of iPhone accessories.

"May I help you?" A salesman had approached Adam.

"Ah, just looking, thanks," Adam mumbled.

When he looked back over at the accessories, the blonde was gone. She wasn't anywhere in the shop. Adam went back out, looking around at the other shops in the side mall, but couldn't see her. She could be anywhere. He wandered out into Rundle Mall proper, searching from one side to the other. As he was looking behind himself, he managed to walk right into someone. It was the blonde. She turned and... it wasn't April.

"I'm so sorry," Adam said.

"That's okay." The blonde smiled back.

"Oh my god, Adam? You totally ran into that girl. You're such a dork."

The voice witnessing his embarrassment was Julie's, and it appeared that Jay was with her too.

"Why are you guys in the city?" he asked.

"Julie thought I didn't have enough torture in my life," Jay said.

"We were shopping," Julie corrected.

"You didn't buy anything," Jay said.

"We went into shops, didn't we? Ergo, shopping." Julie rolled her eyes. "What are you doing, anyway? Other than causing damage to unwary shoppers?"

"Um…" How was Adam supposed to explain following a stranger through the city? A stranger that seemed to have disappeared on him again.

"It's obvious what he was doing, Jules. Haven't you ever seen Adam use his most successful pickup line? The girls fall at his feet. Sure, it's because he pushes them over, but whatever works, right?" Jay said. "She was definitely your type, and she seemed interested. Did you get her number?"

Adam didn't respond.

"Did we interrupt? Sorry," Jay went on.

"Don't be an arsehole," Julie said. "That's not funny."

Jay shrugged, but Adam wasn't sure that he was joking. Maybe Jay wouldn't care if Adam picked up some strange woman. Just because Jay hadn't done that in the last few months didn't mean he wasn't thinking about it.

Yet, Adam had nothing to defend himself with, even if Jay had got antsy about it. What was he going to say, "I wasn't hitting on her, I was stalking her"?

"Where are you guys parked?" he asked instead.

Twenty-Six

JAY HAD JUST got off work. There was no one at home and nothing on the telly, so there wasn't any rush to get there. He'd already purchased the weekly groceries so not much point in sticking around the shopping centre either. What was a boy to do? He sat on one of the benches inside the centre and contemplated his options.

There was a bloke across from him, trying to sell those rubbish do-dads for charity that always seem to be trotted out for some cause or another throughout the year. Jay watched people walk past the man, studiously ignoring his presence. It was kind of amusing, the way they would see him in their path, then quickly glance away and look busy with something or other, like a handbag or phone, so that he wouldn't try to engage them. People were selfish prats, but they didn't like to be faced with the fact that they were selfish prats so they went out of their way to avoid being asked to contribute to the cause rather than having to say no and look like a prat.

After a few minutes, a young man about Jay's age went up to the bloke and asked how much for the flotsam in his cardboard tray. The man did his spiel—two dollars for a pin, three dollars for a pen, five dollars for a tiny bear, whatever. The young guy pulled out his wallet and rooted around in it for a bit. He emerged with a few coins but apparently not enough to actually purchase something.

"Sorry, mate," the young guy said. "I guess I don't have enough. I'm broke. But you can have what's here, as a donation."

"Hang on," Jay said from behind him. Jay had felt sorry for the guy and wandered over while he was digging in his wallet.

"How much do you need?" Jay asked.

"A dollar," the guy said. "I was going to buy the little bear for my niece."

Jay handed over the extra dollar.

"Thanks."

"Don't worry about it."

The two of them walked towards the entrance of the centre, not so much together as heading in the same direction.

"Hey," the guy said. "If you want to get a beer sometime, come over to Birdie—the bar on Hindley Street. My shout."

"I thought you didn't have any money," Jay said.

"Call it employee discount."

"You work there?"

"Yep. But don't hold it against me."

"And do you often go picking up strangers in shopping centres?"

The guy laughed. "Only when I'm new in town and don't really know anyone yet."

"Don't you meet enough people working at Birdie?"

"The drunk, desperate, and ugly, unfortunately."

"You make it sound so enticing."

The guy shrugged. "Beats shovelling shit. I'm Bradley, by the way."

"Jason."

"See you soon then, Jason."

The guy gave him a warm smile and walked off. Jay was unsettled. Had he just been hit on by a guy? Was it wrong that he'd liked it?

WHEN JAY GOT home, he was surprised to see that Julie was in. She was sitting in the lounge room with another girl, and they had a heap of stuff spread out everywhere—paper, textas, books, scissors, glue. They were working on a school project, Jay deduced.

"Hey, sis," Jay said. "Why does the flat look like Adam decided to go back to school?"

"*I* am at school, doofus," Julie replied.

"You doing schoolwork doesn't usually look like a stationery store exploded in our lounge room," Jay said.

"Today it does," Julie replied.

Jay looked down, trying to navigate a path through the mess to actually get into his own flat. He couldn't find one.

"If you don't move some of this stuff in the next thirty seconds, you're going to have boot prints on it," Jay said.

Julie rolled her eyes and gathered up an armful of the junk from in front of his feet so that he could move. Then she kicked a path through the rest so that he could get across the room.

"You're welcome," she said.

Having made it to the kitchen, Jay heard the friend whisper to Julie. It wasn't a very soft whisper, and their kitchen had no walls. Either this chick was exceptionally stupid, or she wanted him to hear.

"Is that your brother?" the girl said.

"Yep," Julie replied.

The girl was silent for a few beats.

"He's cute," she said.

"Adam's his boyfriend," Julie replied.

"Who's Adam?"

"Didn't you just hear me say? It's his boyfriend. Let's just get this done, Chloe, okay?"

Jay snuck a look at the girl. She was staring at him, and when he met her eyes, she gave him a big inviting smile. She was pretty; he had to give that to her. Was filling out her uniform well enough too. Maybe a bit young for Jay, though. And he'd never go after one of his sister's friends. Way too weird and disturbing.

Still, hit on twice in an hour, not bad.

Twenty-Seven

THE FIRST PERSON Jay saw when he got to work the next day was Courtney. She hadn't said more than two words to him since he'd broken up with her dad. Another friendship that had been obliterated because of Jay's actions. He couldn't do anything about Terry—he didn't even know where she was—but Courtney was here, and he could try to fix that.

Jay took a breath and forced himself over to her.

"Hey, Court."

"Hi, Jason. What's up?"

"Just thought I'd come over and say hi... Hi."

"Hi."

"So, how are you doing?"

"Fine, I guess."

"Good."

There was a moment of silence.

"Jason, you don't usually involve yourself in pointless small talk, so again, what's up? I need to get started on my shift."

"Um, I just..."

"Spit it out."

"I guess I just wanted to see if there was a chance we could still be friends. After what happened."

"You mean, after your utter stupidity in breaking up with my dad?" Courtney said. Jay made to say something, but Courtney cut him off. "Look, I know you're in love with this Adam guy. Dad told me. But you broke my dad's heart, I'm not going to be throwing you and your boyfriend a coming-out party, okay?"

"Yeah, but—"

Courtney put her hand on his shoulder.

"No offence, Jason, but I think you and your boyfriend are a couple of dicks," she said.

"But that's what I like about him."

Courtney laughed. "I already know you like dick," she said as she walked away.

A few other people in the store looked curiously at him, but he just stared back, defying them to comment. When he got into the bakehouse, his workmates were giving him the same curious sidelong glances. One of them had obviously heard what Courtney had said. Jay ignored them.

"That's the second chick saying that shit about you," Kevin said.

"And?" Jay said.

"You want to be careful. It's not a good rumour to get started."

"Maybe it's not a rumour," the new guy, Peter, said.

"Well, are you?" Bev asked.

"Of course he's not," Kevin said.

"Then let him answer," Bev said. "Are you?"

"Am I what?" Jay asked.

"Gay. Are you gay?"

"I *am* very happy at the moment. Thanks for asking."

All three gave him blank face.

"Happy. Jolly. Gay. Same thing."

"But do you fuck guys or what?" Kevin asked.

"Are you propositioning me? It does explain why you've always been so interested in my sex life."

"Fuck off. I'm not queer."

"You fuck off. It's none of your goddamn business anyway."

Fuck it, Jay thought. *The secret didn't seem to be much of a secret anymore, and why should he have to lie about it?*

"Actually, yes," he said. "I do have a boyfriend. Yes, we have sex. No, I don't want to talk about it. Just like I never wanted to talk about it when I was dating a girl. Conversation over."

Jay returned to prepping and didn't say a word to his coworkers for the rest of the day. He hadn't intended it to go that way, but none of them said a word to him so he let it lie. It was a very quiet day.

ADAM COULD TELL that Jay was up to something. He was full of that nervous energy that meant he had done something others might consider stupid and reckless, and he was wondering whether to admit it or not. Adam knew the signs by now. Jay would smile but not at anything in particular, and it wouldn't be a normal smile—it would be a small awkward one or a large overcompensating grin. Jay would make jokes but not stop to explain them or laugh at them. And if it was something that could rebound on Adam, as this one obviously was, Jay would keep doing things for him—small things, like pass him a drink without asking—always accompanied by either the fake smile or the half-hearted joke.

"Jase, what is your problem?" Julie asked as Jay was clearing up the dishes from dinner.

"What?" Jay asked innocently, then ruined it by shooting her a large grin. It was like he couldn't decide between lying and ducking out of an explanation or making it so obvious that they would make him explain.

Adam sighed. "Jay, whatever it is, can you just tell us now so we can get it over with?"

"I don't know," Julie said. "Maybe we should have let him do the dishes first. Let him work out his guilt at whatever he's done."

"I'll do the dishes," Jay said, acting hurt that they would think otherwise. He turned his back on the two of them and ran water into the sink.

"Don't worry about it, Julie," Adam said. "It obviously affects me more than you. You can go—"

"No," Julie interrupted. "I want to know what my idiot of a brother has done now."

"Really, you don't have to involve yourself in our dramas."

"What do you think I'm here for?"

"The free rent," Jay quipped from the sink.

"The two of you can never sort any of this shit out for yourselves. Just think of me as your therapist," Julie said.

"Therapists don't tell people what to do, they talk them into working it out for themselves," Jay said.

"So tell me what the problem is and I'll talk you into doing what I want."

"There's no problem," Jay said.

Julie rolled her eyes at Adam. He shook his head back.

"I told everyone at work that I have a boyfriend," Jay announced and turned off the tap. The room felt very quiet without the sound of the water.

"What? Why?" Adam said.

Jay shrugged and started washing, rattling the dishes around in the sink, still with his back to them. "They asked, and it seemed stupid to lie about it. There are already so many people that know."

"Not that many," Julie said.

"Why would they ask?" Adam said.

"Just something Courtney said," Jay replied.

"Oh." Adam could only imagine what that girl would now be saying about Jay.

"What did they say? Your workmates," Adam asked.

"Nothing," Jay replied.

"They must have said something," Julie said.

"Nope," Jay confirmed.

Whatever had happened at work, it wasn't as easy or as pretty as Jay was making out. Adam's heart went out to him. It must have taken a lot of guts to tell those guys the rumours were true.

"Are you okay?" Adam asked.

Jay finally turned around and locked his eyes on Adam's.

"I'm okay," he said with conviction. "Are you okay? With people knowing."

Adam looked into Jay's eyes for a few beats, then said, "Yeah," and smiled. He'd been imagining how it would feel when people knew. In his imagination, it had always been either devastating or wonderful. Now it was a reality, real people out in the world knew, and that felt... normal, like this was the way it was supposed to be.

"What about people who actually matter?" Julie asked. "If you're going to start shouting it to the rooftops, it might be nice to give Mum a heads-up. I think she'll be hurt if she hears it from anyone else."

"Does she speak to Woolies bakers a lot?" Jay asked.

"You know, sometimes I wonder what Adam sees in you."

"I'm studly, obviously."

"If you say so."

JAY LAY IN bed waiting for Adam to start talking. He knew that Adam was working up to it because Adam was lying on the other side of the bed staring up at the ceiling instead of cuddling him like a half-starved boa constrictor. Sooner or later, Adam would roll over and Jay would get moaning in his ear, and not of the sexy variety. But Jay was tired. He wanted to go to sleep and he couldn't do that with his boa constrictor contemplating the ills of the world over there.

"What're you thinking about?" Jay asked.

"Telling our parents," Adam replied.

"Adam, you don't have to tell your parents. Or mine."

"Julie's right. We have to tell them eventually."

"Julie's not always right."

"She was pretty spot on about us."

"Lucky guess."

"If we're not hiding it anymore, it's possible that it would get back to them anyway. How do you think that would make them feel? To hear it from someone else."

"They wouldn't believe it."

"And if your mum asked you directly, like they did today," Adam said. "Would you deny it?"

Jay paused, not sure which was the answer that Adam wanted to hear. He rolled over and put a hand out, feeling for Adam in the darkness.

"Would you want me to deny it?" Jay asked. Adam didn't answer straight away, but when he did, it was firm.

"No," Adam said. "I don't think I would. And maybe that's what these nightmares are really about. My subconscious saying it's the right thing to tell them, even if I don't know what their reaction will be... Besides, we've kept this a secret for so long already, and it felt good to get it out in the open with Julie. She seemed to take it in stride."

Jay snorted. "Jules seemed happier about us than we were."

"You're not happy about us?" Adam asked, moving in closer to Jay.

It was distracting as hell, having a near naked Adam sliding up against him like that, and Jay knew that wherever the discussion was heading, he was about to agree to whatever Adam requested. Then Adam kissed him and he forgot to care.

"I want this to last, Jay. I don't want to be without you, and I don't want to be that old couple that have been roommates for decades and mysteriously never have any serious relationships with women. I want us to be 'us' and not have to hide it."

"Really?" Jay moved away, expecting that tightness he felt in the chest whenever his current partner started talking about the future and permanence. It didn't come. When he considered a future with Adam... well, he had always assumed Adam would be in there somewhere. "I guess we could do that."

Jay could feel Adam's smile in his kiss.

Twenty-Eight

AS THE WEEKEND got closer, Jay began to regret his tendency to agree with whoever had a hand on his dick. Sure, it was a great theory in the heat of the moment, but unfortunately, if he gave his word on something, he was the kind of guy who kept to it.

It wasn't that Jay didn't want his mother to know about him and Adam, necessarily. It was just that they weren't a family who talked about feelings and personal issues. How does one even bring up a topic like that? Oh God, his mother would probably think up one of her weird analogies about love. Jay shuddered to think what she would compare to falling in love with your best friend who happened to be of the same gender. And Adam's parents? They'd always hated Jay—now they'd probably want to move Adam to Alaska or something, away from Jay's evil influence. Of course it would be Jay's fault. Everything always was.

It was all giving Jay a major headache. He wondered if this was how Adam felt all the time. Constantly worrying things over. It was exhausting.

This was how Jay found himself walking into a bar on Hindley Street on Friday evening, on his own. He just needed to forget about it all for a while, and he needed to not bring his worry back to Adam. Adam had seemed surprisingly calm about the prospect of announcing their relationship to his parents the next day. This unnerved an already nervous Jay. He was usually the one reassuring Adam.

"Jason, hi." The bartender smiled at him familiarly, and Jay suddenly remembered why the name of this bar had rung a bell in his head. He had thought he must have heard about it from someone, which was true, in a way.

"Hi... uh." Damned if Jay could remember the guy's name.

"It's Bradley. We ran into each other coming out of Parabanks. You gave me a dollar."

"Sure. I remember." Vaguely.

"Wow. Here I was thinking I was hot stuff, having you come in here to chat me up, and I guess it was just a coincidence, huh?"

"Or maybe I just came in for the free beer."

Bradley laughed. "*That* you remember." He pulled a beer and put it down in front of Jay.

"Thanks. I kind of need it," Jay said.

"Rough day?"

"Not yet."

"Want to talk about it?"

"Spill all my woes to the trusty barkeep while sobbing into my beer? Think I'll pass."

"We'll see how you feel about that after a few more beers."

Jay shook his head. "It'll take a lot of beer for the sobbing. Wouldn't want to cut into your paycheque too much."

"How much beer would it take for 'going home with the handsome barkeep'?"

"Why? Is there one around here?" Jay mockingly glanced over his shoulder.

"Ouch. Not your type, then."

"I... I actually have a boyfriend."

"Lucky him. Is that who you may or may not cry into your beer over later?"

"Not exactly."

"Hmm. Interesting."

Jay shook his head again and glanced up at the TV above the bar. It was showing the Friday night football.

"Oh, no," Bradley said. "You're one of them, aren't you?"

"One of..."

Bradley leaned in close and stage whispered: "An AFL boy. There are so many of them here."

"You *are* in Adelaide," Jay said.

"Ugh." Bradley made a face.

"What are you into then, rugby?"

"Of course. Sport of champions."

"Right. Big ugly guys playing a shoving match."

"How much rugby have you actually watched?"

"How much Aussie Rules have *you* watched? There is way more skill in five minutes of AFL than a whole game of NRL."

"AFL is boring. Have you tried playing that dumb game? Half the time the ball is up the other end of the field and you just stand around watching it."

"I have played. I was best on ground for more weeks than I can count, and I wasn't ever bored."

"You played in the AFL?"

Jay laughed. "Just the local regional league in Ashdon Harbor."

"And I thought for second that I might have a celebrity in my bar. Where is Ashdon Harbor, anyway?"

"You're probably better off not knowing. You're not missing anything, trust me."

"All right."

The conversation and the beer flowed for the next few hours. Jay even paid for some of them. It would have been a good night if it wasn't for his plans in the morning.

Twenty-Nine

ADAM'S PARENTS HAD officially split up almost as soon as he moved his stuff back down to Adelaide. He had been dividing his weekends between one or the other, but he didn't want to have to go through his "coming out" two weeks in a row so he had decided to get both visits over in the same day. He could have asked them if he could see them both together, but that would have implied that there was some big disaster that he had to tell them about, and he didn't want to worry them.

Adam was not going to make a big deal about it. He was just going to mention it casually, and they could make of it what they would. He couldn't control their reaction, so he was trying not to think about it. Besides, it couldn't be any worse than the various scenarios his subconscious had been supplying in his dreams. If he got it over with, he would stop being anxious about it and the nightmares would go away. That was his theory anyway, and it was working well for him so far. Having a plan always made him feel better.

The plan that day was to drop Jay off at his mum's, then go over to his own mother's for lunch and drop his bombshell, then head over to his dad's for the same, and finally go pick Jay up on the way through. Was it weird that the part of this plan that Adam was most nervous about was the last? What would Mrs Porter think of him after Jay told her the truth?

The other unnerving part of the day was that Jay was freaking out. He was trying not to show it, but Adam had sensed the tension in him all week. Then he went and got drunk the night before. Adam would have been angry if he didn't already feel guilty about forcing Jay to go through with it. Part of him wanted to let Jay off the hook all week, but once he had thought it through, he was actually looking forward to being out in the open about their relationship. After this day, Jay wouldn't be able to deny what they were to each other. Was it wrong to want that?

Jay had made Julie promise to come with him for moral support. Julie must have seen how freaked Jay was too, because she agreed pretty readily. Or maybe she just wanted to be there to see her mum's reaction. Adam had to admit that he was not keen on being there for that. But still, it would be better afterwards when he wouldn't have to hide how much he cared for her son.

WHEN ADAM GOT to his mum's, she was pleased to see him, as always. She had made banana cake and a full roast lunch for just the two of them. Adam told her that he couldn't stay too long because he'd promised his father he'd drop by that afternoon. She made a face at that but didn't say anything. In keeping with their general policy about topics they didn't like talking about, his parents tended to avoid even mentioning the other.

Adam didn't want to spend a whole lot of time talking about his relationship with Jay, so he figured he would drop it in at the last minute and then say he had to go. Maybe he would say it as he was going out the door as a by-the-way. That would be kind of pathetic. In the end, Adam was there all of ten minutes before he spit it out. The opportunity presented itself, and he thought that if he didn't say it right then, he would never say it.

"So how are Jason and Julie doing?" Adam's mum asked.

"Good," he said. "Actually, Mum, Jay and I..."

His mother looked at him expectantly, which didn't help at all. Adam turned his gaze to his feet.

"Jay and I are together. As a couple."

"As a..."

"A couple. He's my boyfriend."

"No, he's not," his mother scoffed.

Adam glanced up, but his mother refused to meet his eye.

"He is, Mum. We've been together for—"

"I'm going to go check on that lunch. We'd better start soon if you want to get to your father's later."

"But, Mum..."

"He'll wonder where you've got to if you're too late. He'll blame me for that."

"But, what I said, I'm—"

"No, you're not." She said it firmly, actually looking into his eyes this time. For the last time all day.

The rest of the lunch was excruciatingly uncomfortable. His mother kept asking him about work and the drive up, how the meat was. Any topic that wouldn't include Jay. She was obviously trying to act like the earlier conversation, or attempt at conversation, had never happened, yet was very aware of it. There was a pink elephant in the room, and Adam felt that he shouldn't be enabling her to ignore it, yet he didn't actually want to talk to her about his relationship anyway. Maybe she just needed time to get used to the idea, and then things could go back to normal.

JAY WAS UNCHARACTERISTICALLY quiet all afternoon. Julie was chattering away, trying to cover up for him, but his mother could tell. She would listen to Julie and respond, but Jay felt her gaze on him constantly. Or maybe it was all in his head. When he snuck a glance her way, she wasn't actually looking at him. Ugh, he was totally freaking out.

Jay excused himself from the table and went to run some water over his face in the bathroom. He was sweaty, his heart was beating crazy fast, and his eyes in the mirror were overly large and panicky. Yep, definitely freaking out. He stood at the mirror, breathing in and out a few times. Or probably more than a few. Julie came into the bathroom looking for him, he'd been gone so long.

"Jase, what's your problem?" she said. "You've been acting weird all day. Hell, all week."

Jay spun to face her.

"What's my problem?" he sputtered. "My problem is that you put it into my boyfriend's head that I should come out to my mother."

"So?"

Jay glared at her.

"All you have to do is tell her that you're dating Adam. What's so hard about that? Do you think that she's going to disown you for it being a guy instead of a girl? I mean, you never made a secret of all the girls you paraded around town. What's so disgusting about Adam that you need to be ashamed of him?"

"I'm not ashamed of him."

"Then just talk about it like you would any girl you were dating. It's not any different."

"It's totally different."

"What's totally different?" their mother asked from the doorway. The two of them had been so busy arguing, they hadn't noticed her appear.

"Kissing a boy," Julie replied.

"I think I missed part of the conversation," their mother said, smiling.

Julie shot Jay a look. *Tell her,* it said. He didn't. Couldn't.

"Jesus, Jason. Just tell her. It's not going to stop the world from spinning or anything." Julie was obviously losing patience with him, and Jay was starting to regret bringing her along.

"Tell me what?" their mother asked.

Julie looked pointedly at Jay again, but he remained silent.

"He's in a relationship," Julie said. "It's pretty serious. They're good together."

"That's wonderful. What's she like?" their mother asked.

"He. It's a he," Julie said.

Their mother blinked. "Oh."

"It's Adam," Jay said. "We're... yeah. We're dating, I guess."

"I knew that," their mother said. Without another word, she turned her back and walked away.

Jay shot a look at Julie, but she seemed as puzzled by this reaction as he did. He took off after his mother, dimly registering Julie trailing along in his wake. He caught up to her in the kitchen. She was clearing the dishes off the table.

"Mum..." Jay said.

"I have to go pick up Bernard from the club," she said. "You two will be all right for a while until Adam comes to pick you up, won't you?"

"Mum, are you... Is this okay?" Jay asked.

"Of course," his mother said, pulling him into a hug. "If this makes you happy, then I'm happy for you. Adam, he's..." She trailed off and let go of Jay. "Well, I'd better get down there before Bernard spends his entire paycheque. You kids just make sure that you lock up when you go. Love you."

And then she was gone. Jay was shell-shocked. Julie seemed the same.

"She didn't know, did she?" Jay asked his sister.

"I seriously doubt it," Julie replied.

"Was that how you expected it to go?"

"No. You?"

"Not exactly. Was that a good reaction or a bad one?"

"Um... She didn't disown you," Julie offered.

"She might have just disowned Adam, though. Did you hear the way she couldn't even say anything nice about him?"

"I caught that, yeah."

"Since when is she lacking in praise for Adam?"

"Yeah."

"This sucks."

"Yeah. Sorry."

ADAM'S FATHER WAS confused as to why Adam was there and even more at a loss for what to do with him. He'd already eaten at his mother's, so the guy couldn't feed him.

"How about some coffee?" his dad asked.

"Sure. Thanks," Adam asked.

"Did you bring the paper?"

Of course he had, he was holding it, but Adam didn't say this, just handed it over. He had never understood why his dad was so keen to read it anyway. Like the city version would be more interesting or something.

His dad put the kettle on and started to flip through the paper. Adam was tired and a little depressed from how things had gone with his mother. It probably hadn't been such a hot idea to try and tackle this all on the one day. He really didn't want to come back and do it all again next weekend, though.

"Jay is my boyfriend. We're in a relationship," he blurted.

His dad looked up from the paper and said one word: "Why?"

"Because we want to be," Adam replied.

He had been so caught off guard by the question that he'd responded without thinking. He would have thought that this answer was obvious; yet, it must have satisfied his father. His dad went back to reading the paper, the conversation apparently over.

"That's it? You don't have anything else to say?" Adam asked. "No opinions on the matter?"

"Why should I? It's your life. You can do whatever you want."

The conversation went on as it always did. Adam talked about work, they discussed some of the more outrageous things his dad found in the paper, and they drank their coffee. They didn't talk about his relationship, but with his dad, it felt more natural, not like they were ignoring the elephant in the room, but that it had been acknowledged and it was just there, listening in.

Apparently, it didn't make any difference to his dad whom Adam dated. Come to think of it, he'd pretty much had the same attitude to Adam's girlfriends.

JAY AND JULIE were waiting in front of their mum's house when Adam drove up. He got out, but they were already heading for the car. Had it been that bad, that they didn't even want him in the house?

"How did things go?" Adam asked as they got closer.

"Fine, I guess," Jay said. "Mum told me she loved me, then escaped as quickly as she could. She's down at the club. What about you?"

"Dad basically said it was none of his business, and Mum pretended she never heard me say it."

"Mum said she already knew," Julie added.

"She already knew?" Adam asked.

"No," both siblings said at once.

Jay shrugged his shoulders.

"So was it worth it?" Jay asked. "Are you happy?"

"Yes," Adam said. "I'm glad we don't have to hide anymore."

He took Jay's hand, in front of his mother's house, in Ashdon Harbor, in broad daylight, and it felt just as good as he thought it would.

Thirty

A LITTLE PIECE of advice that Jay needed to remember: when anyone tells you that people need time to get used to something, don't count on it. Jay had assumed that things would settle down at work eventually, but his announcement, or coming out if you wanted to use those words, had effectively marked him as a pariah. The only person who talked to him, outside of the minimal amount necessary to get any work done, was Courtney, and he still hadn't had more than a five-minute conversation with her, seeing that she hated him for breaking up with her father.

He was starting to think of his time at work as meditation. If he got any more introspective, he'd probably end up topping himself. Wasn't the idea of community that you weren't alone enough to put any thought into how much life sucked?

The silent treatment had been going on for almost four weeks. Jay went to work each day and just got on with what he had to do. He didn't try to talk to the others anymore; he didn't even look at them when he could avoid it. How sad is it when you go into work to actually work? Who does that?

He'd been coming in later and later, having trouble dragging himself through the door each day. He'd stopped noticing the stares and whispers. Kind of. What was the big deal anyway? It was the twenty-first century, who acted like this? Hadn't they ever heard of a boy-meets-boy before?

Jay turned from the ovens, his eyes lowered to the ground, mostly thinking about ice cream flavours. Julie had asked him to bring some back, and he had been trying to remember what flavour she had asked for. His shoulder barely nudged Kevin's arm as he passed, but as he did, he heard Kevin mutter "faggot". Jay spun, and for the first time in weeks, he looked at one of his coworkers.

"What did you say to me?" he growled at Kevin.

The others squashed into their tiny cubbyhole stopped what they were doing.

"I said don't touch me, faggot," Kevin said.

"You think it's contagious, that you're going to be attracted to guys if I sneeze on you?"

"No. I just don't want you touching me. Who knows what gives you people jollies."

"Yeah. I'm totally going home tonight and jerking off thinking how sexy your arm felt against my shoulder."

"You want to start something, Porter?"

"That would make you feel better, wouldn't it? Beat the shit out of the little faggot and then go home and have some chicken."

"You're such a freak."

"Hey, you guys—" the new guy tried to interrupt.

"Shut up, Peter," they both replied at once.

The two men were practically nose-to-nose by this point, invading each other's personal space much more than Jay had when he'd bumped into Kevin's arm. Jay raised himself up to meet Kevin's eyes.

"You want to know how I act when I *am* attracted to a guy, Kev? You want to know what to watch out for? What I do when I want someone real bad..." Jay moved in even closer and then shouted in his face: "I kiss them, you fucking moron. And you never, ever, have to worry about me doing that to you."

Jay turned on his heels and performed the mother of all storming outs. He stalked right through the store, probably startling a few early shoppers, but Jay was past noticing or caring. He made it out into the fresh air and started gulping in great big lungfuls. When his breathing evened out, Jay knew that he had to go back and pretend nothing had happened. He didn't think he could.

"Jason, are you okay?"

Courtney had come out to find him.

"I figured you were going to crack pretty soon, but that was..." Courtney trailed off.

"Freakish," Jay supplied. "Gay? Completely fucked up?"

"Option C, thanks. Maybe a little of A, but definitely not B. You didn't look like you wanted to fuck a guy in there. Smash one in the face, yeah. Dice one up into little pieces and sell them in the meat section, maybe. But not fuck one."

Jay blinked at her a few times, his anger dissipating.

"Have you been hanging out with butchers?" He tried to add mock horror to his voice, but his heart wasn't really in it. "I warned you that they'd lead you astray."

"So you did, and I've been good. Scout's honour."

"Were you ever a scout?"

"No, does that matter?"

Jay shook his head. "I'm sorry, Court. You don't need to be dragged into my shit."

"That's what friends are for, isn't it?"

"Are we still friends? I didn't think you were interested."

Courtney shrugged. "Looks like you could use one, though. Besides, I feel like I might be partly responsible for this whole mess. It was my joke that started it all."

"I don't think I can take it anymore. It's not like I was ever really close to most of those jerks. I never thought it would bother me if they stopped talking to me, but... they treat me like a leper. Is it such an awful thing to be attracted to guys?"

"Of course not. They just don't know what to do with you. People want to put others in a box. It saves them having to think about anything too hard. You, my friend, ticked the box for womanising, selfish bastard, and they ticked that puppy in pen. They were so sure they had you figured out. You've been cultivating that image for more than three years. But you've screwed that up with your confession. Where do they put you now? They can't tick gay, you don't fit their stereotype, and besides, you've trolled through 80 percent of the female employees who've been here in that three years. So what the hell are you? They can't acknowledge you without figuring that out."

"You reckon if I'd come into the job with a boyfriend, they'd have accepted me?"

"Sure. Most of them. There are a few homophobic wankers, but probably not as many as you think. Most people think that you're either an arsehole who took advantage of naïve young women to hide your sexuality, or that you're lying to stop more young women from throwing themselves at you. Either way, it's a douchey thing to do."

"And what box have you put me in?"

Courtney laughed. "I know you—I don't have to put you in a box anymore. You have your own box."

"Thanks. That's generous of you."

Jay saw his manager, Gary, striding up to them and groaned. The guy was terminally grumpy, but this time he looked positively livid. Apparently, homicidal bakers strolling through the store was a bad look—who knew?

"Porter, stop making a scene and get your arse back in there," the guy said when he reached them.

Jay and Courtney had sat on a bench just outside of the store. Shoppers were going by them to get into the store but were paying them no attention at all. Adelaide might not be the biggest city in Australia, but it was a city. People tended to ignore you and walk around whatever scene you were making unless you were bleeding. If you were bleeding, they would walk a wider circle around you.

"Give him a break," Courtney said.

"A break is more than he deserves," Gary replied. "You're already walking a thin line, Porter. You don't think I noticed you coming in late for your shifts all week?"

It had been for more than a week, actually, but whatever.

"Chocolate and cookie dough," Jay announced.

"Sorry?"

"That was the ice cream Jules wanted me to get."

"This isn't a joke, Jason. I told you on Monday that you needed to clean your act up. If you don't go back in there now, you're fired. Do you understand that, son?"

Jay sighed and got up. He looked Gary in the eye and said, "Okay." Then he turned his back on the whole scene and walked away.

"Porter," Gary called. "If you walk today, I can't keep covering for you. This is really it."

Jay heard him but didn't care. His apprenticeship was finished anyway, and he'd had quite enough of Woolworths.

WHEN ADAM GOT home from his day in the library back room, Jay had the laptop up on the kitchen bench and had lots of printed-out pages spread next to it.

"What're you doing?" Adam asked.

Before Jay had a chance to reply, Julie came in from her bedroom.

"Hey, Adam," she said. "Do you have a highlighter?"

"Sure. Why?"

"I'm studying for a physics test, and I can't find mine."

"I've got them," Jay interrupted. He held a pink one above his head to confirm his statement.

"Um, why?" Julie asked.

"I'm highlighting stuff, obviously."

"You're printing stuff and highlighting it?"

"What's it look like?"

"But what for? I thought you only used the laptop for porn. Who prints porn?"

"I never use it for porn. I use it to upload embarrassing pictures of you to Facebook."

Adam and Julie had snuck closer to Jay to see what he was up to. The papers all had various notes and doodles scrawled on them in biro, and some of them did have words highlighted. Most of the ones that Adam could see had the word *no* scratched across in large capitals. Julie snatched one up to have a closer look.

"You're looking for a job?" Julie asked.

"Yep."

"Finally sick of Woolies, huh?" Adam said.

"Yep. I quit."

"You what?" Adam said, collapsing onto the stool next to Jay's. "Did you even think about what impact that would have? What about the rent and food and bills? How are you going to afford any of that without a job?"

"We managed before on one wage and Centrelink. We'll survive again," Jay replied.

"How can you be so calm? You don't just quit a perfectly good job, Jay. You don't walk away without putting—"

"Shut up," Jay said. "It was *not* a perfectly good job, and you've walked away from two of them in the past six months. Don't lecture me, Adam."

Jay got up and walked across to the door, grabbing his jacket and keys from the lounge on the way through.

"Where are you going?" Adam asked.

"Out," Jay replied.

He went through the door without a backwards glance, leaving Adam still sitting at the counter with his mouth hanging open.

"What was that?" Adam asked Julie.

"You being a completely useless, pathetic excuse for a boyfriend," Julie replied.

"What? What did I do?"

"Did you even look at him once during your tirade? He looked like shit, and he's been hunched up with this computer for hours. He obviously didn't quit so he could sit at home on the dole or have his boyfriend support him so he can practice his video-game playing. Something happened, Adam. Something bad because he has never liked that job and not once have I ever heard him say he was thinking of quitting. In fact, he usually loved to bitch about it. So, yeah, I think you're a pathetic, selfish prat for not asking him what was wrong instead of making a shitty day one hundred times worse. A boyfriend is supposed to support his partner. A friend will at least commiserate. What did you do?"

Adam's mouth was still hanging open.

"Pathetic," Julie repeated.

Julie gathered up the highlighters and left him to stew in his guilt.

JAY HAD ONLY been gone for twenty minutes when Adam started to get fidgety. Maybe he should try to call Jay, see if he was okay, apologise. Or maybe he should just give him some space until he wanted to come home. Adam wasn't sure what the right move was. He now had it on good authority that he was a crappy boyfriend, so whatever he thought he should do was probably the last thing that he ought to do.

A knock at the door interrupted Adam's train of thought. He opened it to a young woman holding a small tub of ice cream in front of her face.

"Ah," she said. "Not Jason."

"No," Adam said.

"Is he here?"

"No, actually."

"Huh."

Standing in the doorway, Adam felt like he was in some kind of stand-off. He had never met the girl, but she seemed to dislike him anyway. Before the girl could draw on him, or throw the ice cream in his face, Julie breezed past him on the way out.

"Oh, chocolate and cookie dough," she said when she saw the girl.

"Julie?" the girl asked.

"Yeah."

The girl handed Julie the ice cream.

"Jason was supposed to get this for you, but... it was a difficult day."

"Right, thanks," Julie said, taking the ice cream. "And who am I thanking?"

The girl smiled. "Courtney," she said, and Adam immediately understood her attitude.

"Jack's daughter," he said.

"Yes, Jason's boyfriend, I am," Courtney said.

Julie snorted. "Well, thanks for the ice cream."

"No problem. Tell Jason I stopped by... and not to be a stranger." Courtney turned to leave.

"Sorry," Adam blurted out.

"For what?" she asked.

"For how things went, with your father. I didn't mean to, or at least I wasn't—"

"Don't worry about it. It was obvious to anyone who cared to look that Jason was madly in love with you. It couldn't have turned out any different. I just..."

"What?"

Courtney smiled again, but this time it didn't quite meet her eyes. "I wish my dad hadn't fallen so hard for him first. Take care of him, okay? He doesn't like people to know when he's hurting, but he needs you to figure it out and be there for him."

"Like today."

She nodded. "Like today."

"What happened?"

"That's for Jason to tell you. But make him. See you around, Jason's boyfriend, Julie."

Courtney took off, and Adam found himself with a tub of chocolate and cookie dough ice cream in his hands.

"Put that in the freezer for me, will you?" Julie said.

"Where are you going?"

"Out."

"I thought you had to study for a physics test."

"I will. But it's Friday. Who studies on Friday?"

Apparently, he was the only person in the world who ever did.

"Don't be too hard on yourself, Adam. You're both still figuring this relationship thing out, right? You'll do better next time."

"If he comes home."

"Jase'll come home. His bed's here." Julie flashed Adam a grin and disappeared into the night.

Adam wondered what was so great about chocolate and cookie dough anyway. He went inside and rooted around in the drawer for a spoon.

Thirty-One

"JUST GIVE ME the usual," Jay said as he settled himself at the bar.

"Hard day?"

Jay put his head on his hands and groaned.

"Wow. That bad? Maybe I should give you a double."

"A double beer? How would that work?"

"Two glasses?" Bradley grinned, and Jay couldn't help but smile back.

"So, what is the problem?" Bradley asked.

"I got fired today," Jay said. "Or maybe I quit."

"There's doubt?"

"My boss told me that if I didn't go back into work, I was fired, and I didn't go. What would you call that?"

"Uh, deliberately getting fired?"

Jay grunted and took a swig of his beer.

"So, why wouldn't you go back to work?" Bradley asked.

"Who wants to actually work? You know what I mean, it's not like you do a lot of it around here."

"Touché. But I think there's probably more to it than that."

"What, you mean like my homophobic wanker coworker who threatens to punch me in the face if I so much as breathe on him? Or the gossip girls in the front who whisper about me behind my back and think I'm a lying bastard? No, there was no special reason why I didn't want to go back in."

"Sounds like—"

"Sounds like you're trying to be my shrink instead of trying to get into my pants."

"Sorry." Bradley looked contrite. "I could always try to get you a job here? Do you know how to pull a beer?"

"No."

"Perfect."

"You think that getting me a job that I have no skills for is going to make me especially grateful?"

"Actually, I was thinking I could show you how. You know, like in the movies where they practically wrap themselves around the chick when they're supposedly trying to teach them how to play pool or golf or something."

"Who said I'd be the chick in this relationship?"

Bradley leaned over the bar. "Who said anything about a relationship? I'm just trying to get into your pants, remember?"

Another guy up the other end of the bar called out for Bradley to give him a refill.

"Just a sec," Bradley called. "Shit, these people think that I'm here to serve their every whim."

"That is what you're paid for."

"Yeah, but they don't pay me that much."

Bradley went off to serve his other customers, and Jay smiled into his beer. A few more and he was feeling much better. Almost enough to face going home.

"Another?" Bradley asked.

"Sure. But this better be the last one. I should go home before I blow all my savings on beer. I'm going to need them."

"Aw, you're going home. This is the way it always ends. I get you all liquored up and loose, and you take it home to another man. That doesn't seem fair."

"No one said that life was supposed to be fair, my friend."

"Jase," a voice called. His sister had walked in with her friends. She waved them off and then made her way over to him. "Jase, I've been trying to call you. Why didn't you pick up?"

Jay felt in his pocket, but his mobile wasn't in there.

"Must have left the phone at home," he said.

"Typical. You're so hopeless."

"What did you want anyway?"

"Courtney came around."

"What for?"

"Ice cream."

"Okay."

"She said to tell you not to be a stranger."

"Okay."

"Adam was worried about you. You do know he has a boyfriend." Julie said the last to Bradley. "He did mention that at some point while you were busy drooling over him?"

"Jules, he wasn't drooling over me. This is my friend, Bradley."

"And, yes, he did tell me about the boyfriend," Bradley added.

"A friend named Bradley. Why have I never heard of him?" Julie asked.

"I don't tell you everything. It's not like I know all the names of your friends over there."

"Nathaniel, David, Gwen, Sally, and Titch," Julie said, not bothering to point out who was who.

"Titch?"

"I have mentioned them all before because I tell you everything; you just don't listen."

"I wish you wouldn't. Fine. Julie, meet Bradley. Bradley works in this bar at night and toils on a Masters in Psychology during the day. He aspires to one day reach the dizzying heights of being my personal shrink, but for the moment, he's settling for the homely barkeep to whom I tell all my woes. He likes rugby and bad foreign movies that make no sense. Bradley, this is my sister, Julie. She's seventeen."

"Don't serve the minors, gotcha," Bradley said.

"What are your woes, and why aren't you telling them to Adam?" Julie asked.

"Because Adam doesn't have beer." Jay lifted the glass in his hand. "What are you doing here? You're too young to be drinking."

"It's a long story. What happened at work today?"

"It's not a long story."

"Then tell me."

Jay sighed. "Kevin was being a homophobic dick. I walked out and refused to go back. I'm pretty sure I'm fired."

"I thought you quit."

"When your boss tells you that if you don't come back, you're fired, and then you don't come back, it amounts to the same thing, right? Bradley here called it deliberately getting fired."

"Jase…" Before Julie could get out whatever platitude she was going to offer, her friends rushed up.

"Julie, is this him?" one of them said. He was tall and scrawny and was looking Jay up and down like he was appraising Jay's quality. "Is this your brother? He looks perfect. Did you ask him?" The guy turned to Jay. "Thank you so much for doing this. It means so, so much. You don't know how much I was freaking out."

Jay peered past him to Julie who was mouthing "sorry". This did not bode well for Jay.

"Look, whatever Julie promised you I'd do, it's not going to happen today. I'm really not in the mood for favours," Jay said.

"You don't know what the favour is yet," Bradley said behind him.

"You shouldn't even be talking to them," Jay said to him.

"Why? The law says I shouldn't serve minors. It doesn't say anything about not talking to them. What's the favour?"

Julie's friend turned to Bradley then, Jay forgotten.

"There's this guy," he said.

"Isn't there always?" Bradley said in his world-weary bartender voice.

"Anyway, he's a bit older than I am."

"Of course he is." Bradley was taking the piss, but the kid didn't seem to notice.

"I really, really like him, but he thinks that I'm too young for him. That I'm inexperienced. So I kind of made up an ex, an older guy."

"Yeah, that's gonna prove that you're mature enough for him," Jay said.

"He doesn't believe me," the kid said miserably.

"I wonder why," Jay said.

"And the favour?" Bradley asked.

"Julie thought that if her brother pretended to be my ex and acted jealous, maybe Titch would believe me."

"The guy's name is really—"

"Oh God, there he is, coming out of the bathroom. Please help me." The kid flicked his gaze desperately between Jay and Bradley.

"If you like this guy, maybe you shouldn't start by lying to him," Jay said.

"It's too late for that. Please. I really like him. He's so hot."

Jay shot a look at Titch. The guy seemed pretty average to him, and not that much older than the kid in front of them. He shrugged at Bradley.

"What's your name?" Bradley asked the kid as he came out from behind the bar.

"Nathaniel."

"Nate," Bradley said, overly loud. "How could you do this to me? Come into my bar and parade around this new guy. I feel bad enough as it is. I haven't been sleeping, I haven't…" He paused, presumably so that

Titch would think that Nathaniel was talking to him. "I'm not making a scene... Oh, really. You want a scene?"

Bradley leaned over and kissed Nathaniel. It was a long passionate-looking kiss, and the kid was holding onto Bradley's arms like a drowning man with a life preserver. Bradley was certainly providing an educational experience to the little wide-eyed twerp. It was having the desired effect, though. Titch (seriously? It had to be a nickname, right?) was starting to seem mighty bothered by it when Bradley finally pulled back.

"Nate. Tell me that you don't still feel something," Bradley said.

"I don't," Nathaniel replied, in a slightly shell-shocked voice.

"Fine," he said. "But you can't stay here. Just take the slut and get out."

"But—"

"I said get out." Bradley sounded half-hysterical, and Nathaniel was starting to look a little scared of him.

"Come on, Nathaniel. I think we should just go." Titch had come up next to Nathaniel and started leading him out by the elbow.

Titch glared at Bradley over his shoulder as they left. As soon as he turned away, though, Nathaniel mouthed "thanks". Bradley gave the kid a thumbs-up and stepped behind the bar again.

"You didn't have to kiss him, you know," Jay said. "Where that guy was standing, as long as you leaned the right way, it would have looked like you were kissing him anyway."

"But that wouldn't have made you jealous," Bradley replied.

"In your dreams, Bradley."

"I'll see you later tonight then. I have had some wickedly naughty dreams about you."

Jay shook his head and smirked. Then he looked up and saw that Julie was still watching them. Her expression wiped the smirk off his face.

Thirty-Two

"I CAN'T BELIEVE you told that kid I would pretend to be his ex-boyfriend. That's just ridiculous," Jay said as he and Julie walked up to the flat.

She had decided to ditch her friends to drive him home. She said that she didn't trust him to drive with the amount he had been drinking. He wasn't drunk so Jay figured it was more that she didn't trust him to behave himself with the hunky bartender. Not that anything would have happened. It never had before. They just flirted. It was harmless.

"So you think Bradley is ridiculous?" Julie countered.

"I think what he did was. What I can't understand is why you thought *I* would do that."

"It wasn't so much that I said you would. I just said, wouldn't it be good if someone did, and I said my brother had a boyfriend. Nathaniel put the two things together on his own."

"Why don't I believe you?"

Julie shrugged her shoulders.

Jay went to unlock the door of the flat, but Julie put out her hand and stopped him.

"When you say that you and Bradley are 'friends', does that mean in the way that you and Adam used to be 'friends'?" she asked.

"No."

"He wants you to be. He was being pretty obvious about it."

"Then he's shit out of luck."

Jay went to push open the door of the flat, but Julie put her hand up to stop him again.

"You haven't always let a relationship stop you from doing what you want," she said.

"I'm not cheating on Adam, Jules. And I don't want to."

"Good. Don't. Because you'll regret it if you do, Jase."

Julie removed her hand from his arm, and they both went through into the flat. Adam was sitting at the kitchen bench. He spun around when they came in, and they saw that he had Julie's precious tub of ice cream in his hand.

"Hey," she said indignantly. "What's the deal? I said put it in the freezer, not eat it."

Adam looked down guiltily at the tub in his hand.

"You better get over there and commandeer it before you go without your precious chocolate and cookie dough," Jay said.

Julie ran and snatched the tub from Adam. "Shit, how much of this did you eat, Adam?"

Adam shrugged.

"You think I'll like you better with a fat arse?" Jay asked.

"Would that stop you from pissing off to the pub when we get into an argument?" Adam countered.

"No, but it would definitely stop me from coming back. I got no interest in a lard arse."

"What kind of arse are you interested in then?"

"Turn around."

Adam shot an uncertain glance at Julie, but he stood and slowly turned so that his back faced Jay.

"Yeah," Jay said. "That'll do."

"God. Ever heard the expression, 'get a room'? You guys do realise you have one, right?" Julie said.

Jay laughed, then went over and put his arm around Adam's waist, pulling Adam down the hallway. He only managed to get halfway before stopping to kiss. Adam offered up the comfort of the familiar, with a hint of...

"You taste like chocolate," Jay murmured.

"You taste like beer," Adam murmured back.

Jay walked them backwards into the bedroom and closed the door.

"I'm sorry," Adam said.

"For what?" Jay said, concentrating on Adam's buttons.

"For flipping out earlier. Spontaneous decisions make me nervous. I like plans."

"I know, Adam. Don't worry about it. How distracted do you think Jules is?"

"How quiet can you be?"

"Not very," Jay replied, grinning.

As if that was her cue, they heard music start up from Julie's room.

"Problem solved," Jay said.

Of course, it would have been better if the music hadn't been One Direction, but Jules had to torture them somehow. Jay was pretty sure she hated the band too, so the joke was on her. The three of them had done this dance a time or two already, and he knew it wouldn't take long before he'd tuned it out.

After mentally shaking his head at her lame attack, Jay turned his mind back to the man in front of him and the prospect of coming together sooner rather than later. This was what Jay had needed all day. The simple. The uncomplicated.

Once Jay had spoken the magic words that Adam had wanted to hear a few months back, things had gotten back into an easy groove between them. Except this time, Jay didn't have to worry that it would be over any second. Adam wanted to be there. Certainly for the right now, Adam wanted to be there. And the present was all anyone really had anyway.

"Come now, Mr Steady Job, your unemployed plaything needs to prove his worth," Jay said.

"You're going to be paying your way in sexual favours now?" Adam said.

"If that's what Master wants."

Adam made a face. "Don't do that. Just... no."

"No blow job? Not even a handy?"

"No master/slave. It's creepy."

"My brain's too fried to have a discussion with you right now about whether role-playing is creepy."

"Your brain doesn't have to work for your mouth to."

"This is what I'm saying. So strip and get on the goddamned bed."

"Such a romantic."

"Yep. That's me. I'll romance you all night long, baby."

Adam supplied that soft smile for Jay, the one that meant the logical part of his brain was shutting down and he was all in for whatever Jay had in mind. Plus, he was sliding his pants off. That was a good sign too.

Jay's attention was fixed on Adam as his skin became visible an inch at a time. He didn't think that Adam was trying to tease him, but whether Adam had intended it or not, the sight was turning Jay on.

He was about to get very lucky. Then Jay realised that he already felt lucky. He had Adam, and that was a hell of a lot more valuable than a shitty job that he'd never liked. So maybe the day hadn't been so bad after all. Those bastards could go fuck themselves. He was going to fuck his boyfriend.

Thirty-Three

ADAM WAS WALKING back to his car after work when he saw a guy with short blond hair coming the other way and had that vague feeling of having seen him somewhere before. It took Adam a few more steps before he realised where he knew the guy from. It was Steve, April's cousin. Adam turned around so abruptly he almost smacked into the teenager behind him. He knew the kid was snickering about him but didn't stop to apologise.

"Steve," he called.

Adam jogged and caught the guy's arm. Steve shook him off but stopped walking.

"Hey, Steve. It's Adam. April's boyfriend. Ex-boyfriend. Have you heard from her?"

"Mum hears from her every now and again."

"How is she? Is she okay? Is she still in Adelaide?"

"Seems to be all right. And no. She went to Sydney. She didn't tell you?"

"No. It was... Sydney?"

"Yeah. Her dad lives in Sydney."

"I thought April wasn't in contact with him."

Steve snorted. "Told us that kind of information was all online now. Wasn't hard to find him."

"Oh."

"Do you want me to give her a message or something?"

Adam thought for only a second.

"No," he said. "Thanks."

He turned back towards where he had parked the car.

"Hey, whatever-your-name-is," Steve said.

"Adam."

"Whatever. What was with you two anyway?" Steve gave him a hard stare, reminding Adam of the threat he had made if Adam ever hurt April. "April didn't say much."

"She didn't say much to me either. Just that she didn't want to go to Canberra."

"I guess she just needed to see her dad after..."

"Yeah."

"See you round."

Steve walked off, leaving Adam standing alone in the city thinking about April, again.

ADAM KNEW HE should let it go. He had Jay, and he was happy. April was history. Yet... he found himself thinking about her, a lot. It was like a movie that you missed the last fifteen minutes of and always wondered what happened at the end. He'd done the same thing with Gabby, obsessing about the break-up to the point where Jay probably wanted to kill him. It had taken almost a year before he stopped thinking about Gabby.

Adam tried to keep his mind busy, but no matter what he did, he couldn't stop thinking about April with her dad in Sydney. He could understand why she'd want to find the man. He could even accept that she was so messed up that she would leave without saying goodbye. But why hadn't she contacted Adam once she had herself sorted in Sydney? Had their relationship meant so little to her that she could just forget him like that? Like Gabby had done when she took off to Melbourne.

ADAM HAD ASSUMED that finding the Williams in question would be harder than April's cousin had made it out to be. Williams was a pretty common name. He'd thought there would be a lot listed for Sydney. Turns out, the White Pages site online showed five listed within Sydney city itself and another thirty in the surrounding suburbs. That was kind of doable. Of course, if April had meant the outer suburbs of Sydney, the search might get more complicated.

April would have had the luxury of knowing her dad's first name, which would have been helpful in narrowing down the search. Adam had to do it the old-fashioned way. He started calling them during his lunch break at work, picking one of the thirty-five at random. If he could find her Dad, Adam might find April. Even if she wasn't staying with her dad, the guy would at least know where she was.

Amazingly, he hit pay dirt on the third number. A teenage boy answered the phone, and when Adam asked to speak to April, the kid said that she was at uni. Adam gave the kid his name and number and waited for April to call him back.

After a week of waiting, Adam called the number again. This time, he called after work, thinking the later time might mean that April was actually home. The same teenager answered. He went off to get April, and Adam was left hanging on the other end of the line, watching the minutes tick by. When the kid finally picked the phone up again, it was to say that April wasn't there.

"When do you think she'll be back?" Adam asked.

The kid was silent for long enough that Adam wondered if he was going to answer at all.

"Look," the kid said. "If I were you, I'd stop ringing here. You should save your money. April doesn't want to talk to you."

"She said that?"

"Yeah."

"What did she say?"

"That she didn't want to talk to you."

"She didn't say why?"

"What do I care why? It's her life. If she changes her mind, she'll call you. I gave her the number."

"Oh. Thanks."

"Yeah. See you later, man."

The kid hung up, and Adam realised that getting any kind of closure might be more difficult than he'd hoped after all.

OR NOT.

A few weeks after that phone call, the closure Adam had been searching for was hand-delivered to his house. April showed up on his doorstep one night, saying that she was in town for a week or so visiting her aunt and sisters.

"And you thought you'd check in to see if Adam was still here?" Jay asked, as annoyed at April's presence as he ever had been.

"I knew he was still here. He told my brother. I came to see why he's been calling my house constantly," April replied.

Jay shot Adam a look that went from surprised to furious in a split second.

"Maybe I should just leave you two to catch up then," Jay said.

"Jay..."

Jay waited, but Adam didn't know what to say to make his boyfriend less pissed off at him. When Adam remained silent, Jay stormed out, probably heading to the pub again. Adam knew that he should have stopped Jay, but if he went after his boyfriend, April would disappear again and he really needed to talk to her. He didn't want to spend any more time obsessing over what he had done wrong to screw up their relationship. He kept thinking that if he could just figure that out, he could let it go and move on. And maybe he wouldn't make the same mistake again.

So he invited April in for coffee instead. Jay had finally talked him into buying one of those fancy coffee machines.

"How was Canberra?" she asked. "You did go?"

"Yeah. For a while," he replied. "It was okay, but I missed everyone back in SA."

"So what are you doing now?"

"I work at the public library in the city. Mostly cataloguing, getting the stock ready for the shelves, that kind of thing."

"And how is it going? Do you like it?"

"It's all right."

"You sound really enthusiastic."

"What about you? You found your dad?"

"And a half-brother. Even the step-monster isn't so bad." April laughed. "It's good, though. I really like it there. I'm doing a Bachelor of Arts. We're studying gothic literature. All these books that I never would have read otherwise."

April told him about every class she was taking in a glossy overview. Adam hoped that she was actually enjoying the classes, and her family, as much as she was saying and not just trying to convince him that she was doing okay.

When the coffees were ready, Adam led April back to the futon.

"Sorry about Jay," he said.

"It's fine," April replied. "I've got a boyfriend back in Sydney. In case Jay was worried about me trying to steal you back or something."

She pulled out her phone, found the photo she was looking for, and showed it to Adam.

"What do you think?" she said. "Hot, right?"

Adam glanced at the picture but didn't really take in any details about the guy.

"I'm not gay, April," he said.

"Is that what you wanted to tell me?" April asked, putting the photo back.

"No. I just..."

"I never said you were."

"I know."

"Are you still sleeping with him? Jay."

"We're... Jay's my boyfriend now."

"Well, congratulations. You're not gay, just have a boyfriend."

"It's Jay. It's not like... I'm not attracted to any other guy."

"Why did you really want to talk to me, Adam? And don't say that you just wanted to see how I was doing. That's bullshit."

"I just... I wanted closure. Don't you?"

"What is there to close? You slept with someone else, and I left. It seems pretty closed to me. Or it did before you started calling me."

"I guess I just wanted to know why you left. What I did wrong. It was really just Jay? There was nothing else? I mean, we seemed to be okay before you left. I thought we were okay."

"You can't be serious. Adam, it wasn't real. *We* were never real."

"How can you say that? What we had, it felt real to me."

"Did it? To me, it always seemed like you were only half there. I thought you were shy or that you were just different to other guys. But that wasn't it. You were always half with him. I must be a little slow to take that long to figure it out, but I did figure it out. When it was waved in front of my face. That day, when I walked in on the two of you, it wasn't the first time you'd been with him, was it?"

"No."

"Yeah, I figured. I must have been so... Maybe I didn't want to see it."

"It doesn't make what *we* had less real."

"Now you're just being silly. I appreciate that you were there for me when I needed you, I'll always be glad of that, but come on. Did you really expect me to just go with you to Canberra and pretend everything was fine? It wasn't fine. Trust me, loving someone feels better when they love you back."

"I did love you."

"If you loved me, you wouldn't have done that to me."

Adam opened his mouth to say something but realised that he had no defence for what he'd done. She was right, of course. If he had really wanted to be with her, he should have been able to stay away from Jay.

"If I offered to get back with you right now, what would you say?" April asked.

"That isn't why I called you."

"So you wouldn't be tempted, for just today, for old time's sake, and no one else ever had to know?"

"No. I wouldn't."

"See? That's the difference. You love him. Whatever you were trying to get from him by using me to make him jealous, you obviously got it—"

"I wasn't using you."

"I may be slow, but I'm not stupid. Maybe you didn't realise that was what you were doing, but it was."

"No. I wanted to be with you, April. I cared about you. Jay and I, it wasn't... he was always dating girls, different girls all the time."

"That must have pissed you off. Wanted to give him a dose of his own medicine?"

"No. I just wanted something that was mine. He never was."

"But you couldn't stop whatever it was you had with him, because you were in love with him."

"That pretty much covers it, yeah."

"Dammit, Adam. I don't want to feel sorry for you. I've been building up a lot of resentment over what happened."

"I'm sorry."

"Accepted. Are we closed now?"

"I don't know, I guess."

"Great, because I'm exhausted." April sat back and sipped from her coffee mug. "I'm kind of glad you called actually. I didn't want to hate you."

"Me either."

"Don't do it again, though. It's kind of stalkery."

"Says the girl who I found waiting for me on my front step the day after meeting her."

Thirty-Four

JAY'S DAY HAD been pretty crappy before April showed up. He had looked up every job in Adelaide on Seek. He was either not qualified or not interested. He'd never cared what he was doing before, but now he kept thinking that if he had at least liked his job at Woolies, it wouldn't have mattered so much that his coworkers were arsehats.

And then there was April.

Jay couldn't believe that Adam had gone behind his back and chased her. After everything... He should have seen it coming, though, shouldn't he? There's no such thing as a happily ever after. That's just not the way the world works. And he was stupid enough to be taken in, just for one second. Because it was Adam.

Fucked if he was going to hang around and watch that bitch wrap Adam around her little finger again. He'd grabbed his wallet and headed out. All he wanted was to get shitfaced so he couldn't think anymore. So he wouldn't see her smug, ugly face telling him that Adam had asked for her.

Bradley greeted him with a huge grin when he walked in to Birdie. Ah, the pleasure of going somewhere where everybody knew your name. The important people, like the guy holding the drinks, anyway. Jay grinned back and settled himself on his usual stool at the bar.

"Hey, man, haven't seen you around in a couple of weeks," Bradley said.

"I think if the bartender gets worried when he hasn't seen you, it's probably a sign you have a problem," Jay replied.

"How's the job search going?"

"Abysmal."

"Aw. I have something that might make you feel better."

Bradley sauntered off, to get a beer Jay thought, but he didn't come back for a long time and when he did appear, he didn't have any beer. He had a tall, stocky man walking with him instead.

"This is the guy," Bradley said to the man with him. "His name's Jason, he can cook, and he's looking for a job. You can cook, right?"

"Sure," Jay said.

The other man sized him up and nodded.

"Fine," he said. "Come on back. Anything would be better than Eddie. Well, hurry up, then."

Jay looked at Bradley quizzically, but Bradley just motioned him around to the section of bar that raised up and then pulled him through to the other side.

"You wanted a job, right?" Bradley said.

"And this is a job doing what exactly? I was a baker not a cook."

"It's basically an assistant to Trev. You can chop and stir, yeah? You'll probably be fine. I mean, look around you, how complicated do you think the food here is? And Trev isn't going to care what you do at home, as long as you do what he tells you when you're here."

"I didn't even know this place had a kitchen."

Bradley pushed Jay towards the door into the kitchen. Jay stumbled in that direction, mumbling thanks to Bradley over his shoulder.

TREVOR WASN'T MUCH of a talker. All Jay heard for the next few hours were gruff directions and admonishments to be quicker, stir harder, chop smaller, that kind of thing. Surprisingly, though, Jay was enjoying himself. It wasn't taxing work, and the place wasn't overly busy, so it wasn't stressful. At the end of the night, Jay wasn't even tired, not like he had been after his shifts at Woolies. But it had successfully kept his mind from thinking.

"Not bad," Trevor said to him as they were clearing the kitchen. "So, are you actually looking for a job, or did Brad just want to shut me up?"

"I'm looking," Jay replied.

"I think you found one if you want it."

"Cool. I do."

"Come back tomorrow afternoon at four. We'll talk about shifts."

"Okay. I'll see you then."

When Jay emerged from the kitchen, Bradley was waiting for him on the other side of the bar.

"Whoa," Jay said. "Me behind the bar and you in front of it. This is some bizarre alternate universe. What did you do to me?"

"I facilitated your return to the land of the employed. How does it feel? Careful, it might make you dizzy at first, you better take it easy."

"Good idea." Jay ducked under the bar and joined Bradley. "I am feeling a bit dazed. Trevor offered me a job, starting tomorrow."

"Great. We should celebrate. I've got beer back at my place," Bradley offered.

"We're in a bar."

"Yes, we are."

"There's beer here."

"There is."

Bradley held Jay's gaze, not pushing but leaving the suggestion out there. Jay knew what he should say.

"How far is it?" he asked instead.

BRADLEY'S PLACE WAS smaller than Jay's, but he had a big comfy couch. Jay settled into it as Bradley handed him a cold beer.

"Congratulations," Bradley said, clinking the top of his bottle with Jay's. "May you last longer than Trev's previous slave."

"Cheers," Jay said, taking a long swig. "It'll be good, working together."

"Absolutely. I'm fabulous, so I could totally see how you'd think that."

"Shut up. You'd have to be better than the last lot of tossers."

"I suppose it won't be too horrible seeing you all the time."

"You're a good friend."

"Is that all?"

"Yeah," Jay mumbled, picking at the label on his bottle. "Where's your flatmate tonight?"

"Went to some gig. He won't be back till at least two or three am. What about your boyfriend? Is he going to be calling any second wondering where you are?"

"He's with his ex-girlfriend."

"You're shitting me... You're not. What the fuck is that about?"

Jay shrugged. "I don't know. She said he called."

"Does he want to get back with her?"

Jay looked up and caught Bradley staring intently at him. "I don't know," he said quietly.

"That's crap. If I was with you, I wouldn't go off chasing rainbows."

"'Cause I'm such a catch."

"Yeah. You are. You're gorgeous, Jason. You know that, don't you?" Bradley brushed his fingertips across Jay's cheek. "I've wanted to kiss you since the moment I met you. Have you even thought about it?"

"Yeah."

Bradley leaned in, slowly, giving Jay every opportunity to stop him. Jay didn't. The kiss was all warm, soft lips and wet tongue. Jay *had* been curious about what a kiss between them would be like. He now had his answer. Pretty damn good. No wonder that little twerp in the bar had looked so shell-shocked from this.

Jay's body was full of enthusiasm for the way the night was going. His mind, on the other hand, was insisting that he stop and think about what he was doing. He ignored his mind and ran his hand up the back of Bradley's shirt. The man was smooth, velvet skin on top of hard muscles. Jay felt his arousal building.

Bradley pulled at the button on Jay's jeans, sliding down the zipper and moving his hand past the waistband of Jay's underwear.

"Wait," Jay said, jumping up from the couch.

"Am I going too fast?" Bradley asked.

"I can't do this," Jay said, buttoning his jeans back up.

"We can slow things down if you want. Have another beer."

"I'm gonna go."

"Don't, Jason," Bradley said, standing up to join him.

"I love Adam. I can't do this."

"He's probably sleeping with his ex right now."

"I'm not going to do this, no matter what happened with them. I'm sorry, Bradley, I shouldn't have come."

With that, Jay turned and walked out. His dick wasn't particularly agreeing with his decision, but tough, it felt like the right one.

Thirty-Five

"JASE." JULIE SAT on his bed and shook him until he batted her away. "Jase, wake up. Mum's here."

"What?" Jay mumbled, still half-asleep.

"I said, Mum's here. She's actually here, in Adelaide, in the flat, in the lounge, right now. Get up! This is historic."

Julie disappeared again, and Jay tried to make sense of what she had said. He groaned and forced his body up. Jay wasn't sure what to expect from a visit at this point, but he should probably be awake and dressed for it.

Adam wasn't on the other side of the bed. Jay was relieved as it meant that he could avoid figuring out how to deal with the events of the previous night a little longer, just as he had been relieved that Adam was asleep when he'd gotten home from Bradley's. Then he felt guilty for feeling relieved that his boyfriend was absent. Then he felt guilty for having gone to Bradley's in the first place. All in all, it was probably not a good time for his mother's first visit.

When Jay ambled into the main living area, his mother was, indeed, standing bewildered in the middle of it.

"Mum?"

"You only have two bedrooms. I suppose I should have realised something when Julie said that Adam had moved back in. Two bedrooms. Why didn't I know that your flat only had two bedrooms?" his mother babbled.

"Because you've never been here before?" Jay replied.

"I thought you *did* know about Adam and Jase," Julie said.

"Oh, well, yes. Jason, come and sit down. Why don't you make a coffee; you look like you need one," their mother said.

"Which is it? Should I sit or make coffee?" Jay said.

"I'll get the coffee," Julie offered. "You want one, Mum?"

"Thanks, honey. That would be nice," their mother said.

Jay sat down on the futon and gestured for his mother to do the same.

"So, not to sound ungrateful or anything, but what's with the visit?" Jay asked.

"I wanted to see how you were doing. Both of you."

"You never have before."

"Well... I think I probably didn't react very well when you told me... the last time you were in Ashdon."

"When he came out, you mean," Julie put in from the kitchen.

"Hmm. Jason, I don't want you to think that I love you any less."

"I didn't," Jay said.

"Good. Adam's a nice boy."

"Yeah."

"Are you... You're in love with him?"

"Yeah."

"That's wonderful. Really it is, Jason. I'm happy for you. Where is he, anyway?"

"I have no idea."

"He went to get milk," Julie said from the kitchen. "Nobody wanted milk in their coffee, right? Because we don't have any."

"Oh," their mother said. "What's new with the two of you?"

"Jay quit his job," Julie said, bringing the coffees over.

"I got another one," Jay said.

"When did you get a job?" Julie asked.

"Last night. In the kitchen at Birdie," Jay answered.

"That bar in Hindley Street?" Julie frowned.

"Yeah."

"Do you like it?" his mother asked.

"I've only worked there for one day, but yeah. It's not too bad."

The front door opened then, and Adam came in with a bottle of milk. He said hello and smiled brightly at Jay's mother. She mumbled hello back and rose from the futon.

"I'd better get going. I don't want to take up too much of your time," she said.

"You just got here," Julie said.

"I'm sure you have a lot of things to do," their mother said. "I'll see you soon."

She was running away again. This was getting ridiculous. Jay let her get outside of the flat before catching up to her.

"Mum, wait," he said.

"I really have to go, Jason," she said.

"No, you don't. Stop being weird."

"I don't know what—"

"Yes, you do. You didn't even look at Adam back there. He's always been your little golden boy, now he's beneath your notice? What's your deal?"

"I wasn't—"

"Mum," Jay warned.

"I just... It's strange. Thinking of you, and him. I never... I'm not against men who... are intimate with other men, but... it never occurred to me that you would be..."

"You don't want your son to be a fag," Jay said.

"That's not what I said, Jason. I want you to be happy. I just... I don't know what to say to him anymore."

"No. You don't get to do that. For years you've been spouting all that bullshit about the wonder and rarity of love. If it's so special, you should be goddamn happy that I found it. With anyone. He's the same person he was before. And if you think less of him that he loves me, what does that say about how much you value me?"

"Jason..."

"Am I so unworthy of love?"

"Of course not. I was just... surprised. Give me a little time to wrap my head around this. That the two of you are..."

"Fine. But do it in his presence. His own mother will barely look at him since he told her about us. He shouldn't get the same thing from you as well. He didn't do anything to deserve that."

"Okay. I'll try."

The two of them headed back into the flat and made a big effort to act like everything was normal. It wasn't completely successful, but Jay gave his mother points for trying.

THE GUILT AND doubt swirling in his gut was preventing Jay from enjoying having Adam in his bed. In their bed. God, he hoped it was still going to be their bed.

Adam had not addressed Jay's storming out the night before. Not even a word. But it was all Jay could think about. Was he really what Adam wanted? Because after what had happened with Bradley, Jay was certain Adam was what he wanted.

He pulled away from Adam and sat up. He was usually all for ignoring problems and avoiding talking about feelings, but he didn't think he could do it this time. The truth of what he'd almost done was eating at his soul.

"What's the matter?" Adam asked, sitting up too. "Are you upset about April? You know that nothing happened, right? I wouldn't... I just wanted closure, that's all. To figure out what made her leave. I should have told you. I would have, but I didn't know she was coming. She wouldn't return any of my calls. I thought she was—"

"I kissed someone last night," Jay interrupted.

"What?"

"I was really pissed at you about April. And just... hurt."

"So... you hooked up with a stranger?"

"It was Bradley. The guy from Birdie. And we didn't... It was just the kiss."

"What happened?" Adam's face was stone—still and hard, coldly judging Jay's indiscretion.

"He wanted to celebrate the new job. So I went back to his place—"

"You went back to his place? So you were going to... You were going there to fuck."

"No. I don't know. But I couldn't. As soon as it started, it felt wrong. I'm sorry. Adam, it won't ever happen again. I don't want it to. Adam?"

Jay waited, his heart squeezed tight by an invisible fist, constricting more with each second ticking by without an answer.

"You really didn't go through with it?" Adam said finally.

"I really didn't. It's different this time. We're different. I promise, Adam. All I want is you. That's what you want too, isn't it?"

"Yeah. Of course. I should have come after you last night. I knew you were upset about April. I have no idea what I'm doing. That's why I wanted to talk to April, figure out why I keep screwing things up with everyone I care about. I don't want to screw things up with you."

Jay pulled Adam in against him again.

"I guess neither of us is perfect," Jay said. "But I love you anyway."

"I love you too," Adam said.

At the words, the fist around Jay's heart let up a little.

Thirty-Six

WAS ADAM KIDDING himself to believe Jay when he said things would be different this time around? Jay had been quick enough to jump into Jack's bed the previous year, not to mention the numerous girls that had been in and out of the flat before that. Why would things be different now?

Jay was obviously attracted to the guy from the bar. What was he like? Was he better looking than Adam? Funnier? Smarter? Adam had no clue what Jay even saw in other guys. But then if anyone had asked him why he was attracted to Jay, Adam was not sure he could have answered either. Jay was just Jay. He affected Adam in a way no man had ever done. More strongly than any girl had done either. It wasn't logical, it was just fact.

Adam sighed and switched the TV off; he couldn't concentrate on it with all this running through his head and with Jay off "working" with the would-be seducer. He glanced over at Julie, who was doing her homework up on the bench that surrounded the kitchen.

"Julie, do you know anything about this guy that got Jay the job at Birdie?" Adam asked.

"He's a total tosser," Julie said.

"You've met him?"

"Yeah. I went into this bar with some friends—long story, and don't look at me like that, I didn't drink anything—anyway, Jase was there talking to the bartender. He said they were friends."

"Is he good-looking?"

"Why? What did Jase tell you?"

"Is there anything that Jay *should* be telling me?"

"I thought it was weird that Jase had never mentioned him if they were such close friends."

"And?"

"Well," Julie said reluctantly. "It was pretty obvious that the guy had a thing for Jase, but Jase didn't seem to care. I told him it was going to end up being a problem..."

"He kissed Jay."

"That bastard."

"Did he know that Jay had a boyfriend?"

"Oh, yeah. He definitely knew. I'm gonna kick his arse." Julie got up and started towards the door.

"You're going over there now? What's that going to achieve?" Adam asked.

"It's going to make me feel better."

Adam hesitated. "I don't think..."

"Hey, you wanted to know what he looked like."

"I did," Adam admitted, "but I'm not going to—"

"Whatever. Come on."

IT TOOK A while to find the place. Julie was bad with directions, and as she kept reminding Adam, she had only been there once before.

Adam's heart sank when Julie confirmed that the guy behind the bar was the one they were looking for. He might not be an expert in what makes a man attractive, but even Adam could tell that this guy would make girls swoon, or maybe that would be boys in this case. He was male-model handsome, boy-band pretty. Adam had nothing to say to this guy. Julie grabbed his hand and pulled him up to the bar anyway.

"Hey. Julie, right? Jason's sister." The guy beamed at Julie. "I'm Bradley, I'm the one—"

"I know who you are. This is Jason's boyfriend." Julie pointed at Adam, her finger digging into his chest. Bradley's smile wavered slightly, but he held onto it.

"Adam. Jason's talked about you a lot," Bradley said.

"If he's constantly talking about his boyfriend, why did you stick your tongue down my brother's throat?" Julie demanded.

"He did stop talking about Adam long enough for that," Bradley said.

"You're such a wanker," Julie said.

"Did your brother not mention that he actually kissed me back? That he willingly came back to my place? I didn't force him to do anything. If he was considering sleeping with me, he obviously isn't happy at home."

"Yes, he is. He and Adam are perfect for each other."

Julie's hands were clenched into fists at her side, and she looked about ready to punch out the bartender.

"No offence to Adam," Bradley said, "but he doesn't look that special to me."

"You obviously don't know Jase," Julie said. "He is never going to dump Adam for you, so just back off."

"And what does Adam have to say? Aren't you going to tell me to stay away from your man as well? That's why you came, right?"

"No," Adam said. "I came to see Jay. I trust him. If he was going to sleep with you, he would have done it last night."

"When you were off with your ex-girlfriend, you mean."

"You were what?" Julie asked. "Why haven't I heard this part of the story?"

"Yeah, Adam. Why hide that part of the story?" Bradley mocked.

"Nothing happened between me and April," Adam said.

"Fucking April. No wonder..." Julie trailed off when she remembered why they were there. "That doesn't excuse you from taking advantage of my brother."

"He's a big boy, Julie. He can make his own decisions," Bradley said.

"And he did," Adam said. "He decided he didn't want you. Now, are you going to take our order?"

Bradley eyed him, trying to decide whether to keep arguing or not perhaps, but Adam just stared back at him calmly and settled onto a barstool.

"What do you want?" Bradley asked.

"A beer. But give it to me unopened. I don't trust you not to spit in it."

Bradley gave Adam the beer and took his money, then found himself very busy up the other end of the bar for the next twenty minutes.

Adam had come to a realisation while he and Julie were talking to Bradley. He did trust Jay. Jay had never lied to Adam, and if Jay said that he wasn't going to sleep with anyone else, Jay really believed it. He'd had the opportunity to sleep with this implausibly handsome guy and he hadn't taken it. That would have been unthinkable a year ago. Jay never turned away from temptation—until now. And it was all for Adam.

Adam couldn't keep the smile off his face.

JAY HAD SAILED through another night in the Birdie kitchen, no worries. It had been a bit awkward seeing Bradley again, but he'd made it pretty clear to the guy that what had happened between them could not happen again. He thought it was all going to work out.

Jay let out a sigh of relief when he opened the door into the bar and Bradley didn't immediately jump on him. Even better, the first thing Jay saw when he came in was Adam sitting with Julie. Adam was smiling from ear to ear.

"What're you guys doing here?" Jay asked.

"Just thought you might need some supervision," Julie said.

"I wanted to see your new workplace," Adam said, ignoring Julie's response.

"Not much to see," Jay said. His eyes swept the room, trying to think of something worth pointing out.

"Adam had a little talk to Bradley," Julie said. "Made sure he won't be bothering you again."

Jay raised his eyebrows at Adam.

"She's making more of it than it was," Adam said.

"What did you say to him?" Jay asked.

"Just that I trusted you and that I didn't believe you'd sleep with him. For some reason, he thought I was going to warn him off or something." Adam looked pointedly at Julie, letting Jay know that she was somehow the cause of this.

"Same difference," Julie said.

"What did you think, Adam was going to come in and punch the guy in the face?" Jay asked his sister.

"Julie almost did it for me," Adam said, amusement ringing through his voice.

"Jules," Jay growled.

"Well, you should have heard what he was saying about Adam. He totally deserved it," Julie said.

"You're exaggerating," Adam said.

"What did he say?" Jay asked.

"That Adam didn't look like anything special," Julie said. "But it was the way he was saying it, like Adam was nothing. He's a jerk, Jase. I don't think you should be friends with him."

"Leave him alone, Julie," Adam said. "Jay can choose his own friends. As long as they are *friends*."

"I think I can handle ditching the pathetic one-night stands," Jay said, "as long as *you* stop escaping to the land of politicians and porn, or somewhere equally idiotic."

"Deal." Adam held out a hand to shake on it, but Jay pulled him into a kiss instead.

Their first public kiss. Adam was right; being open about their relationship did feel pretty damn good.

Those few short months without Adam had been the worst in Jay's life. He was willing to sacrifice nights of meaningless sex with near strangers if it meant that he got to keep Adam around. Adam was his best friend. And, Jay was finally ready to admit—what he had with Adam, it was Love. And not just because that was the word that would make Adam happy, or convince his mother to see them as serious. Jay felt the truth of the word every time he looked at Adam. There was no other way to describe it.

Jay hated it when his little sister was right.

About the Author

Michelle Ogilvy was born and bred in Adelaide, Australia. In primary school, to alleviate the boredom of putting spelling list words in sentences to explain their meaning, she started weaving them all into stories. She hasn't been able to shake this writing thing ever since.

Her day job involves working on health data collection tools, which resulted in her first publication, in a medical journal. For about a year, she worked as an editor for the department, but eventually she realised that her writing at home was enough time spent alone concentrating on words on a computer screen and she went back to her old job. It's still a lot of time spent staring at a computer, but there's at least more interaction with actual humans.

Twitter: https://www.twitter.com/MichelleOgilvy

Also Available from NineStar Press

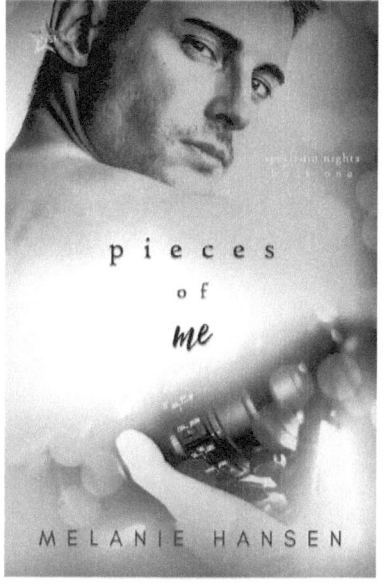

www.ninestarpress.com

www.ingramcontent.com/pod-product-compliance
Lightning Source LLC
Chambersburg PA
CBHW050036180626
46810CB00002B/750